Her life was likely never to be quite the same again.

While Lydia wouldn't grieve leaving the soulless, gilded prison of her father's house, the place where she had always been largely invisible and barely tolerated, she was entering into a union with a man she did not know, or ever hope to understand.

The open, optimistic, impetuous, fiery and charming Owen of her youth was gone. He was still thoroughly charming, at least he had been right up until he had proposed marriage to her, and clearly still impetuous if their unexpected and hasty elopement was any gauge. But the optimism and openness were no more. All the fire had been dampened, instead replaced by the cynical, emotionless businessman who played his cards close to his chest.

Author Note

A year ago, I asked my followers on social media what sort of story they would like to see next. I had two ideas. Both of which I liked a great deal. The first was a marriage-of-convenience story involving a governess and an earl, and the second an enemies-to-lovers story that centered around the heroine's misdeeds in the past before the hero went off to war.

Assuming my followers would be as excited as I was about these two stories, I stupidly put it to a vote—where all my best-laid plans unraveled like knitting.

You see, my followers had another idea. Because clearly my job wasn't hard enough already, they wanted me to write an amalgamation! An enemies-to-lovers marriage-of-convenience story!

But I listened, threw my other two perfectly good ideas out of the window and went back to the drawing board. Therefore, there is no governess in this book. The hero isn't an earl, either. The heroine doesn't have a checkered past and nobody went to war.

Now my story involves the explosive end to a forbidden first love, a former stable boy turned convict and an aristocratic heroine sold to pay her family's crushing debts...

VIRGINIA HEATH

——

The Scoundrel's Bartered Bride

HARLEQUIN®
HISTORICAL™

Recycling programs
for this product may
not exist in your area.

ISBN-13: 978-1-335-50557-6

The Scoundrel's Bartered Bride

Harlequin Enterprises ULC
22 Adelaide St. West, 40th Floor
Toronto, Ontario M5H 4E3, Canada
www.Harlequin.com

Printed in U.S.A.

When **Virginia Heath** was a little girl, it took her ages to fall asleep, so she made up stories in her head to help pass the time while she was staring at the ceiling. As she got older, the stories became more complicated—sometimes taking weeks to get to their happy ending. One day she decided to embrace her insomnia and start writing them down. Virginia lives in Essex, UK, with her wonderful husband and two teenagers. It still takes her forever to fall asleep...

Books by Virginia Heath

Harlequin Historical

Miss Bradshaw's Bought Betrothal
His Mistletoe Wager
Redeeming the Reclusive Earl
The Scoundrel's Bartered Bride

The Wild Warriners

A Warriner to Protect Her
A Warriner to Rescue Her
A Warriner to Tempt Her
A Warriner to Seduce Her

The King's Elite

The Mysterious Lord Millcroft
The Uncompromising Lord Flint
The Disgraceful Lord Gray
The Determined Lord Hadleigh

Secrets of a Victorian Household

Lilian and the Irresistible Duke

Visit the Author Profile page
at Harlequin.com for more titles.

For my wonderful little writing group.

Who always make me feel better when
a story has me tearing my hair out.

Chapter One

Mayfair—November 1817

'I heard an interesting rumour about you today, Lydia.'

Just the sound of his deep voice cutting through the music and incessant chatter of the ballroom behind caused her step to falter. She'd seen him earlier. Of course she had. Shaking hands with the great and the good. Smiling. Charming. The most striking man in the room. Because Owen Wolfe was hard to miss no matter how much she always tried to and had a way about him which vexingly drew the eye. But tonight she wasn't quite herself, so hadn't diligently avoided him with the same dogged determination as she usually did.

Wasn't quite herself!

An understatement. Tonight she was reeling and in no fit state to spar with him—although hell would have to freeze over before she ever allowed him to see how much he affected her. How much he had always affected her, dratted man, regardless of how worryingly prophetic his comment was. She stared back towards the dancing couples twirling on the crowded floor dispassionately in order to centre herself before flicking her eyes coldly back to his, hoping against hope she projected a blandness she did not feel.

'Then gossip and scandal must be painfully thin on the ground if I am the current topic of it. And it is *my lady* to you.'

Gossip was inevitable, she supposed, although surely the news could not have spread so soon? Not when she had only found out herself this very afternoon and had only been shamed into agreeing to the proposal with great reluctance moments before she strapped on her brave face and came here as was expected. A last resort, her brother had reassured her. Only if all else failed...

Although what the else was, she still had no earthly idea seeing that the Bartons were rapidly running out of options.

And credit.

Ignoring the sudden tentacles of dread at the daunting prospect which loomed before her, she tossed him her most irritated and imperious glance as she sailed past, avoiding the urge to run away as fast as her legs would take her to the sanctuary of home where she could lick her wounds in private. Coming here had been a mistake—one borne out of sheer denial that her life was about to thoroughly implode.

He, of course, was leaning against a pillar with his customary, casual arrogance, strong arms nonchalantly crossed. Effortlessly elegant. Aggravatingly handsome. Smug blue eyes far too intelligent for his own good—but then again, for all his many and hideous faults, Owen Wolfe had always been exceedingly clever. Even as the lowliest stable boy in the Barton mews on Berkeley Square all those years ago, his canny intelligence had shone like a beacon.

'It's true, then?' Despite her haste to be shot of him,

this cloying ballroom and the new, oppressive weight sat squarely and solely now on her shoulders, his long legs easily fell into step alongside hers. 'Your father really is auctioning you off to the highest bidder, *my lady*?'

Yes. Because things had apparently become that dire and debtors' prison loomed. Something he undoubtedly knew because he had the vexing habit of knowing almost everything well before everyone else nowadays.

'Is that the *actual* rumour?' It took every ounce of pride and fortitude Lydia possessed to shake her head in mock exasperation and to not allow the stunned despair and outrage to show on her face. 'Gracious.' She flicked open her fan for good measure and gave it a curt waft while another part of her died on the inside. 'Well, I suppose while the gossips are talking utter nonsense about me, they are giving another poor soul a reprieve.'

'You are truly getting married?' He shook his tawny head in disbelief, his lying eyes appearing concerned when she knew better than to trust them no matter how much her heart still wanted to believe he possessed genuine human emotions. 'And all these years I had convinced myself you were waiting for me.'

He enjoyed reminding her they had a past.

As if she would ever forget it, when the sorry truth was she remembered it as if it were yesterday.

She had been away all summer with her mother. The day they returned to Berkeley Square, when the carriage door opened, Lydia found herself looking into the bluest eyes she had ever seen, set in the most handsome face, too. He smiled at her and took her hand...and *bang!* The rest of the world disappeared as time literally stood still, because her tender young heart had apparently decided, there and then, it had found its mate.

'You flatter yourself. But then you always had an inflated sense of your own worth and ideas far above your station.' She knew reminding him of his roots would grate and was rewarded by the sight of his perfect jaw lifting defiantly, just as it always had when he was put back in his place by one of his betters. She paused before skewering him with her glare, making sure she was looking directly down her nose and letting every ounce of her heartfelt disapproval show.

'What are you doing here anyway? I cannot believe you are an *invited* guest. More likely you are wholly unwelcome and entirely uninvited—which explains why you were lurking in the shadows behind that pillar... *As usual.*' Or at least it had been usual in the two years since he had unexpectedly returned to Mayfair and the clocks had momentarily stopped once again. Too many clandestine pillars and tree trunks at too many cloying entertainments and society gatherings, when by rights, the owner of one of London's most famous gambling clubs should remain in the gutter where he deserved to be.

He smiled, unoffended, yet the way her traitorous pulse quickened at the sight mortally offended her. Of all the men of Lydia's acquaintance, only *he* had ever had that effect on her.

'The shadows have always appealed to me more than the chandeliers—although if you'd care to dance, I might make an exception?'

As if at his command and to taunt her further, his mouth curved into a knowing smile as the orchestra played the first strains of a waltz. Lydia rolled her eyes, letting the irritation show. She was in no mood for his practised flirting. Those deceptively twinkling blue eyes masked a soul as black as pitch.

'I had thought the Duke and Duchess of Aveley were more discerning in their choice of friends, as you are the absolute *last* person I would have expected to see within a mile of this illustrious place. What with your reputation…' She let the implied accusation hang, hoping it, too, would gall. They both knew what he was—regardless of the romanticised version of the tale which was doing the rounds. He might well have earned a pardon, but the sordid truth of his crime was unpardonable.

'Yet here I am. An official guest. I was even allowed through the front door. Would you care to see my invitation?'

'I would much prefer to see the back of you. For ever this time.'

As cutting final barbs went, it was a pathetic effort, but under the circumstances all she had. Yet as lacklustre as it was, it seemed to do the trick. He was most definitely not beside her as she stalked to the door. Nor was he behind her. She knew that for certain because she always seemed to sense him. Only Owen Wolfe made her skin prickle with awareness—to the complete disgust of her better judgement. She was almost through the door when he spoke again, just loud enough that she could hear, and ruined her escape.

'The smart money is on Kelvedon.'

Lydia stopped dead as the walls closed in. 'I beg your pardon?'

'The Marquess of Kelvedon…' He pushed himself from the pillar he had lounged against and sauntered towards her. 'Big belly. Bald head. Hideously foul breath. Old enough to be your grandfather…'

'I know who he is!' The prospect of her father marrying her off to that decrepit old lecher just to pay off a few debts was preposterous. That couldn't be what she had been bullied into agreeing to?

Surely?

While she was prepared to concede keeping a spinster daughter properly attired Season after fruitless Season was indeed expensive, as was keeping her *ad infinitum* while she languished on the shelf gathering dust, clearing her debt to the family by marrying her off to an old lecher seemed a high price to pay. Even for her callous sire.

'And you are entirely wrong!' Dear Papa might well expect her to finally do her duty, he had been loudly emphatic in that demand, but not to that extent. Or more likely he wouldn't have given it a passing thought. Daughters weren't sons—something he had reminded her about tirelessly for as long as she could remember.

'He's certainly rich enough and his blood is certainly blue enough. Those are the main criteria anyone who is anyone in *polite society* cares about, are they not? Especially *your* father.' Those insightful blue eyes were cold now and they both knew why. There was no love lost between their former employee and his employer. Too much water under the bridge. So much that the bridge had long been swept away in the raging torrents of the flood.

'*As usual*, you are completely wrong.' She turned on her heel to leave, suddenly desperate to challenge her unfeeling father and hear him denounce the rumour himself to put her racing mind at ease. And where was her brother? Her eyes nervously scanned the dance floor. He would defend her, too, if she pushed him hard enough. She might well be largely invisible to her sire most of the time but Papa sometimes listened to Justin and she was fairly certain there was no way he would countenance her marrying an old man.

'Am I?' She did not need to look at him to picture his smug expression. She knew it too well. 'I dare say the smelly Marquess has enough money to clear your family's oh-so-carefully hidden but rapidly mounting debts. Your pompous and pious family will be quietly bailed out—exactly as they want—and old Kelvedon gets to manoeuvre himself a little closer to the King…exactly as he wants. Everybody wins…except you, of course, Lydia. But you will do it regardless because that is exactly what any *loyal* blue-blooded, spineless daughter would do in the face of complete family ruination. You will do as they say…without question…*as usual*.'

His assessment sailed perilously too close to the truth for comfort, making her more uneasy about her future than she had been only a few minutes ago. It was all so sudden. All so final. All so hideously unfair. But what else could she do? This year's failed crops and flat market had put them all in a precarious position. Money did not grow on trees and an estate along with a house in Mayfair was expensive. Justin needed her help to save things and she wasn't about to abandon her only brother in his hour of need. They might not be as close as they had been when they were younger, but she was a Barton and Bartons did what was expected. If the only choice was Kelvedon…

The oppressive air in the ballroom was suffocating her, the noise pounding in her head in disjointed time to her hammering heart. 'With an imagination as vivid and as fanciful as yours, you really should write for the scandal sheets, Mr Wolfe.'

'You used to call me Owen.'

Something she did not need to be reminded of. It had been merely the tip of the iceberg of things she never should have done with the lowliest and duplicitous of stable boys all those years ago. Thank God nobody else knew of her shame. 'I was practically a child then!' He had been convicted on the same day as her seventeenth birthday.

'So was I.' He gave her the merest hint of a smile, then

shrugged his now ridiculously broad shoulders. 'Eighteen is hardly a man.'

She did not need to think of that intoxicating young fellow, so full of dreams and full of life. The one who saw the sixteen-year-old her when nobody else did and listened when nobody else cared. Or at least gave the appearance of it. 'I was ridiculously naive then—fresh from the schoolroom! And you always did have a silver tongue! It's a pity I didn't discover it was forked much sooner.'

He sighed and shook his head. 'Are you determined to hate me for all eternity, Lydia? Because I don't hate you… although Lord only knows I probably should.' And there it was again. That flash of humanity in his eyes which wormed its way past her defences and made her want to believe it. *Idiot!* She loathed herself for that weakness. Loathed him more for taking advantage of it. 'It's been ten years.'

Ten years, two months and one day to be precise, when one dreadful moment in time changed everything. One second she had been blithely hurrying down the path to her future when the path disintegrated beneath her feet and there suddenly was no future. Or at least not the one she had wanted. Her heart still didn't want to believe it. Her head still struggled to comprehend how one moment, one ominous tick of the clock, could possibly change everything.

'Hate assumes I care enough to be bothered when I am indifferent, Mr Wolfe.' A complete pack of lies. Everything about him set her emotions off-kilter. Always had. Always would. Nobody else had ever quite measured up and now she was about to be punished for her fickle heart's foolish desire because of the sorry truth of it. An arranged marriage. To a very wealthy man who might well be the dreadful Marquess of Kelvedon—because he certainly met all the criteria, exactly as Owen said.

Another dreadful moment in time. Another path crumbling beneath her feet. Another future, albeit a lesser one, gone, too, in the blink of an eye.

The walls began to close in, but she looked down her nose defiantly.

'Go back to your shadows, *Mr* Wolfe—they suit you so much better than the chandeliers.'

Lydia did not wait to see his expression. She slammed through the door and into the frigid garden, then tore across the lawn. The Aveley stables were housed on the same mews as her own. In two minutes she would be home and she could think. Perhaps miraculously come up with a plan to save her family and the estate and all the workers who depended on it which did not involve marrying a lecher. Not that marrying a stranger at such short notice was any better. A loveless marriage had never been what she had envisioned. The same foolish and romantic heart which had once loved Owen Wolfe so completely before he broke it, still yearned to love unreservedly once again and be loved in return. It still craved passion and excitement and laughter and joy.

But needs must and beggars could not be choosers. It was her turn to replenish the Barton coffers after taking from them so freely for years. Her father was adamant she must do her duty and her brother was doomed if she didn't. Damned if she did. Damned even more if she did not.

With hindsight, Lydia cursed herself for being too picky. In the seven Seasons she had been out, there had been no end of suitors and several advantageous proposals, meaning she could be safely married by now and not burdened with this unpalatable chore. Yet she had turned them all down politely because none of them had ever made her

heart soar the way she knew it could. She had been waiting patiently for *the one*—only to realise too late she had
compared every titled gentleman to the hollow, calculating
stable boy who had ruthlessly used her, then betrayed her
when he had shown his true colours. Colours she should
have seen if she hadn't been so besotted with him to look.

The truth of it made her blood boil.

Her heart would never soar again. There would be no
other *one*. No happily ever after. Just a marriage of convenience to a man she would probably never love. And if
it was indeed Kelvedon, she wouldn't be able to stand the
sight of either!

Heaven help her.

The Aveley grooms stood to attention as she marched
past. She didn't pause to greet them as she normally would.
The tears were too close to the surface and she couldn't
trust them not to fall. The mews was crammed with carriages, coachmen and stable hands played cards around
overturned barrels as they waited for the ball to end. She
wove around them, pushed past, her sights set on the bless-
edly silent Barton mews just a few yards away.

'Lydia...' She felt the unexpected touch of his hand
on her arm all the way down to her toes and froze. She
frowned at it before directing the full force of that frown
at him. For a big man, he moved with impressive stealth.
A predator. Like his namesake the wolf. Except he was
every disarming inch a wolf in sheep's clothing, prey-
ing on the weak and the stupid. And she had been both.
A veritable lamb to the slaughter! And of course, he had
to have stopped her here to witness her unshed tears and
her patently obvious utter defeat—in the place where it all
started—to rub salt into the reopened wound. An ironically
fitting end to the second-worst day of her life.

'What could you possibly want now?' Her words were

clipped, as hostile as she could make them, the urge to slap his handsome face simply because it existed causing her to clench her fists until her nails bit into her palms.

'If I am right about Kelvedon… If you need…anything…' those clever blues eyes were uncharacteristically stormy now, drawing her in, luring her to trust him as his grip loosened and she felt his thumb caress the bare skin of her forearm as if he cared '…you know where to find me.'

'I won't.' She tugged her arm away, remembering exactly how foolish she had been all those years ago each time he touched her, when she had believed he cared and how shamelessly he had used her on the back of it. 'I wouldn't come to you if you were the last man on earth and my entire world had fallen apart!'

Which it was likely to do at any given moment.

Chapter Two

'Are you sure there is nobody else in the running?'

This wasn't the news Owen had wanted to hear because it certainly would not put his racing mind at ease. Not after he had seen the horror in Lydia's eyes first-hand when he had been the one to inform her of her fate.

He wasn't proud of himself for doing that either. It had been churlish, bordering on the vindictive, borne out of some petty desire to put her in her place after she had tried to put him in his. He had learned to ignore those who looked down their nose at him, enjoying the challenge of winning them over and then happily taking their money when they lost it at his gaming tables. Unfortunately, all bets were apparently off when it came to her. With her he was constantly all at sea and nearly always without a paddle. Never quite in control when he diligently controlled everything else. Lydia vexed him—far more than a ghost from his past should.

'Not unless they are keeping their cards very close to their chest and are still negotiating.' Randolph shrugged his shoulders. 'Which I am reliably informed there is no evidence of. He's dined at the house twice this week already and has been the family's *only* guest. It's definitely

Kelvedon.' His best friend and business partner paused and watched him closely for his reaction. 'Why else would he have made an appointment to meet with the Bishop of London yesterday? He's procured a special licence.'

Owen nodded curtly and pretended to focus on tying his cravat in the mirror in case the sudden burst of rage at this news gave him away.

This was all happening so blasted fast he could barely keep up with it all, and worse, he had no earthly idea why he was compelled to keep up with it all in the first place. It wasn't as if he wanted the vixen. Not in that way any more at least. Lydia was dangerous to his liberty and his sanity. Why should he care who she married? She wasn't his problem, thank the Lord.

Even so—poor Lydia.

He wasn't entirely sure what he felt for her beyond a combination of anger, hurt, nostalgia and fascination—but nobody deserved that fate, no matter what they had done. The Marquess of Kelvedon was a leering, sweating pig of a man more than double her age, renowned for his wandering hands. Owen had had to warn him twice in as many months to keep his filthy paws off the hostesses in his club. Once more and the lecher would be barred from Libertas for life no matter how much he spent at the tables. The thought of those hands mauling her...

Irritated at his unhealthy preoccupation with a woman who did not deserve his concern, his sudden inability to control his swirling emotions and his own ineptitude at tying a neckcloth, he tossed the third ruined strip of linen on the bed and snatched up another one.

'I hate these things!' His continued obsession with the minx was unhealthy. It was one thing when he'd been a green eighteen-year-old lad who'd worn his heart on his sleeve and only saw what he wanted to see, another entirely for a grown man of almost thirty who knew exactly what she was! He had been sport. Nothing more. A dirty secret. Someone to flatter her ego and practice her wiles on, then someone to discard and deny all knowledge of simply to save her own precious reputation!

He wound the fabric clumsily around his neck and tried again, not holding out much hope for success and conscious he was at risk of arriving late to the opera—a social faux pas in a society that put too much stock in ridiculous rules which put appearances over people.

'Why the blazes is the measure of a gentleman determined by the knot in his cravat? And in this time of industry and brilliance, why the hell hasn't some enterprising fellow invented one which is pre-tied and prettified and only needs one tiny, invisible hook to secure it around the collar?' The fourth tie joined the third on the floor as he grabbed the last one from the dresser and shook it at Randolph. 'I will never understand it!'

His diminutive friend rolled his eyes and dragged a chair over, making short work of climbing onto it, then slapping Owen's fingers away from the task to take over himself. 'That's because you have no patience. Temper won't get it tied…' He shot him a pointed look before busying himself with the knot, his stubby fingers performing miracles Owen's enormous digits were incapable of. 'Although I suspect your hot head tonight is less to do with your cravat and more to do with a certain lady…' He ignored Owen's instinctive scowl. 'Who I must say you seem uncharacteristically obsessed with of late. Well…more so than usual…'

'And what is that supposed to mean?'

'That despite your several thousand and convincingly emphatic assertions to the contrary over the many, *many* years I have known you, I am starting to think you are not quite as over Lady Lydia Barton as you might want us all to believe.'

'That is utter nonsense!' And a little too close to the truth for comfort. She still had some inexplicable and irrational power over him, which was exactly the crux of the problem when the only person Owen ever wanted to have power over him until hell froze over was himself. 'I loathe the wench! And with good reason!'

Which went no way at all to explaining why he had made her business entirely his business all week so that Randolph was already smirking in that smug way he did when he was convinced he knew something Owen didn't. 'However...' he did his best to look matter-of-fact '...she is well connected and well thought off among the *ton*, so it makes sound business sense to keep up with the gossip. You, more than anyone, know the importance of keeping an ear to the ground. It is always useful to know the state of our clientele's finances. Especially as Kelvedon is such a *good* customer.'

Randolph's fingers paused and he blinked in obvious disbelief. 'A pathetic excuse which might work well with the masses, Owen—Kelvedon is a hedonist who will never give up his vices, even for a bonny wife like the lovely Lady Lydia, so his continued patronage at Libertas is assured. Your interest in her is entirely personal. Do not deny it.' His nimble fingers returned to the task in hand. 'Her impending nuptials have made you jealous.'

'Have you been on the brandy?' Was he jealous? Frustrated? Curious? A week since he'd heard the first rumours and Owen still wasn't entirely sure how he felt beyond unsettled. Or perhaps it was panicked? He'd certainly awakened in a cold sweat last night after a particularly bad dream featuring both Kelvedon and Lydia behind a locked church door while the desperate dream version of himself failed to ram the thing open with only his shoulder.

'Gertie thinks you still love her.'

Owen rolled his eyes, appalled at the suggestion. As if he were that stupid! That masochistic! That pathetic. He didn't beg for crumbs from his supposed betters any longer or allow matters of the heart to overrule the sound judgement of his own pragmatic head. Loving Lydia had lost him his liberty… Maybe. 'Gertie is mistaken.'

'Is she?' Randolph stepped back to admire his work and grinned. 'In my experience, there is a fine and precarious line between loving and loathing. It would certainly explain your current obsession. And your recent foul mood.'

'Trust me, the line between myself and that woman is wider than the Blue Mountains and just as impassable! She fed me to the lions, if you recall. Watched me arrested and dragged off to gaol and never uttered a word in my defence!' When she could have vouched for his character and probably given him an alibi. He remembered that fateful moment as if it was yesterday. Her shock. Her disgust. And then her silence. 'You get over all foolish notions of love pretty quick after that happens, I can assure you.' Nor did you get over the sense of powerlessness that came from being a nothing and a nobody. Or the lack of control over your own life.

Randolph ignored both his denial and his murderous expression to carry on prodding the surprisingly open wound regardless. 'Gertie reckons once a heart has been pierced by Cupid's arrow, there can be no going back. The deal is done. The die is cast.' His friend used far too many gambling metaphors. 'The heart always wants what the heart needs.'

'Your wife is a hopeless romantic.' He jabbed his finger to Randolph's chest, immensely uncomfortable with the turn the conversation had taken, but with no clear or coherent reasons justifying why his interfering friend was wrong. 'If I am obsessed with anything, it's finally seeing that family get their comeuppance!' He stalked away to grab his evening coat and shrugged it on. 'It's petty and it's beneath me—but I fully intend to enjoy it. After everything, I deserve that at least.' If he told himself that often enough, he might actually come to believe it.

'You're not the vengeful type. You pride yourself on being the bigger man. It's your most piously nauseating trait.'

'There is nothing nauseating about doing the right thing and I *am* usually the bigger man—but the bad blood between me and the Earl of Fulbrook and his lofty brood is intensely personal. I might not be the type to seek my own revenge, but I'll be damned if I won't enjoy it if fate dishes them their just deserts for me! Keeping abreast of the soon-to-be Marchioness of Kelvedon ensures I get to enjoy the spectacle fully from a seat at the front.' For good measure, he waved his finger in his friend's disbelieving face.

'And while I will admit once upon a time I might have foolishly allowed my heart to have been pierced by Cupid's blasted arrow, I soon got over it and then wrapped the damned organ in armour in case the blighter ever tried to point his bow in my direction again!' Owen marched to the door. 'Thanks to you, I'm late for the opera!'

'What do you care? You hate the opera. And you are only late because you insisted on hearing about your lady love's wedding preparations…'

'She's not my blasted lady love!'

'And as Gertie also says, if you have to shout—you're wrong.'

'Go to hell!' He fully intended to slam the heavy oak door as hard as he could.

'It's a great shame, though, isn't it? I mean regardless of what happened to you… Which is obviously unforgivable…but I wouldn't wish Kelvedon on anyone. Not even my worst enemy.' Which was the single most niggling thing keeping Owen up at night. Kelvedon was hideous. Inside and out. 'Word on the street is he's a bit handy with his fists as well as his hands.'

'What?' Against his better judgement, Owen turned around as his conscience pricked further. 'Define handy.'

'Only that he is renowned for his temper and his poor barren first wife was often seen with bruises…before she mysteriously fell down those stairs…' Randolph shook his head, his face a picture of concern. 'You've got to feel for the girl even though you despise her.'

'I don't completely despise her.' That was the problem. 'Loathing isn't despising. And being a decent sort, I do feel some compassion for her.' If Kelvedon ever laid a finger on her… Now he felt compelled to do the right thing. Being the bigger man really was a nauseating character trait. Blasted Randolph! Giving him another worry to add to the churning mix of emotions he couldn't currently control and apparently couldn't ignore.

'I'm late!' And it was probably best he extricate himself from the situation before his irritating friend added anything else to the seething cauldron bubbling in his gut.

'I know you loathe her and everything, but being a decent sort who always does the right thing unlike the rest of us *mere* mortals…perhaps you could help her in some way?'

Owen had offered her his help the other night—Lord only knew why. She had turned him down flat. Thank goodness. 'I sincerely doubt there is anything I could offer Lady Lydia Barton that she would take.'

'I'll wager she would! If it was a toss up between you

and the odious Kelvedon, for example… I know which of you I'd rather marry if I was desperate.'

Owen paused mid-step and simply gaped. 'Have you gone completely mad?'

'It would save her from a fate worse than death. And you are partial to doing good deeds. Almost daily, in fact. You are annoying selfless. It's one of the main reasons my Gertie adores you. She says you have a giant heart made from solid gold.' A description which always made Owen uncomfortable, largely because he preferred to keep that unfortunate character trait a secret in case it was exploited again. But Randolph and Gertie were family, and his best friend was a master at finding things out, so they knew.

They also knew absolutely everything about his doomed romance with the vixen and how it had left him shattered, too. Because he had stupidly confessed everything on a number of occasions after a little too much alcohol—back in the days when he had never dreamed of ever seeing English soil or the blasted Lady Lydia Barton again.

He bitterly regretted those heartfelt, damning conversations now as they were obviously the root cause of Randolph's current meddling. Ammunition of the worst sort because Owen had provided it.

'I donate to the poor! I don't marry them!'

'Still… I know the way your noble mind works. It might be worth thinking about…for your own peace of mind…'

'It isn't.' The very thought was preposterous. 'I have no need of a wife, I've never wanted one and, if I did, it certainly wouldn't be her! I've already spent seven long years in purgatory thanks to that woman. What you're proposing is a life sentence!'

'Perhaps…'

'*Perhaps!* There is no perhaps about it. We loathe one another.'

His friend waved that away as if it were an inconsequential detail easily surpassed when it was the whole crux of his preposterous idea. 'I wouldn't dismiss it out of hand. You are a rescuer at heart, so it will make you feel better about her tragic circumstances if nothing else...'

'Believe me—I am not *that* charitable.'

'That's a shame.'

'Not for me it isn't.'

'Because the more I think upon it, the more I see the concept has some merit...'

'Merit?' Owen folded his arms and shook his head. 'I cannot wait to hear this! Your flights of fancy are always entertaining. This one surpasses all of the previous ones by a country mile.'

'Well, it does have merit.' Randolph jumped off the chair and came towards him. 'Firstly, your cynicism about love and marriage is what makes it so perfect! We can take all the conventional aspects of it, all the emotion, all the anxiety and all the sighing out of the equation and make it purely about business. She's an *earl's* daughter.'

'So?'

'It stands to reason you being married to a member of the aristocracy, especially one as well thought of as her, will open doors for us. And, as you yourself only just stated, it makes *sound* business sense to keep up with the gossip, to know the state of our clientele's finances—especially when it comes from such a reliable source. She's from within their own ranks, Owen!' There was an almost maniacal gleam in Randolph's eyes now as he waved his arms around expansively. 'One of the elite! Just think of all the enlightening little pearls we shall glean first-hand!'

'Good grief...' Owen shook his head, unsure whether to laugh or scream. 'You're an imbecile. I've gone into business with a three-foot imbecile.'

'I'm three-foot-six.'

'What difference do six paltry inches make?'

'A lot in certain places if you haven't got them. Although fortunately I have.' His friend winked saucily. 'That's why the ladies have always loved me... But I digress. Where was I? Oh, yes...and secondly...' Randolph ticked the next ludicrous point off on his upstretched hand. 'With all the rumours flying around about her impending marriage and the prospective unsavoury and thoroughly repulsive groom, the *ton* have a lot of sympathy for her now. They all know what Kelvedon is and they'll all work out why he was foisted upon her, too. You stepping in and graciously saving her from a fate worse than death can only serve to enhance your reputation and the meticulous intricate myth which surrounds you.'

'The myth?'

'The wealthy man of mystery. The ruthless man of business. The poor boy made good. The hero who never fails to step up...' He shot him a pointed look at that one. 'The charmer... The aloof gatekeeper... The man you dare not cross...'

'Oh, good Lord!' Owen flicked open his pocket watch and yawned. 'Surely you are done?'

'The returned convict... The wronged man who was transported for a crime he didn't commit...'

'I *was* transported for a crime I didn't commit!'

'Semantics.' His outrage was dismissed with a genteel flick of the wrist. 'All I mean is nobody outside of these four walls quite knows who *Owen Wolfe* really is. This would certainly put the cat among the pigeons and confuse and intrigue them all over again. Libertas will be the talk of the town again! Just think of the romance of the tale! Her family banished you to the other side of the world—' he swept out one arm theatrically '—yet instead of seeking revenge as any normal human being cruelly denied their freedom would, you rose above it and rescued their daughter out of the goodness of your heart.'

'I thought I was supposed to be mysterious and a little bit ruthless?' The pair of them had worked hard on cultivating that image and, much as it pained him to make Randolph right again, it was working wonders for their business. 'Suddenly playing the good Samaritan would go against the grain.'

'*Au contraire*, my handsome and cynical friend! It adds yet another layer to the conundrum that is *Owen Wolfe*. A delicious layer which hints at that heart of gold beating loudly beneath the aloof and impenetrable business exterior. One which appeals to the feminine mind...'

'Libertas is a *gentlemen's* club.'

'All the ladies will be swooning and clambering to invite you to the *many* entertainments you have thus far been excluded from—because it is the ladies who organise these things, Owen—and with those invitations comes fresh *male* customers. Fresh *rich* male customers.' He wrapped his palm around his ear like a shell, knowing the lure of money was Owen's nemesis. 'I can hear the glorious tinkle of coin already.'

'Imbecile.'

'Face it, my friend, everybody loves a hero, especially such an intriguing and enigmatic one as you are shaping up to be—and we'll make a fortune on the back of it. You marrying her is a business opportunity!' He threw out both arms this time. 'A glorious business opportunity!'

'Yet I am surprisingly ambivalent about it.' Owen turned to leave, only to feel his friend's strong grip tugging his coat tails. 'A lifetime shackled to a woman who hates me simply to utilise her connections in society sounds like a living hell. For me, that is. Not for *you*, of course. And the truth is, I am not *that* concerned about her welfare.'

'And thirdly...'

'Lord, give me strength.' Owen threw his own hands in the air. This was all going from the sublime to the ridiculous. So typically Randolph. He pulled his coat away from the lunatic's strong grasp. 'You're delusional. Completely mad. Why am I even still listening to you? Why the hell do I *keep* listening to you?' He tapped his temple, bending at the waist to look his friend dead in the eyes. 'When you've clearly gone soft in the head. I knew all the sun in the Antipodes would do you damage in the end. I repeatedly told you to wear a hat. Why did you never wear a hat?'

'And thirdly...' said Randolph, undeterred by the insults and plainly enjoying himself. 'She's always been the itch you couldn't scratch. If you marry her...' he drew a saucy hourglass in the air with his hands while raising his eyebrows suggestively '...then you can scratch it whenever you want to!'

'Go to hell!'

Owen did slam the door this time and was halfway down the winding staircase when he heard Randolph's smug voice on the landing.

'The heart always wants what the heart needs, Owen. And I suspect, regardless of all the armour you've strapped on since, you might want to visit the surgeon because the tip of Cupid's arrow is clearly still wedged in yours.'

Chapter Three

Owen did not dignify that with a response, entirely because he couldn't think of one which didn't have him stamping his foot in denial, but silently seethed as he briskly stomped the mile to Covent Garden, hoping the chilly November air would calm his temper in time.

Blasted Randolph needed to mind his own business!

Except he had to concede it was entirely his own fault for making it his friend's business the second he had heard the first hint of the rumour.

He had known that was a mistake the moment he had asked and witnessed the intrigued glint in his canny friend's eyes. But what other choice did he have? Nobody could gather information like Randolph. Nor did anybody know him quite as well as his friend did. In the absence of proper clarity, because Lord alone knew Owen couldn't see the wood for the trees himself, and with Randolph's meddling wife's interference, it was hardly a surprise his friend was putting two and two together and making five. One of these days he was going to strangle Randolph and enjoy doing it!

Cupid's blasted arrow!

It would be laughable if it wasn't all so tragic.

Owen hadn't been hit by an arrow. An arrow was too delicate a weapon for the havoc she had caused. It had been a thunderbolt which had knocked him sideways the first time he had set his eyes upon Lydia all those years ago. It had been only his second day in the Barton stable when her carriage had rolled in. He had fetched the steps as he had been instructed, opened the carriage door and… *Boom!*

The spell was cast and all rational thought evaporated.

She smiled at him, took his proffered hand briefly and the earth seemed to shift on its axis. Then for a while all was utterly perfect in his world, simply because she was in it.

Until it all crashed around his ears and he was hauled off by the constable and sent to the other side of the globe in irons against his will, completely powerless to stop it and his tender heart and all his ridiculously romantic illusions about love and Lydia shattered completely.

Randolph and Gertie knew all of that. Every last sorry detail. Which was why they could make such fine sport of it at his expense.

But what Randolph and Gertie did not know, what nobody knew aside from Owen, was that he had been hit by another damn thunderbolt the second he clapped eyes on her upon his return to England!

And this one had knocked him backwards, sent him flying, then left him winded and dumbstruck. Until he finally battled through the mire and found the wherewithal to rationalise his wholly unexpected and monumental response properly. Something which had taken the last year and a half to achieve and still wasn't fully formed in his mind—but it was close. Close enough that he had started to feel better about it.

Before news of her impending marriage had churned him all up again and confused the hell out of him.

Rationally, Owen needed to take this past week's events out of the equation to focus on the absolute truths he now understood plainly. Only those would calm him down and hand control of the situation back to him. It wasn't love this time. He knew that for sure. And perhaps it hadn't been love all those years ago either? With maturity and experience came a level of understanding about the way things were between a man and a woman which he'd not had a clue about at eighteen. What had slammed into Owen that second time was lust. Lust as primal, all-consuming and as carnal as any he'd ever felt for any other woman—and all because Lydia possessed every one of the feminine attributes which specifically called to him as a man. It was as if all his desires and fantasies had been rolled into one being, made expressly for him by nature, to his specific design. On the outside, Lydia was the woman of his dreams. What flesh-and-blood man could fight that?

When she had been sixteen he had wanted to kiss her. Now she was all woman in every sense of the word, his body wanted to possess her. It was that basic and that simple.

It was that same lust which had made him continually seek her out in the months since. It did not take a genius to work out her impending marriage signalled the end of all hope of ever slaking it. Not that he had dared try. He did not like the way Lydia made him feel. The power she had held over him was as destructive as it had been disastrous. And if she made him feel all at sea from a distance still now, he feared he would drown if he ever got too close.

Therefore, Randolph and the fanciful Gertie were entirely wrong. He didn't *still* love her, but he *had* always wanted her. That was his truth and his curse. Because Lady Lydia Barton was his own personal siren, calling him to the treacherous rocks he knew only too well and determined to make him suffer while he was pummelled ruthlessly against them.

He was so infuriated by it all, he almost collided with a handcart as he turned into Piccadilly, then only narrowly avoided backing into a hackney as he swerved too close to the road for comfort.

Urgh! More pointless philosophising to fire his temper when he needed to stop going around and around in circles! His face was aching with the force of his frown, when he needed to be charming and just a little bit mysterious and aloof with just a hint of ruthlessness and danger thrown in for good measure. The public face of the mythical Owen Wolfe.

He scrunched up his features to relax them as he stalked into Covent Garden and only just managed to smile as he walked through the theatre doors to greet his illustrious host. The Earl of Grantley was a good customer and a supremely well-connected one.

'Owen!' The Earl pumped his hand enthusiastically. 'I was beginning to despair of you ever arriving!'

In a city where it wasn't what you knew, but who you knew, it was these connections, these invitations, these occasions, which had seen his business and his fortune double in size in only six months. And with money came power. After spending most of his life at the mercy and whims of others, he was finally the master of his own destiny. Something which had taken ten long years to achieve and which he would protect until his dying breath. This was a much better use of his time than pontificating over Lydia.

'My apologies…urgent business, I'm afraid.' Unfinished business which would soon be well and truly finished. And he would welcome its end!

'Not to worry and entirely understandable. A success-

ful and popular man such as yourself must be pulled every
which way.' Grantley reminded him of a puppy. So happy
to see him. So desperate to please. 'At least you are here.'
The young Earl clearly considered his presence a coup. As
did several others who watched impressed in the crowded
lobby. Proof at how much effort he and Randolph had put
into his public persona to cultivate the myth. 'Allow me
to introduce you to my other guests.'

A bevy of eager young gentlemen bounced on their
feet as they surreptitiously looked him up and down. They
had all doubtless bent over backwards to secure this in-
troduction. They all knew membership to Libertas only
came via a personal invitation from the owner, a strategy
which Owen had initially had his doubts about when Randolph had suggested it, but which had absolutely worked
to their advantage.

That was the fundamental element of the dance they
had choreographed.

Nobody wanted to be in a club anyone could join and,
as he knew to his cost, it was human nature to want what
was repeatedly denied to you. Therefore, when he sent out
just one invitation the next morning to the gentleman who
had impressed him or irritated him the most, he knew it
would only spur the unlucky four on to court him harder
in the future—just like the over-keen Grantley. Libertas
in the heart of well-to-do Mayfair, like White's, Almack's
and indeed the King's Royal Court, was the domain of the
elite. The most exclusive of exclusive gaming clubs for the
most preferential and superior of clientele. And Owen intended to keep it that way.

With no more pointless distractions.

'This is Hugo Brent, heir to the Viscount Warley, Sir
Peter Tyne of the Charteris family...' Taking a mental
note of all the names and pragmatically evaluating their

provenance and potential value to his business, he shook five pairs of hands and made small talk, his mind struggling to stay focused, but spiralling back to her regardless.

Blasted Lydia…

Ten long years. Incarceration. Deprivation, hunger and back-breaking work on the other side of the globe. Injustice. Terror. Total heartbreak and the blackest despair. Owen had beaten it all, yet still the allure of Lydia held the power to hold him captive. It made no sense and he loathed it. Almost as much as he wanted to loathe her—but couldn't.

Marry her! That was the absolute last thing he wanted to do, when he would rather never see her again. He didn't want to have to constantly think about her either. He didn't want to feel compelled to seek her out whenever fate provided him an opportunity or an excuse to do so. Owen did not want to be that unworthy smitten stable lad any longer. And he certainly did not want to keep wanting her either. She hated him and he hated that he didn't quite hate her. Therefore, what was the point in even thinking about it? His obsession with Lydia was as unhealthy as it was irrational.

'And this is my sister… Lady Annabel St John.'

A sultry pair of green almond eyes locked boldly with his, then when he took her proffered hand she squeezed his fingers in obvious invitation. 'Mr Wolfe… What a pleasure it is to finally meet you. I have heard so much about you this past year I simply had to cast off my widow's weeds and come tonight.'

And in that one sentence, he knew exactly where he stood. A blessed relief on the back of all the shifting quicksand that was Lydia.

'Lady Annabel…' He kept his gaze firmly on hers as he brought that bold hand to his lips. Took in the lovely face, the fine figure, the knowing glint in her eye as he lingered over the kiss. 'The pleasure, I can assure you, is all mine.'

Ruthlessly, he suppressed the pang of guilt which always accompanied any flirtation with another woman. He had nothing to feel guilty about! If he was riddled with unspent lust, here was a prime opportunity to relieve himself of some of it. Lady Annabel was clearly ready, willing and able and Lydia was *not* his problem. A mantra which he had repeated often this past week when his brain continued to mull over her predicament and suggested he was somehow responsible for it. She was shallow and cowardly and not worthy of his concern. Kelvedon was welcome to her and she him. A loveless marriage to a wealthy peer was hardly as horrendous a punishment as seven years' hard labour in Botany Bay for a crime he did not commit!

The call came for them to take their seats and without waiting for him to offer it, Lady Annabel took his arm proprietorially. 'I insist you sit beside me, Mr Wolfe. I have so many questions.'

'Such as?' At her encouragement, they lagged behind the others as they made their way to the Earl of Grantley's private box.

'Well, to start with…' Taking advantage of the privacy of the narrow staircase, Lady Annabel smoothed her other hand up his biceps. 'I wanted to know if all the scandalous rumours about you are correct?'

'Probably.' He dropped his voice to a whisper. 'Do you mind?'

The lusty young widow laughed the breathy laugh of a woman who knew how seductive she was. 'On the contrary, Mr Wolfe… I cannot resist a scoundrel.' In case he missed her implication, she positioned herself closer, until he felt the soft press of her ample bosom against his arm as they continued up the stairs.

If he played his cards right—and he already knew he had been dealt a hand of kings—he would warm her bed later. A prospect which should have excited him more than it did thanks to another unwelcome image of Lydia, looking as perennially hurt and disappointed in him as she had the day he'd been dragged away from her father's house clapped in irons.

He almost growled in frustration at his brain's inability to put the past behind him where it belonged, but instead forced a charming smile as he helped the earthy Lady Annabel into her seat and lowered himself to sit beside her. When she shuffled closer so that their bodies touched from hip to knee, then used the shield of her programme to disguise her hand as it brazenly stroked his thigh, he decided to seize the moment and to hell with his stupid blasted brain and damned Lydia!

She really was *not* his problem and in a few short weeks, he would be rid of the allure of her for ever, too. In fact, now he was rationalising it alongside the tempting prospect of pastures new, in a funny sort of way her impending marriage was probably the best possible thing which could happen.

It drew a line in the dirt.

A decisive halt to their relationship.

A fresh start which would finally release him from her thrall to channel his pent-up lust elsewhere and perhaps quickly to become Owen Wolfe, the legendary ladies' man...

Now that was another layer to his mythical character he wouldn't mind adding.

He was sick and tired of feeling disloyal if he as much as glanced another woman's way when he should be glancing here, there and everywhere with unburdened impunity! Wouldn't that be a splendid reward for all his years of hard work and suffering? And so much better than Randolph's ridiculous suggestion.

In fact, he would start tonight and continue as he meant to go on. Once the wench was well and truly hitched, he would throw himself into the endeavour with the same determined vigour as he'd thrown into becoming the master of his own destiny. Something much more agreeable to ponder tonight than the unresolved ghosts of his past.

Already he was feeling better. Already the temptation that was Lady Annabel St John was starting to give his body other ideas. Much better ideas than the ridiculous one Randolph had just peddled. He would not waste a second on feeling guilty or feeling pity for the woman who so openly despised him.

No, indeed!

And while he was warming the luscious Annabel's sheets, nor would he give a passing thought to the disturbing images of Lydia similarly ensconced in Kelvedon's.

Enduring the smelly Marquess's hands on her body was nowhere near as awful as feeling the lash slice your back or the constant chafe and dead weight of your chains around your ankles as you languished helpless in the bowels of a ship headed nowhere. Owen had had to make the best of his sentence just as she would have to make the best of hers. At least she had the peace of mind her punishment served a higher cause. Owen's had served to rob him of seven long years he would never get back. Something Lydia's mute betrayal had had a hand in. Perhaps if she had stepped forward? Stood up for him…

'Can I tell you a *shocking* secret, Mr Wolfe?' His new companion's lips grazed his ear as she practically sighed the question into it. 'I abhor the opera… I only came here tonight for you… Do *you* mind?'

'On the contrary…' Owen smiled and was about to

allow his own hand to cover Lady Annabel's unsubtle one on his leg when the atmosphere around him seemed to shift and he almost groaned aloud.

He did not need to see her to know she was here.

Every nerve ending positively fizzed with awareness.

Nor did he need to search for her frantically in the crowd. His eyes were instinctively drawn to her the moment she entered the box, just as they were always drawn to her whenever she was close by.

Which meant he saw the Marquess of Kelvedon enter directly behind her and saw, too, the hauntingly pained expression in her eyes when the old lecher placed his hand possessively on her elbow to guide her to her seat, then the utter disgust when he slipped it down to pat her bottom. Lydia brushed it away like a gnat, but it didn't stop him, forcing Owen to watch Kelvedon's ugly face contort into a cruel scowl and his filthy hand to head back forcibly towards her body as the auditorium dimmed.

Chapter Four

Despite the steaming hot bath she had insisted upon the moment they returned last night, Lydia had deemed it necessary to order another this morning and to request all the bedding be changed and her night rail boiled because she felt so dirty and soiled.

Kelvedon made her nauseous. Everything about him disgusted her, from his uneven brown teeth to the creaking corset he wore under his coat. But the thing which disgusted her the most was the way he continually touched her. He had squeezed, then groped her thigh so many times during the performance, she was certain his horrid hands had left a greasy stain on her silk gown and each unwelcome touch, no matter how swiftly or vehemently it was rebuked, made her want to gag.

Worse, as he pawed her, his breathing became erratic, heavy and laboured and the blatant lust in his beady eyes was horrifying. He was looking forward to their wedding night. She knew that because he had seen fit to tell her not once, but three times while the theatre lights had been dimmed and her brother could not see or hear what he was doing.

But Owen Wolfe had seen.

His gloating eyes had been on her all night, doubtless enjoying the sight of her with the very man he had predicted she was being sold to. It was humiliating in the extreme and, somehow, his presence made the ordeal of the evening worse. Especially because he was sat beside a very beautiful woman. Very closely beside a beautiful woman who had gazed at him longingly all evening like a starving dog outside a butcher's window, waiting for the perfect moment to pounce.

Yet another bitter blow she had not been expecting and one which cut her to the quick.

Before she had bolted for the carriage and wept bitter tears into her powerless brother's handkerchief, the hideous Marquess had insisted on kissing the back of her hand. It had been a sloppy kiss. A lingering torture. One which had left a sticky patch of spittle clinging to her skin. Despite all the hot water, and the stiff brush she had taken to it which had made it red and raw, that hand still did not feel like her own.

And even though her dear brother was still hopeful he could convince their father to consider someone else as her husband, to widen his search for a better suitor, she couldn't help wondering how she would ever cope with the ordeal of the marriage bed if just the man's touch could make her feel so hideously violated? Unless she procured some laudanum and rendered herself incoherently non-sensical on her wedding night and was spared from ever remembering it at all.

The past five days had been horrific. After barely digesting the fact she had to marry for the sake of the family and fast—the man she loathed above all others had been the one to tell her who she was to be shackled to. That Owen had known it was Kelvedon before her father had deigned to tell her had been a humiliating and bitter blow. Yet when she had challenged her father, he had been dismissive in his acknowledgement.

Kelvedon was a marquess. A respected peer and politician. He was wealthy and he was agreeable to the speedy marriage the Barton coffers required because he was in dire need of an heir and desirous of a wife young enough to provide him with one. Of *course* there was no other groom being considered. Why would there be? She should be grateful to be marrying so well after all her fickle years languishing on the shelf, refusing wealthy peer after wealthy peer. Grateful to Kelvedon for rescuing her from that shelf and grateful, too, to her father for finding her such a good catch at such short notice when she was long past her prime.

Not that he was the least bit grateful that her speedy marriage to a groom no other woman wanted also brought him a swift ten thousand. That was by the by. Her duty.

In desperation, and she was not proud of herself for this self-centred and selfish outburst, she had argued it made better financial sense if Justin married. Not only was he five years older, he was the heir to an earldom and quite a catch. He could command a dowry of twenty thousand at least. And it was his inheritance after all. All for his ultimate benefit.

Papa had practically had a fit at that, which his physicians had expressly warned against since his heart had turned bad. He was so incensed at her question he had gone purple and his lips an ominous blue. How dared she?

How dared she?

The marriage of a future earl with such close connections to His Majesty, no less, was much too important to rush! The right wife needed to be found and Lydia could hardly expect her brother to appear impoverished and begging for a wealthy woman. That would lead to them being

short-changed in the settlements! Whereas her brother
would not have to appear desperate once Kelvedon had
paid for her, because he wouldn't be desperate. Refusing
to marry him not only jeopardised the estate and everyone who depended on it—it sabotaged her brother's future as well.

That, rather than her father's plight, had been the
clincher. So she had agreed to it all under duress, in case
her father's heart gave way on the spot because of her in-
solence, thoroughly ashamed she had tried to save herself
by sacrificing Justin, when he had quite enough on his
plate already trying to manage the mess her father had
made of their finances. Feeling pious as well as beaten,
she decided the only way to cope with it was to be matter-
of-fact. It was what it was and she would make the best of
it. It wasn't as if she had a choice.

But since her agreement, everything had been planned
around her. Earth-changing things were decided for her
without either her presence or her input in the decisions
and she was apprised of them when her father saw fit. Or
when Justin came to seek her out, his expression filled
with pity and remorse, as he passed across those details
neither her sire nor her aged new fiancé thought important
enough to concern her with.

That was how she knew the settlements were being
signed today. In fact, they were probably being signed right
now as she sat here in her bathtub, pathetically trying to
blot it all out and pretend it wasn't happening. The panting, groping, odious Marquess had procured the special
licence, a bland and insipid bridal gown she had neither
been measured for nor chosen had arrived yesterday and
in just three days Lydia, Justin and apparently her ailing
father would all travel to Kelvedon's estate several hours

east of the city where the wedding was to take place in his private chapel.

In view of the haste of the affair and the dubious circumstances, the announcement would not go into *The Times* until that fateful morning because her advantageous marriage was to be a private affair with no pomp or ceremony.

That was one detail she was relieved about. She could not fake happiness or celebration and was determined not to try. She had been bought and sold like a piece of meat, with no consideration of her feelings or concern for her happiness, to pay her father's debts. If her sacrifice wasn't the only thing which would prevent her brother from inheriting complete chaos and ruination, too, she wouldn't be doing it at all. But of course her father knew that, which was why he had ruthlessly used it as leverage.

The only act of recourse available to her at this late hour, the only futile act of rebellion, was her utter disdain for the proceedings and the two callous old men who controlled them. She might well be doing her duty exactly as a Barton daughter was expected to do, but she fully intended to be the most disgusted and disappointed bride who ever walked down the aisle as a mark of protest. Let Kelvedon see from the outset exactly what he was getting for his money. A chattel, yes, but not a submissive and willing one. She fully intended to make him as miserable as he made her, for as long as they both should live.

Beyond that, she couldn't bring herself to think about her future, despite Justin's assertions her intended was old enough and unhealthy enough he wouldn't last long and she'd be free soon enough in the worst conceivable scenario.

That was easy for him to say when it was those daunting intervening years which terrified her the most. So much so that, until further notice, she only wanted to contemplate the present and cope with living in it hour by hour. And this hour, and very probably the next, would be spent here in this bath.

'My lady! You are wanted immediately in His Lordship's study.' Her flustered maid dashed in wide-eyed and snapped open a towel. 'We must make haste.'

'Does he know I am bathing, Agnes? And therefore indisposed?' At least her marriage would release her from her father's dictatorial demands. A tiny glint of sunlight in the darkness until she remembered she would be her husband's to order around instead.

'I don't think he cares, my lady. And in case you were thinking of defying him and taking your time, you should also know there has been an argument. A huge one. Between His Lordship and your brother. Your brother is fuming.' That didn't sound good. Justin wasn't one for arguing with their father. Or anyone for that matter. He always bowed down to pressure. 'I would even go as far as to say I've never seen him so angry.'

'Do we know what they were arguing about?' Lydia grabbed the proffered towel and began to rub herself down briskly while Agnes rushed around like a whirling dervish collecting undergarments and stockings.

'Your name was heard by the footman stationed in the hallway. And more than once, too, so I'm told.'

'Oh, dear.' Fresh dread settled in the pit of Lydia's stomach as she dressed. Justin was clearly having little luck fighting her corner this morning as he had promised and, with the sands of time rapidly running out, it appeared her fate was sealed. Her brother wasn't one to shout, unlike Lydia who was always too fiery. It was one of the reasons Justin sometimes managed to break through their father's stubbornness when she only ever met deaf ears. For Justin to be fuming and to have raised his voice, things had to be dire, when normally he would surrender swiftly and back away.

Their father did not like to be crossed and, knowing Papa, he'd have brought the wedding day forward as a punishment to the both of them for having the audacity to attempt to defy him.

While the maid laced up the back of her gown, Lydia gathered her damp hair into an unceremonious knot and clumsily pinned it to her head before flying out the door and into the vipers' pit.

She skidded to a halt outside, took a deep breath to steady herself and then knocked.

'Enter.'

Her father was sat behind his desk, looking fearsome despite his increasing frailty, yet suspiciously calm all things considered, whereas barely suppressed rage positively rippled off her brother in waves as he stood ramrod straight next to his elbow.

'There has been a development.' Never one for pleasantries, her father got straight to the point. 'A counter-offer.'

'I don't understand?' Her eyes flicked to Justin's for clarification and with gritted teeth he shook his head. 'From someone else?'

Please God let it be someone else!

'Someone else...'

Lydia's relief was so palpable, she slumped into the nearest chair. She wasn't going to marry a lecher. The miracle she had prayed for had occurred.

'Someone entirely unsuitable!' Her brother's fist slammed on the table, popping the bubble of relief before she had had a chance to enjoy it. 'Someone I cannot believe was allowed through the front door, let alone granted an audience!'

'He offered significantly more than what Kelvedon did for her!'

'Then let us use that as a bargaining chip and get Kelvedon to raise his offer!'

Lydia reeled back, stunned her brother would even suggest such a thing when he knew how much Kelvedon disgusted her.

'Getting ten out of him was like drawing blood from a stone!'

'Let me try, then... Perhaps I can convince him?'

Had Justin gone mad? He wanted to negotiate with the Marquess? Sell her to a man he knew she could not abide the sight of? 'I do not want to marry Kelvedon, Justin! Under *any* circumstances!'

The panic in her voice brought her brother up short and his expression instantly collapsed in remorse. 'I know, poppet...but the alternative...' He looked bilious. Pale. Scared.

'The alternative is a *lucrative* one.' An unspoken message passed between father and son, one she was clearly intended to be excluded from. 'It would be foolish to dismiss it and I am no fool and nor should you be. I insist we take it.' For the first time her father looked rattled, as if he, too, was frightened of the new candidate. 'As I see it, we have no choice in the matter anyway and it is agreed in principle already.'

'You never should have entered into a negotiation with *him*! And certainly not without me there!'

'The papers are being drawn up as we speak, Justin.' Her father said this with such finality, as if she wasn't in the room at all. 'Be advised I fully intend to sign them— irrespective of whether you agree with my decision or not. Until the earldom is yours to thoroughly ruin, what I decide still goes.'

'We would look like idiots! The laughing stock of the *ton*.'

'There are ways around that.'

'Kelvedon is a marquess! A respected peer and politician!' Words that she had heard her father use on her now came forcibly from her brother's mouth. 'The settlement papers are already signed! The Marquess could sue!'

'Not if we are clever about it.'

'He is in well with the government! Powerful in the Lords! We cannot afford to *alienate* him! You would jeopardise all that for a villain with the morals of a snake?'

'It is not in jeopardy. Lord Kelvedon need not know we are considering another.'

'You would sell your daughter—my sister—to a monster for a paltry few thousand pounds?'

A monster? The relief at there being another candidate was rapidly turning into a panic that she was heading for a worse fate. 'Who is he?'

Both men ignored her. 'In the long run Kelvedon is a better prospect...'

'It is the short run which concerns me most!' Her father raised one bony hand and snarled at her brother, 'Do you want to lose this house, Justin? Do you want to inherit an earldom consigned to our dilapidated estate in Cheshire? Hundreds of miles away from this city and the many entertainments you love *so very much*. Because there is not much joy to be had in Cheshire, I can tell you!'

They were about to lose the house? This house? They had given her no clue things were that dire. Debtors' prison for a little while rather than all-out destitution. Again Lydia stared pointedly at her brother, hoping he would clarify exactly what was going on, who the new villain of the piece was or at least hear him state for the record he would happily rusticate in Cheshire for ever and live on a diet of dried beans if it saved his sister from marrying either a lecher or a monster, only to watch him deflate as if all his fight was gone.

'No.' Just like that her brother backed down, his temporary bout of uncharacteristic bravery clearly over.

'Then stay out of this! You've done *quite* enough already, boy!' Another odd look passed between them, one which had Justin staring at his feet like an admonished child. 'Do you think I like this? I am livid, Justin! Livid! The nerve of the scoundrel beggars belief, but we have *no choice*. Not any more at any rate!'

Remembering she existed, her father finally turned to her, cold and matter-of-fact once again because it was the only emotion he could ever muster around Lydia.

'The offer is annoyingly conditional at this stage. The gentleman refuses to proceed unless *you* are in complete agreement with the terms and insists on hearing that agreement from your own lips in private. I am entrusting you to see that is done today, Lydia.' He glanced back down at his papers, dismissing her in his customary way, but she saw his shoulders slump as he suddenly looked very old. 'He is expecting you and I need not remind you the house of Barton is depending on you.'

Justin's pale face and downcast expression put fear into her soul. That he would rank Kelvedon above whoever the new candidate was spoke volumes in itself. 'Am I to be told who *he* is or must I guess?'

'It is Wolfe, Lydia.' Justin's eyes were desperate as they darted nervously to their father and back again. 'Owen Wolfe. And you *can* say no.'

Less than two hours later, her carriage pulled up outside Libertas. Or at least she assumed it was Libertas because there were no signs or clues that it was. To all intents and purposes, this grand building on the corner where elegant and refined Curzon Street met its neighbour, the more egalitarian Half Moon Street, was much like any other Mayfair town house. Significantly bigger, perhaps, because it occupied a corner plot so she could not see the back of it and was not joined in any way to the residences butted closely against it.

The four cream-stucco storeys were perfectly proportioned and symmetrical whichever street you happened to be standing on. The uniform windows were framed in stark white cornices decorated with intricately moulded garlands hanging beneath each sedately painted sill. Subtle black railings flanked the perimeter from the pavement, the only gap in them giving way to a huge set of double doors, painted in shiny ebony and adorned with just two enormous brass door handles in their centres which were slightly hexagonal in shape.

All in all, hardly the den of iniquity Justin had painted it to be. But then again, an elegant facade, whether it be on a house or a man, could be deceiving.

Still, and to her great consternation, the prospect of the man within appealed more than the aged groom her father had picked out. Owen vexed her, alternately made her furious or caused her to question her own sanity and consistently left her off-kilter—but at least he didn't turn her stomach. Far from it, heaven help her, not that she would ever admit as much to her brother. Or anyone else for that matter. Owen's continued hold over her was Lydia's intensely private shame to bear. He'd ruined her chances of ever settling for another man when he returned. Devil take him!

'All built from his ill-gotten gains, no doubt. A leopard doesn't change his spots no matter how much nonsense and misinformation he peddles around town.' Justin shook his head in disgust. 'When they locked him up, they should have thrown away the key.'

But they hadn't. They'd pardoned him. He had left the Antipodes lauded for his heroism by the governor of New South Wales himself. The moment he had set foot on the dock in Portsmouth stories had multiplied in the newspapers of the gross miscarriage of justice he had suffered at the hands of the English courts.

Had she known he was coming home, she would have done her best to avoid him. But he had appeared out of nowhere in Hyde Park one afternoon as she took her daily ride, looking even more handsome than he had when he had left, and the years they had been apart disappeared in a puff of smoke alongside the entire world around them.

He had wanted to talk and like a dolt she'd listened, hoping he would be remorseful for what he had done and eager to apologise. The traitorous female part of her which had once been completely in love with him wanted to hear him explain why he had done it, to fall on his sword and beg for her forgiveness and reassure her he was not that greedy, self-centred and duplicitous boy any longer, but a man who had never got over choosing greed above the one true love of his life.

But he was innocent, he had said, and not the least bit sorry for all the pain he'd caused. He also said he would prove it—but two years on she was still awaiting that proof and was furious at herself for spending at least the first six months praying he would find it.

What an idiot!

When every fool knew once bitten, twice shy.

It was only then she faced the harsh reality she had so desperately wanted to deny: that Owen Wolfe was nought but a charming liar and she must completely harden her heart against him.

Despite that, she had greedily read about Libertas in the gossip columns over the past year and listened to more gossip about the place among the ladies of her acquaintance. They all spoke of it like forbidden fruit. Decadent, luxurious…exciting. All words she would always associate with the man who owned it, because that was exactly what he had been when she had been foolish enough to succumb to his charms. Because that was how he had made her feel. His goodnight kisses had been decadent. Being basked in his attention had felt luxurious and their doomed and short-lived clandestine romance had been beyond exciting—before it all went to hell in a handcart, of course. Yet still he intrigued her despite it all.

Dratted man!

'Have you ever been inside?'

Justin shot her a horrified look. 'I wouldn't darken the scoundrel's door! At least not under any normal circumstances. This will be my first and hopefully my last visit here! The man repulses me.' He huffed out a sigh of regret and squeezed her hand. 'I'm sorry, Lydia…that was tactless of me. Obviously, if you do the unthinkable and agree to his insidious proposal, then I will make the best of things.'

Easy for him to say. He wasn't going to be the one shackled to him for life. And with Owen it would be for life. He was young and robust and unlikely to keel over at any moment like the dissolute Marquess of Kelvedon.

'However, for your sake I hope you do find the courage to turn him down.' Courage? What had Wolfe threatened to frighten her father so? Papa hated him. They all did. 'After all he has done to our family… When our mother lay dying…' He let the sentence trail off. Neither of them needed reminding of Owen Wolfe's crimes. 'I would sleep easier knowing he wasn't your lord and master. That is all.'

'You would prefer it to be Kelvedon?' Lydia could barely say the man's name without wincing.

'Of course not! He is not much better.'

'But you *do* think him better?' Which gave her a peculiar sinking feeling in her stomach.

'He is not a thief or a liar or a convicted criminal. With Kelvedon what you see is what you get. With Wolfe…well, who knows?' He gestured to the building with his gloved hands. 'How else does a motherless ragamuffin from a workhouse, an illiterate stable boy, a barefaced lying, swindling, cheating crook get all this?' Unfortunately, Owen was all those things and more. Her head knew that even while the irrational feminine part of her seemed keen to ignore it. 'He's been back…what? Two years? And he can afford to buy this grand house, start a lucrative club from scratch—and then still have enough left over for you?'

It did beggar belief, she supposed. The sums involved were astronomical.

'And with money which was not legitimately earned, I'll wager.' Justin continued to say the exact things which troubled her conscience. 'That is not a man I want to entrust my only sister to, no matter what our father has to say. It is clear to me he only wants you for revenge. That he will make you suffer because he was stupid enough to get himself caught.'

Certainly food for thought, but unpalatable whichever way you viewed it. The archetypal rock or hard place. Wolfe or Kelvedon? A shameless criminal who had an irrational hold on her or a disgusting but honest lecher? Neither appealed, but regardless of what her heart said, she would heed her brother's counsel. 'Papa will not be happy if I turn him down.'

'Is Papa ever happy?' Justin shook his head and smiled without humour. 'Leave him to me, poppet. I will be by your side to take all the blame once the deed is done and work my fingers to the bone to see we never have cause to regret turning down this dirty villain's money!' Usually averse to conflict and weak in the face of adversity, he suddenly seemed passionately determined to fight. Then his fierceness crumpled, replaced with pure remorse. 'You've been put in an impossible situation, Lydia, and I wish things could be different. I've been racking my brains trying to come up with another candidate... Another way to fix things...'

It was her turn to squeeze his hand. 'I am sure you have done your best, Justin.' Once their father's mind was made up, only a miracle would change it. 'It means the world knowing you are looking out for me.' That should make her feel better, but didn't. Poor Justin held no sway. Not when Kelvedon loomed once again and there was absolutely nothing now to be done about it. 'Come... Let's get this over with and then we can suffer the inevitable explosion from Papa together.'

She held his arm as they took the three marble steps together and hugged it tight when he knocked on the imposing front door, trying to remember she was a Barton and Bartons did what needed to be done.

It was opened straight away by the biggest man Lydia had ever seen. He was so tall, they both had to crane their necks to look up at him, so wide he practically filled the frame. He was dressed like a butler, but this man resembled no butler she had had the misfortune of encountering. His nose had been broken at least once and reset badly, as it had partially collapsed on the bridge and then veered off to the right. Both his front teeth were missing and etched into the skin of his cheek next to his right eye were three black ink tears. He looked every inch the criminal she suspected he was and somehow that strengthened her resolve. This *was* a den of iniquity. Filled to the brim with crooks, cheats and ne'er-do-wells. Owen's kind, not hers.

'Lady Lydia?' His accent was as coarse as his features, marking him as a man from the gutter as she suspected. She nodded, trying not to appear intimidated by this enormous brute of a gatekeeper. 'Owen's expecting you.'

Owen.

An equal, not a master.

Odd.

He stepped aside, but when they both went to pass, the brute halted Justin with one meaty hand. 'Owen wants to speak to her alone.'

'I am afraid that will not be happening… The very suggestion is highly improper. My sister needs an escort and that escort will be me.'

'Then I've instructions to send you both packing, my lord.' The brute planted his feet wide and crossed his arms. 'It's the lady on her lonesome, sir—or neither of you, I'm afraid.'

'Then it will be neither of us!'

'It's all right, Justin. I can do this myself.'

Lydia let go of his arm decisively and offered him her best brave smile when he looked about to argue. She wanted to do this. Needed to do it for the sake of her own pride. Whatever Owen was up to she wanted no part of it, was sick to the back teeth of the hold he had on her. While she might be for sale, she wanted to let him know not at any price.

'Wait in the carriage. I shan't be long. Owen Wolfe doesn't frighten me.'

If anything, this rude and eye-opening welcome to his dastardly domain merely made her decision to defy her father easier and to hell with the consequences.

Chapter Five

'She's here! I've instructed Slugger to bring her up.'

Randolph was bouncing with joy at this news, while Owen's heart was beating nineteen to the dozen at the prospect. Of all the stupid things he had ever done in his life, surely this was the most idiotic? He still couldn't quite believe what he had started and wasn't entirely sure why he'd been compelled to do it beyond a nagging sense it was right despite the plentiful and dangerous evidence to the contrary.

He wanted to blame Randolph for planting the seed in his head, but knew that wasn't fair. The wretch had been correct—he was a rescuer at heart and he had been hell-bent on rescuing her. In fact, he'd been a man possessed since last night, on a mission he didn't fully understand beyond the need to get it done and to hell with the consequences. Only now that she was here, those consequences were lining up like hungry paupers at a soup kitchen demanding to be fed.

He had offered to marry Lydia.

And if she accepted it was going to cost him most of the profits he had earned from Libertas since it opened.

Two things he knew already which were going to give

him nightmares. The first because of all the bad blood and baggage which no amount of lust or noble intentions were going to bridge. They were little better than strangers now, if one ignored the animosity, which of course they wouldn't. And the second because it threatened every belief he held dear. Money equalled power and power equalled control. His fortune was his armour. The bigger it got the more impenetrable it was. It didn't matter that he would probably earn it all back in about six months. For six months he would be without the means to fully protect himself if the need arose and that made him feel vulnerable and exposed. Thank goodness there was no chance of her saying yes.

She hated him.

For the first time in a decade he was ridiculously grateful for that fact.

'Shall I fetch some tea for us all? Me and Gertie are dying to finally meet her.'

'No tea. And no to *us all*. This is between me and her and I will do it without your interference.' Randolph would try to talk her into it. Just as he had talked to him. The only difference was a big part of Owen had wanted to be manipulated. The mad, glutton-for-punishment, stupid part of him.

'Well, that's hardly a warm welcome, now, is it? This is going to be her home—don't you want her to feel welcome in it?'

'This is business, Randolph. I couldn't care less if she feels welcome or not.' Owen grabbed his friend by the shoulders and turned him around, then began to march him to the far door in the back of the office which led to the private set of rooms beyond. 'This meeting is to discuss terms.' He might intend to be blasé about her refusal, but still he had no intention of doing it in front of an audience. 'If she is agreeable to mine, you can meet her later. If not, I see no point in making the acquaintance.'

'Even though it was my idea?'

'Especially because it was your idea.' Once this awkward and pointless meeting was over, he really was going to strangle Randolph. He'd been the one to put the flea in his ear and make him behave more irrationally than he had been already.

Marry her! The idea has merit! She's always been the itch you couldn't scratch!

Clearly just the seasoning his seething, bubbling cauldron of emotions had needed to make it boil over! For twelve hours he had been an irrational mess, possessed by an evil demon who had controlled his mind and suffocated all logic. Already, thanks to the furious stupor he had been in the grip of, Owen was three thousand pounds poorer and he knew without a doubt he would never see that hard-earned money again.

Three thousand pounds gone.

Pouf!

He was still reeling from the stupidity of the most ridiculous investment he had ever made.

He might as well have piled the banknotes on his desk and set the damn things alight!

'Can't I at least fix your cravat? That limp rag around your neck is hardly impressive…' Owen pushed him through the doorway and made sure he turned the key in the lock, imprisoning his meddling partner securely in the residential wing of the house, before he straightened his cuffs and glanced at his watery reflection in the windowpane.

His cravat was a disaster and he wouldn't care. He had no reason to impress Lydia when he was nobly offering to save her bacon and she would rather marry Kelvedon than let him save it.

Slipping on the mask of indifference he had last worn when the Earl of Fulbrook had begrudgingly granted him an audience at the crack of dawn this morning, Owen walked to the other door, the public-facing door, and tugged it open and almost jumped out of his skin because she stood inches from his face on the threshold.

'Is this your perverted idea of revenge?' As was usual nowadays, she was frowning at him as though he was something unpleasant trailed in from the street and stuck to the carpet.

'And a cheery good day to you, too.'

'The answer is no.'

'To what exactly?'

'To everything!' Her gloved hands exploded in the air. 'To all of it!'

'So you know everything and all of it already, then, do you?' Because he would lay good money she did not know the half of it.

'I know you are a thief and a liar! A scoundrel who stole my mother's jewellery while she lay dying in her bed! One who used me to shamelessly do it!'

'How many times do I need to tell you I never stole a single thing from your family?'

Twenty? Thirty? But since his first day back in London when he had expressly sought her out and tried to explain he was innocent, she had refused to hear any of it. *'Show me some proof,'* she had said with a look that could curdle milk. *'Some irrefutable and tangible proof, then I'll hear you out.'*

'I saw it with my own eyes, Owen!'

Something he was still no nearer to being able to explain despite trying his damnedest. He had left his tiny four-foot-by-six-foot room above the stables at dawn to do his job exactly as he always did and when they dragged him back there a few hours later, the damning evidence was concealed in his mattress and small cupboard. A battered silver locket, six paste brooches and three ugly silver candlesticks. None of it worth taking.

'You were caught red-handed.'

'To have been caught red-handed, Lydia, I would have had the damn jewels in my grubby fist at your mother's jewellery box in her bedchamber.' He had argued the same at the trial, too—not that it had got him anywhere. 'I was convicted with circumstantial evidence. Somebody planted those things in my room. I don't know who and I don't know why…'

It had tormented him. For almost a decade, the mystery had eaten him from the inside. He had racked his brains for years as to the culprit and their motive, needing to understand why he had been singled out when he was certain he'd had no enemies at eighteen, driving himself mad trying to work out what he could have possibly done to make somebody hate him so much.

All the days, weeks, months and years when he had been falsely imprisoned, he had plotted how he would uncover the truth upon his return and exact his revenge by seeing proper justice done. It was one of the things which had kept him from giving up, curling into a ball and allowing the punishing climate and dreadful conditions of Port Jackson to claim him as they had so many others. Near daily he'd even fantasised about how he would march up to the Earl of Fulbrook's front door, demanding a public apology, imagining how sweet a moment that would be and envisioning Lydia's reaction. Her sorrow for her mistake. Her relief… Her tears of joy as she begged him for forgiveness for ever doubting him. His benevolence as he proved he truly was the bigger man by instantly forgiving her so they could live happily ever after…

That part of his fantasy always irritated him. The blasted woman still had a hold on him and probably always would.

But despite his best efforts to unmask the perpetrator and after spending a great deal of hard-earned money on the quest, he was frustratingly still completely in the dark aside from the nagging suspicion it had something to do with her.

He had always felt it was something to do with her.

'And where is your proof?'

'I don't have it…' Nor was he searching any longer. After six months of fruitless investigation and despite the wily Randolph on the case, too, Owen had been either forced to give up or go insane with the constant frustration and the impenetrable dead ends.

Mostly he tried to bury it nowadays and move forward—except just the thought of Lydia always sent it jumping back to the fore. Undoubtedly because when he had first returned to England and sought her out to apprise her of the true facts, she had shaken her head pityingly at his version of events and said she had *hoped* he had come to apologise after explaining what had pushed him to do such a terrible thing because she wanted to understand and she *wanted* to forgive him.

Forgive him!

That monstrous insult still stuck in his throat.

'Oh, for goodness sake! Don't you ever tire of trotting out that lie?' His insistence on sticking to the truth always had the power to enrage her and by default him, too.

'It's not a lie.' It always took all his self-control not to spontaneously combust on the spot, although today he barely managed it. His teeth ached with the effort it took to appear calm. 'Whoever did it robbed me of seven years.'

'You stole her pearls, Owen! Her great-grandmother's pearls! While she slept! Have you no shame? No morals? She loved them so much. They were the only things she ever wore!' And here they went again, going round and round in unrelenting and never-ending circles, both furious at each other and with no end to that in sight. 'I'd rather marry Kelvedon than suffer a lifetime with you!'

An emotion dangerously resembling jealousy cut through the hurt and the anger of the injustice he had suffered and instantly clawed at his gut. 'Then marry him.' It took every ounce of his strength not to shout, 'See if I care.'

'I shall!' She spun in her heel.

'Even though his very presence disgusts you.' His tone might sound reasonable, but he couldn't stop himself pacing. Couldn't fully mask his exasperation. Here he was, determined to rescue her, and Lord only knew why when she wasn't worthy of the effort, and she was too blasted stubborn to let him!

'I know you, Lydia. I *know* that is how he makes you feel. I saw it with my own eyes only yesterday. I watched you baulk as he touched you.' An image he couldn't shake from his mind. 'His touch makes you sick to your stomach.'

'The thought of your touch makes me sick to my stomach, too!'

That hurt.

Exactly as it was supposed to. It took all his stubborn pride not to react and when he didn't, she couldn't resist throwing another poison dart.

'I wish I could erase every single one of them from my skin! I came here to tell you I'd rather be dead than marry you.'

She did haughty so well.

'And it is *my lady* to you! Not Lydia. Never call me by my first name again!'

The relief he expected to hear at her vociferous refusal did not come. Instead came a sort of calm panic which took control of his tongue. 'You are not even curious to know what I know or hear why I proposed such a ludicrous offer in the first place?'

He watched her dark eyes narrow slightly as doubt set in. 'We are agreed on something at least. It is ludicrous.' She marched passed him, then turned and stood ramrod straight in the centre of his office, the imperious icy glare down her nose doing little to conceal her obvious curiosity. 'You have five minutes.' As he was about to close the door on her ultimatum, she had the gall to tap her foot. 'And not a second more.'

'Then you might as well leave now, *my lady*.' Owen crossed his arms and leaned back against the frame, determined to call her bluff and enjoy doing it. He was sick and tired of her putting him in his place and damned if he would pretend to brush it off in his own blasted office. 'Visitors to Libertas dance to my tune, not the other way around.'

'Then this *is* revenge. Exactly as I suspected. Tell me, *Mr Wolfe*…is it as sweet as we are all so often told it is?' The question came out in a hiss. 'Does it make you feel inordinately smug to witness my family's downfall? Or are you merely inordinately smug as a matter of course nowadays?'

The tenuous grasp on his emotions almost snapped then and he very nearly slammed the heavy door shut in a fit of outraged pique. Instead, he settled for one deep, calming breath which did little to ease his barely suppressed and roiling temper. 'This isn't revenge, Lydia. Revenge suggests I had a hand in their downfall, when this mess is entirely your feckless brother's and pompous father's fault.'

'Do not insult my family!'

Owen held up his palm to stay her. Neither man was worth his respect, let alone her sacrifice, but she would blindly stand by them till the bitter end regardless—but she hadn't cared enough to stand by him. Even after the initial shock had worn off, he'd hoped she would come to her senses. Remember she loved him as he had loved her and realise he was incapable of the callous crimes he had been accused of.

'Much as it would delight me to lay claim to the lofty Barton family's *mighty* fall from grace, because heaven knows I suspect both your father and brother thoroughly deserve it, I never sent them spiralling into debt, nor did I have any part in their scurrying to court the richest peer willing to bail them out at short notice. All I am guilty of in this whole sorry debacle is of knowing who your dreadful betrothed was before you did and stupidly offering you a chance to escape him.'

'This is a noble sacrifice, then?' She clasped her hands in front of her face and sarcastically batted her eyelashes. 'Borne out of your selfless desire to rescue a damsel in distress.' Those expressive brown eyes narrowed again and she stalked towards him, waving her finger. 'Exactly how gullible do you think I am? I know you, too, Owen!' That finger prodded him in the chest. 'You are up to something!'

'Well, of course I am up to something! You didn't seriously think I would offer something as monumental as marriage unless there was something in it for me, did you?'

She opened her mouth to speak, then closed it again, blinking back at him, confused. Owen decided to take that as a good sign—although good for who at this stage he wasn't entirely certain. Things weren't exactly going according to plan. He was supposed to have waved her off happy when she refused his proposal, not try to discuss her decision or sway it. Or inhale her perfume. Why the blazes was he always seduced by that perfume?

But by her temporary silence, at least he had regained control of the argument.

'Why don't we sit?' He needed the barrier of his desk between them. A solid oak barricade separating him from the intoxicating scent of the sultry jasmine she had always favoured. He could never smell that damn flower without thinking of her. Neither could he escape it. A version had grown rampantly wild in Port Jackson, he was convinced simply to torture him. 'Then we can discuss business.'

'*Business?*' She stared at him as if he had gone mad as he led her to a chair and continued to glare as he sat himself opposite and found himself staring back.

Where to start? He was blowed if he knew where this was going. Fortunately, she threw him a haughty bone.

'What could *you* possibly know that *I* do not?'

'I know that Kelvedon's money wouldn't make much of a dent in the debt.' Owen opened the drawer in his desk and took out the sheet of foolscap containing all of Randolph's diligently acquired findings and slid it across the table. 'These are the most pressing debts we know about.'

He watched her scan the list, her eyes widening here and there at the sheer scale of them. Alongside long-outstanding amounts owed to a vast array of shops, merchants and tailors from Bond Street to Cheapside, who were sick and tired of waiting for payment, there were several loans still owing to four separate banks. All other debts aside, those loans totalled an eye-watering six thousand pounds in their own right. Owen and Randolph had purchased and luxuriously renovated Libertas with significantly less.

When she finally looked back up at him, clearly dumbstruck, he felt bad that he was yet to tell her the worst.

'There's more, I'm afraid.' He handed over the parchment which had gained him the audience with her father. 'Three years ago your father mortgaged the house in Berkeley Square. For over a year, he has failed to pay even the interest, let alone any of the principle sum, and has refused point blank to engage in any conversation with the gentleman who lent him the money as to when he will repay the debt.'

Doubtless Fulbrook thought the Cheapside merchant far beneath him and content to wait *ad infinitum* because he was a peer of the realm. 'In desperation, the gentleman concerned began legal proceedings to take possession of the property as he has every right to do under the law. The case was due to be heard in a fortnight...' Although the merchant would have no need of the law now that Owen had doubtless made his year by purchasing the rotten debt from him.

Pouf!

Three thousand pounds...gone just like that.

'Papa intimated we were about to lose the house...' He watched her gaze fix on the underlined mortgage total with resignation. 'But I had no idea things were this dire.'

'There are also your brother's debts.' Her head snapped up.

'What?' He could tell by her expression this came as a complete surprise. 'Justin owes money, too?'

'I am afraid so. He owes six months to the Albany for his bachelor lodgings...' a ludicrous situation to have got himself into when his father had an enormous house on Berkeley Square he could have lived in for free '...and has separate tailors' bills and other incidentals outstanding.' Justin Barton also allegedly owed money to some very unsavoury characters. Men who preyed on the desperate. He couldn't categorically prove that yet, not with *irrefutable* and *tangible* proof, so kept it to himself. 'They add at least another thousand. Maybe more.'

Definitely more.

The trouble with borrowing money from unsavoury characters was they tended to play their cards very close to their chest unless they were all done waiting for payment. A few were shouting very loud and would undoubtedly insist their debts be paid first and foremost or would seek reimbursement via other methods. Owen suspected there were many more who could throw their hats into the ring if they too became impatient. Until they did, those dubious *gentlemen's agreements* would be hard to trace.

'I did not realise my brother had debts, too.' This news seemed to bother her. 'Mind you, I wasn't aware of my father's until recently either.'

'I don't suppose it is something which is discussed around the dinner table.'

'Or with daughters.'

He saw her dark eyes cloud and felt for her. Clearly her father's uninterest in her had not improved in the years since he'd left the Barton residence. Lydia had always been largely ignored, which had been the single biggest reason he had been able to befriend her in the first place. They had both been alone in the world, both deemed insignificant by everyone else and at best a means to an end. Something Owen would no longer stand for now he was master of his own destiny, but clearly Lydia's situation and her own self-worth had not improved else she wouldn't be considering Kelvedon.

The whole sorry situation and her family's solution left a bad taste in his mouth. What had those near-sighted supposed gentlemen expected? Her brother's ratcheting debts on top of years of her father's slapdash misman-agement and flagrant overspending were bound to come back to haunt them all sooner rather than later. Any fool could have seen that a mile off. Belts should have been tightened years ago; pennies should have been diligently looked after to save the pounds. Instead, the Barton men had preferred to bury their heads in the sand for the sake of appearances rather than facing their financial problems head-on. Private opera boxes and copious pairs of Hoby boots were a ridiculous extravagance when the family was strapped for cash.

Selling off Lydia to bail them out of trouble was not only grossly unfair—it was, in Owen's humble opinion, ultimately pointless.

The Earl was too old and pompous to change his ways and his heir was too weak-willed to do what was really nec-essary either. The money they got from Lydia was merely a stay of execution if neither man fundamentally changed their ways. Where Owen came from, credit in any form was never an option, so it had never occurred to either him or Randolph to spend beyond their means or attempt to purchase anything without first saving up the funds. Yet another stark difference between her world and his he would never truly understand.

'Obviously these are just the London debts. There are probably more in Cheshire...' He hadn't meant to say that. In thinking out loud he was in danger of rubbing salt into the wound and, more worryingly, inadvertently giving her more solid reasons to say yes to his ill-thought-out proposal which he had made in the irrational heat of the moment.

'Exactly how much are we talking about? In total.' The defiant ice queen was gone, replaced by a pale and defeated version of Lydia he didn't want to witness when he had always adored her spirit.

'I estimate it to be at least fifteen thousand—assuming I have uncovered everything.' Which in less than a week, and even with the tenacious Randolph on the case, he likely hadn't.

'I see.' She stared down at her hands. 'The Marquess of Kelvedon's money really isn't enough, is it?'

'No.'

Only her eyes lifted. All the usual heat in them missing. 'And what have you offered?'

'Ten... Alongside the immediate settlement of all the outstanding mortgage debt.' A necessary lie now that the deeds were his lock, stock and barrel. He had shamelessly used it as leverage with her father to get what he wanted, but which he wouldn't use on the daughter. Owen wouldn't blackmail her into marriage. Irrespective of his wasted three thousand, she either did it willingly or not at all.

'Why?'

A fair question and one he really did not know the true answer to beyond the overwhelming compulsion to save her.

'I see a business opportunity.'

Owen had to fight the urge to stand up and pace again or even run a frustrated hand through his hair at the lie because he would never admit to the jealousy, confusion and sense of responsibility which was eating him from the inside.

'You are an earl's daughter. A well-connected earl's daughter with a great many society friends and acquaintances. You would give me the veneer of respectability I would never be able to achieve on my own. That opens doors... Brings in new clients... More money.'

'You expect me to believe this is about money now and *not* revenge?' She shook her head and laughed without any trace of humour.

'Everything is about money.'

He almost added money equalled power and power equalled control—but stopped himself just in time. It gave her too much of an insight into the insecurities he would likely never be able to shake and did not want anyone to be able to exploit ever again. 'But perhaps there is a little bit of revenge in the mix, too. Hardly a surprise all things considered—and I am only human.'

Except he hadn't particularly enjoyed wielding that mortgage deed this morning and informing the pompous Earl of Fulbrook that he could evict him from the house whenever he saw fit if he didn't give Lydia the opportunity to consider his proposal. He had been too concerned with her welfare to savour the irony of the moment.

'Your father is keen to keep on the right side of your current fiancé, especially as the settlements have been signed, therefore we will have to elope before your engagement to Kelvedon makes the newspapers. If you are agreeable, tonight makes the most sense, I suppose.' Events were rapidly spiralling out of his control and he hoped at least managing that detail would make him feel less... adrift. 'It will cause a bit of a scandal, I'm afraid, but in many ways that works in my favour.'

'It also works in my father's.' The disappointment at her sire was unmistakable in her tone. 'He can entirely blame me for causing it and publicly lament my usual wilfulness while appearing completely blameless in front of his precious Marquess. Before he shamelessly pockets your money, of course, and slaps himself on the back for making such a favourable deal. I assume he gets that money as soon as the unpleasant deed is done—not before.'

Owen nodded. 'Call me sentimental—but I really do not trust your father as far as I can throw him.'

'And we are supposed to forget the past and simply

spend eternity together? Blithely build a home and family on non-existent foundations?'

The pang of something dangerously resembling longing caught him off guard before he ruthlessly dismissed it. She still hated him. The thought of his touch still made her sick to her stomach.

'If you think I am offering you a proper marriage, in every sense of the word, Lydia, think again. I want neither of those things.' Not any more at any rate.

'Then what are you proposing?'

If only he knew! He barely recognised himself right now and had no clue where this was going. 'A business transaction. Nothing more, nothing less. Your connections in society, your expertise in navigating it and your public support and endorsement in exchange for my thirteen thousand pounds.'

'My public support?'

'Balls, entertainments, invitations. Beyond these four walls we behave as though we are a doting couple.'

'And within them?'

The sticky bit. The bit he was least convinced by and most at odds with. 'I propose we stay well away from one another.'

At this, she seemed to relax, which shouldn't hurt but did. Much more than Owen bargained for.

'Beyond that, will I be granted any freedoms or are these four walls all I can expect?'

What a ridiculous question! Unless she really did think him a monster? Really did hate him to her core?

'You are not a prisoner, Lydia. As long as you stick to the terms of our arrangement, I have no interest in where you go, what you do, or who you do it with.'

Owen regretted the last assertion as soon as it left his mouth. Certain things would bother him. A few would send him insane. He knew that with the same certainty as he knew he was currently, and apparently wilfully, walking blindly into perhaps the biggest catastrophe of his life.

Out of his control.

Likely uncontrollable, too.

Both things scared the hell out of him. Thanks to blasted Randolph and his own nagging conscience, he was in the middle of the Pacific again, only this time, in a rickety, leaking old rowboat in the midst of a roaring tempest. Madness. Total, utter, preventable madness. In fact, he should abandon the idea immediately.

'That is my offer. Take it or leave it.'

And because his stupid heart was racing at his own inability to stop himself from walking headlong into disaster and all the potentially disastrous ramifications if she miraculously agreed, it was his turn to tap his foot. 'You have five minutes. Not a second…'

'Yes.'

The floor shifted beneath his feet.

'Are you sure?' Owen felt sick as fear warred with incredulity. Relief with panic. 'You do not need proper time to think about it?'

Because he did. He suddenly needed to think of a damn good way to untangle himself from this mess before the relentless quicksand sucked him under.

The far door suddenly flew open accompanied by the ominous rattle of cups and an innocently grinning Randolph. It didn't take a genius to work out the menace had been listening at the keyhole at the same time as he'd been picking the blasted lock.

'Who fancies some tea?'

Chapter Six

It had been way past midnight when the carriage finally trundled into the inn at Gretna Green. In view of the lateness of the hour, the exhaustion of the travellers after nearly four whole days on the road and the lack of any genuine haste or fear of any family members chasing them as was the tradition with most usual elopements, Owen had decided against rousing the local smithy from his slumber and had taken rooms instead so the pair of them could rest.

Lydia, however, had got precious little sleep. It was hard to drift off when you were stood on the edge of a metaphorical cliff and about to leap headfirst into the unknown. For the last few days she had been focused solely on the chore of getting through the wedding, when the wedding was the least of her problems now that her for ever was about to begin.

Her life, as she had always known it, was likely never to be quite the same again. While she wouldn't grieve leaving the soulless, gilded prison of her father's house, the place where she had always been largely invisible and barely tolerated, she was entering into a union with a man she did not know, had probably never known in truth, nor ever hope to understand.

The old open, optimistic, impetuous, fiery and charming Owen of her youth was gone. He was still thoroughly charming. At least he had been right up until he had proposed marriage to her and clearly still impetuous if their unexpected and hasty elopement was any gauge. But the optimism and openness were no more, all the fire had been dampened, instead replaced by the cynical, emotionless businessman who played his cards close to his chest and refused to allow her to see what he was thinking.

Despite spending all of four days together, they had barely exchanged more than two dozen words because he never shared the fast coach he had provided for her lacklustre escape, preferring to ride alongside on his own.

Even when they stopped at the frequent staging inns to change the horses or when they set up camp in one overnight, he kept himself to himself, honouring his promise of them staying well away from one another. Lydia rode alone, ate alone and took herself to each strange bed alone, depressed he knew her situation was so desperate he did not even bother having a man stand guard overnight because he was supremely confident she would still be where he had left her in the morning.

Such were the terms of their peculiar arrangement, she supposed, and her particular and slightly uncomfortable bed to lie in.

All alone.

Although whether or not that was part of their arrangement to avoid one another she was yet to discover. The marriage bed, like so many other things, had not been discussed at all. Perhaps they would be discussed today, once the deed was done and it was too late to turn back? He might have said he was not offering a proper marriage in every sense of the word, but he had not really clarified what that meant. Men were a slave to their urges—or so her mother had said one day when Lydia had discovered her father kept a mistress—and if that was the case, then surely he would expect the conjugal rights the law made explicit for husbands?

She wasn't entirely sure what she thought about that. Awkward, definitely. Nervous, understandably, yet unbelievably curious. She and Owen had done things all those years ago—some quite scandalous things, truth be told—but not *that* thing. And as much as she had claimed a desire to erase all those illicit kisses and inappropriate caresses from her mind, to herself at least she would be honest about those memories. His touch had been divine.

Perhaps a little too divine because she had been only too happy to allow him to be a little bolder each time he had crept into her bedchamber. Enough that she would have been thoroughly ruined if anyone had ever found out. Owen had been her delicious secret and within the hour he would be her husband and everyone would know about them.

Lydia stared at her reflection in the mirror for a final time, sighed at the sensible woollen travelling dress and decided she would have to do. It was not at all the wedding dress she had always envisaged for herself, but then again neither was the wedding, so what difference did it make? Within minutes she would be married by a blacksmith in front of two complete strangers and within hours she would be headed back on the interminable road to London.

Putting on the pretty frock she had packed on a silly whim for the occasion seemed both foolish and inappropriate. It was not as if her groom would care. He hadn't even bothered to check on her this morning, preferring to ferry messages backward and forward via the innkeeper's wife. The last had stated he was waiting downstairs. Lydia had made him wait a full fifteen minutes despite being dressed and ready out of sheer stubbornness.

A tiny, pointless and pathetic act of rebellion which she sincerely doubted he had even noticed.

With a sigh, she opened the door and descended the narrow stairs to the taproom below.

'What kept you?' Clearly he had noticed and had been pacing while he waited, which gave her some comfort. She could tell by the slightly dishevelled state of his hair he wasn't quite as in control of his emotions as he wanted her to believe. Hair he still ran his hands through when he was impatient or irritated. The only two emotions she seemed to have no trouble eliciting from him nowadays when all he cared about was getting his own way. 'I only paid the witnesses for the hour.'

'As I doubt it will be a long service, you are likely guaranteed to get your money's worth.'

His tawny eyebrows drew together momentarily before she watched him consciously smooth them out. The action made her wonder if he was not as cool, calm and confident about what they were doing as he tried to convey. It did not make her feel any better knowing he had grave doubts, too. Surely he could see this was doomed to end badly. 'I suppose we'd better get it over with.'

'Yes. I suppose we should.' She expected he would offer his arm and found herself frowning at his back when he didn't. He hadn't touched her once since the meeting in his office. Not even to assist her into the carriage. Starting as he meant to carry on? Who knew? Lydia certainly didn't.

He paused in the courtyard, waiting for her to catch up, and walked alongside her, leaving a telling gap of at least three feet between them as they went in painful silence towards the austere-looking blacksmith's shop in the centre of a crossroads. The crossroads somehow more symbolic this morning than the prospect of smithy because the ceremony was no longer what worried her. It was everything else.

Owen opened the narrow black door and waited for her to pass through it without meeting her eyes.

She sensed him behind her as she took in the scene, trying and failing not to feel overwhelmed by it all. The space was every inch a working blacksmith's, with no flowers or pomp or ceremony. One of the four walls was dominated by the thick chimney breast and the huge bellows used to keep the fire roaring. The others held various tools hung haphazardly from ancient, bent and rusty nails. Then there was nothing else except the battered and aged tree stump in the centre of the room which held the anvil they would take their vows over, two scruffy locals who were being paid to be their guests and the blacksmith in his sooty leather apron. All three were smiling in a manner which implied they believed she and Owen were a pair of star-crossed lovers desperate to be together no matter what. Another miserable aspect of this whole sorry but calculated debacle.

'Mr Wolfe—what a pretty bride ye have!' The smithy nudged Owen playfully. 'No wonder ye have brought her here in haste. I'd be keen, too, if I had such a bonny fiancée.' Another nudge, this one accompanied by a wink. Then, to her utter mortification, he turned to her. 'And ye, lassie, are lucky to have found such a handsome man. The pair of you are destined to make such beautiful bairns...' He dropped his voice to a whisper and winked again. 'Unless a bairn is the reason you are here?'

'No...um...bairns.' Another not-inconsequential detail they were still to discuss. 'Yet.' If ever. The prospect of never made her suddenly sad.

'Or at least not that ye know of, eh?' The blacksmith laughed at his own words, nudging Owen conspiratorially, and she felt her cheeks heat at the bawdy insinuation. 'But better to be safe than sorry. That's what I always say. Are ye both ready?'

'Yes.' They said it simultaneously and the three locals grinned again, assuming the emphatic response was down to excitement rather than sheer embarrassment.

'Then let's deal with the necessary legalities before we get to the vows, shall we?' His grinning face bobbed between them. 'I can see you are both beyond the age of consent so no need to ask you that. Is your name, sir, Mr Owen Wolfe and do you hail from Half Moon Street in London?'

'That is correct.'

'And you, missy? Are you Lydia Catherine Emily Olivia Jane Barton from Berkeley Square?'

'I am.' Although she was surprised Owen had known all her names so thoroughly to be able pass them on. There were so many of them she could barely keep track of them herself. They were all even spelled correctly on the certificate in front of the smithy, so clearly her husband-to-be wasn't the illiterate stable boy any longer. Just as he wasn't a lot of the things she remembered any longer.

She had started teaching him to read before his arrest at his insistence. He had always dreamed of bettering himself and saw learning to read as an essential step. He must have continued those studies somewhere, yet when one considered where he had been that feat could not have been easy, and she was strangely proud of him for doing it in spite of the difficulties. He also now had the business, the fortune and, in some quarters, the respect he had always wanted. With the added veneer of an earl's daughter for a wife, she had no doubt the sky was the limit for him. Regardless of how he had achieved it all, his single-minded determination was impressive. Or calculated and ruthless, depending on your point of view. Lydia's fell squarely in the latter.

'Are you both unmarried and free to enter into this union?'

They both nodded and watched him scratch the details down with a tatty quill on the cheap paper. 'And did ye both come here of your own free will and accord?'

Another nod. Duty and opportunity. Undoubtedly the two most depressing reasons to marry. 'Then let us proceed. Take your good lady's hand, Mr Wolfe…'

Stiffly, she offered it and, just as awkwardly, he took it. However, the second he did Lydia instantly felt odd, only too aware of the comforting heat and size of his, although bizarrely better about what they were about to do.

'Owen Wolfe, do you take this woman to be your lawful wedded wife, forsaking all others, keep to her as long as ye both shall live?'

'I will.'

Was that a catch in his voice? Nerves? Emotion? Regret?

'And do you, Lydia Catherine Emily Olivia Jane Barton, take this man to be your lawful wedded husband, forsaking all others, keep to him as long as you both shall live?'

As long as you both shall live…

Eternity!

Lydia found herself gripping Owen's hand tighter. 'I will.'

Then all of a sudden there was a ring. A simple, plain gold band which had the power to send her pulse rocketing and made the blood pound in her head so loudly the blacksmith's next words seemed to come disjointed from afar.

She felt Owen's hand slide the ring on her finger and heard his voice loud and sure. 'With this ring I thee wed, with my body I thee worship…'

Lydia's heart skipped a beat and the room instantly became very warm.

'With all my worldly goods I thee endow, in the name of the Father, Son and Holy Ghost. Amen.'

Auctioned, bought and paid for.

No longer her father's chattel, but her husband's. No longer a Barton, but a Wolfe.

Lady Lydia Wolfe.

A name, she realised, which felt inevitable. One she had practised long ago with various-sized quills and ink in the privacy of her own bedchamber until she had perfected the signature. She remembered burning them, too, the same day he broke her heart, then mourning the loss of him keenly for months afterwards despite hating him for what he had done. Yet, with all that, she had never truly got over him—which was a sobering thought.

She heard the tremor in her own voice as she clumsily repeated what the blacksmith instructed. By the way his blue eyes turned stormy, so did Owen. Then their convenient anvil priest smiled at his paltry congregation.

'For as much as this man and this woman have consented to go together by giving and receiving a ring, I therefore declare them to be man and wife before God and these witnesses. In the name of the Father, Son and Holy Ghost.' The blacksmith and the witnesses beamed at them. 'Amen.'

Lydia saw Owen's Adam's apple bob as he stared straight ahead and realised she was struggling to swallow herself now the sheer enormity of what they had done was only just beginning to sink it. But his hand wrapped around hers was sure and steady. Comforting. Safe.

Safe? Where had that come from when only a moment ago she had thought him ruthless? Yet safe was what she felt and bizarrely relieved, although what about she had no earthly clue.

'Now comes the bit when you kiss her.' The smithy

nudged the groom and all at once a veil of dense awkwardness descended. Owen hesitated, blinked and then, as if he was only doing it on sufferance and would rather be doing absolutely anything else instead, bent to kiss her. Although it was so quick and the contact so minimal it hardly constituted a kiss at all and once again Lydia was strangely disappointed, acknowledging to herself she had always revelled in his kisses before and had perhaps been anticipating doing so again. Nobody had ever kissed her like Owen Wolfe.

Chapter Seven

Another icy droplet of rain found its way under Owen's collar and trickled painfully down his spine to join its companions already gathered in the waistband of his now sodden breeches. It had been pouring since sunset, which meant it had been pouring for at least four hours already and the angry storm clouds which periodically gave him a brief glimpse of the full moon suggested the rain wasn't likely to stop any time soon.

Ahead, his two loyal coachmen were hunched in their own greatcoats uncomplaining, although they were undoubtedly soaked to the skin exactly as he was. So far, he had made them drive past five cosy-looking inns which were perfect to spend the night in. He didn't have the heart to make them drive past the one looming in the distance, no matter how much he wanted to. It wasn't fair to make them plough through the night just so he could avoid it. Because this wasn't just any old night.

This was his wedding night.

And wedding nights usually promised certain things.

But there was no putting off what was undoubtedly going to be one very awkward conversation any longer. Fate was conspiring with the elements against him, and his begrudging bride hadn't been able to stretch her shapely legs in hours.

Resigned, yet still dreading it, he kicked his horse on ahead and flagged the coachman to pull in, feeling like a coward for hoping this particular inn was miraculously full and he would be granted a reprieve of another few hours more.

But of course it wasn't, because nobody in their right mind traversed the Great North Road this late at night in the middle of November in a deluge.

Before his carriage rattled into the stable yard, Owen sought out the innkeeper and paid in advance for the three rooms. One for his men and one each for himself and his new wife.

'Coming back from Gretna, are you?'

Owen nodded curtly, in no mood to make conversation.

'We get a lot of honeymooners here.' The man grinned knowingly as he handed him the keys. 'Fear not—' He wiggled his bushy eyebrows for good measure as he slapped Owen on the back. 'The beds are sturdy, my friend. Even with a big fellow like you…'

As he said this, Lydia came in and paused mid-step, her eyes widening at the comment she had quite clearly overheard. Owen knew exactly what she was thinking. It was along the same lines of what the innkeeper was thinking, and probably his men, too.

The wedding night.

Which was most definitely not going to happen.

Owen had assumed as much days ago when she had informed him the thought of merely his touch made her sick to her stomach. Such an emphatic declaration had hardly boded well for unbridled passion. Rather than imagining a stoic and reluctant Lydia tolerating the unseemly intrusion, it had been easier to blot the spectre of the marriage bed out of his mind to mentally reinforce the terms of their original agreement. A public facade and complete private avoidance.

But then he had stood beside her at the anvil, felt her squeeze his hand, felt the air around them shift. To his complete surprise, he hadn't needed to choke the damn vows out at all because in that charged and surreal moment he suddenly meant them. Each and every one of them! For a few ethereal seconds, as they stared at one another, hand in hand, it was as if fate had brought them full circle to exactly where they were always meant to be. Together. Undoubtedly nearly a decade too late and by the most convoluted route possible, but they were there and that was all that mattered.

Then he had watched her expression change from a little overwhelmed to downright petrified and he realised she did not feel at all the same way about their union. To her he was still the heartless thief and would likely never forgive him for the crimes she was convinced he had committed. If anything, and to confirm his suspicion, she had looked ready to run before her blasted duty to her feckless family forced her into staying. At best, she was marrying him on sufferance. A harsh reality not dissimilar to being plunged headlong into an ice bath and all at once he had felt both foolish and furious. Enraged at the inexplicable hold she held over him and how easily he could still be bewitched when he was around her.

What an idiot! What a huge mess! And now they were stuck with each other. Her with the utmost reluctance and him more than a little bit devastated at that insurmountable fact. If only he had the evidence. The undeniable proof she had asked for...? His teeth ground together as the usual anger simmered, because evidence or no, she should have believed him.

'Can I fetch you both a bit of supper?' The innkeeper smiled at Lydia who only stared back, her feet rooted to the spot like a fox caught in the light of a lantern. 'There's some stew left and perhaps even enough of my wife's meat pie to share between the two of you.'

'Either would be good,' Owen answered for her. A meal delayed the awkwardness. Sitting across the table from her in view of the few intrepid evening drinkers who were propping up the bar gave him somewhere impersonal to reassure her he wouldn't be darkening her door tonight or any time soon. As much as he would love to scratch the itch which seemed to constantly plague him, he couldn't bear the thought of scratching it like this. The guilt would destroy him.

So he would tell her straight she was off the hook. With a potential audience there would be no scene. No histrionics or impassioned declarations. The conversation would need to be conducted in quiet voices with the minimum of fuss. Dispassionate and impersonal and thoroughly depressing. He would instigate it, be matter-of-fact and he would pretend he could not see the sheer relief at the reprieve he had tossed her despite just the thought of it being unsettling to him.

'Then I shall fetch it right this minute.'

The innkeeper scurried off and Owen took himself to the most private-looking of the tables near the window. He pulled out a chair for her and felt himself wince when she walked slowly towards it like a condemned man on the way to the gallows.

Lydia sat primly on the very edge of her seat, her knees pressed together tightly as if protecting her virtue already from his perverse and base urges. Part of him wanted to shout at the implied insult because while he might well have a great many overwhelming urges where she was concerned, he could damn well control them and shame on her to even think he couldn't. Another part wanted to reassure her everything was going to be all right, to vanquish, then extinguish the abject fear he could see shining in her widened eyes and make her feel better.

Always the rescuer, just as Randolph said. Sometimes Owen hated that innate trait which ran so strong in him that even the harsh existence in Antipodes couldn't knock it out.

'I suppose there are a few important matters we still need to discuss.' God, this was awful. His throat was dry, his tongue suddenly too big for his mouth. 'Some parameters and logistics...' He sounded like an engineer planning a new bridge or an umpire at a cricket match. 'What I mean is...'

'Your dinner is upstairs waiting for you!' The innkeeper seemed to appear out of nowhere and for some inexplicable reason his announcement made him stare at the battered wood of the tabletop willing the food to appear here where he had planned to nonchalantly choke it down.

'I'm sorry?'

'It is being laid out as we speak in your private dining room, sir.'

'I didn't order a private dining room.' The very last thing he wanted was a private dining room or any other private room come to that which also happened to have her in it.

'It is part of your suite.'

'I didn't order a suite either.'

'You most definitely did, sir.' The smile was a tad patronising this time, tinged with annoyance. 'Two rooms for you and your new lady wife.'

'When I requested two rooms...' Several of the intrepid drinkers stopped staring into their flagons to watch the entertainment, making Owen's toes curl inside his boots as he dropped his voice to a whisper. 'I meant two *bedrooms*.'

The innkeeper's patronising smile gave way to one of pity as he focused his gaze on the wide-eyed bride and then slowly back to what he feared was an equally wide-eyed groom. 'Well, isn't that a novel request…what with you both fresh from Gretna and all.' Then to Owen's complete mortification, he decided to offer them some sage marital advice in the loudest whisper ever known to man.

'It's only natural to be nervous, Mr and Mrs Wolfe— but delaying it 'tis only going to make the nerves worse now, isn't it? Why don't I send up a bottle of good brandy to go with yer dinner? Help you both to ease into the pro-ceedings…'

As Owen willed the floor to open up and his brain to come up with a suitable response which did not leave him looking like either a pathetic specimen of a man who couldn't do what was expected or a lust-fuelled clod who had clearly put the fear of the Almighty into his blushing bride, he saw two of the intrepid drinkers abandon their stools to edge nearer. The openly curious men made no secret of the fact they were eavesdropping and were po-sitioning themselves to spectate properly on his utter hu-miliation, expressions of curious anticipation written all over their weather-beaten faces.

'Or I have some sherry if the lady prefers it? Not that there is anything wrong with a man drinking the stuff, too, if that's what pleases ye…'

'Just the dinner will suffice.' Owen had had quite enough of being thoroughly emasculated in public. With a mortifying screech, he pushed his chair from the table and grabbed Lydia's hand. 'Come, Wife!'

Come, Wife? What sort of thing was that to say? He winced as he tugged her towards the stairs, forcing himself not to take the blasted things two at a time in his desire to escape. Worse, if indeed things could get worse, his enormous hands couldn't muster the ability to open the door properly once they got to it. The two spectators were now stationed at the foot of the stairs grinning as he fumbled with the blasted latch—which meant he practically flung it at the wall in his bid to open the damn thing when it finally gave way. The door responded by hitting the plaster with a resounding crash which punctuated the brittle silence spectacularly to further entertain the amused patrons below, who made no attempt to muffle their laughter in the slightest.

He stalked in, only to see the slightly stunned but smiling face of what he assumed was the innkeeper's wife as she placed down the last plate of steaming vegetables on an intimate table set for two. The only candles lit in the room came from a pretty candelabrum set just off from the middle of the table, leaving the besotted newlyweds ample space to gaze adoringly at one another across the lace tablecloth and even hold hands if they had a mind to.

'Will you be wanting me to bring up some dessert later, sir?'

'No!' He practically barked it. 'Thank you.'

'Then I shall bid you both goodnight...'

The woman glanced back over her shoulder to the wide-open door of the bedchamber beyond with a grin. The big, sturdy canopied bed dominated the space, mocking him, the covers neatly turned down on each side of the mattress in case they were too overcome with passion to have the wherewithal to manage that themselves.

'I've already turned down the covers.'

She winked at him as she breezed past and then, to Owen's horror, did the same to Lydia before pulling the door closed with an ominous click.

Keen to take back control of the situation, while slowly dying on the inside, he found himself marching into the bedchamber and snatching up a pillow, then wrestled off one stubborn blanket, before marching back and tossing them both decisively on the floor next to the table.

'I'll sleep in here!'

Her only reaction was to blink. 'On the floor?'

'I've slept on worse!' Because he was still nowhere near in control of his emotions, he heard himself clarify the arrangement with extreme belligerence. 'And I shall spare you the need to barricade yourself in, madam! I have no desire to visit your bed, Lydia! *Not* tonight and *not* ever!' Despite knowing that if he had to resort to shouting he was wrong, he shouted the last part anyway. 'Ours is a marriage in *name* only! And you'd do well to remember that!'

The obvious thing to do after such an impassioned declaration was to storm out, only thanks to the taproom filled with nosy onlookers downstairs and the enormous bedchamber in front of him, he had nowhere else to go. Lydia, damn her, made no move to leave the room either.

'Now you have got that off your chest, can we eat? Or are you going to start throwing the food around next?'

'You want to eat?'

Flabbergasted, he watched her pull out a chair and sit before she lifted the lid of a tureen and took a sniff. 'As tempting as it is to join you in a tantrum, because Lord only knows I am as horrified by our situation as you are, I haven't eaten anything since luncheon and I am starving.'

'Oh…'

She dunked the ladle in the stew, filling it to the brim. 'Shall I dish some up for you or do you still need to wave your arms around some more?'

Then to his utter horror she started to laugh. He had a

sneaking suspicion it was at him and that made him feel even more ridiculous and belligerent.

'I don't see what's so funny.'

'Do you not?' Her eyes drifted to the pile of bedding on the floor, then flicked back up at him. 'The innkeeper? His wife? Those two drunkards who had all the subtlety of a pair of bricks? The Chinese-puzzle door latch? The cringeworthy marital advice?' Her lips twitched again as she returned her attention to serving the stew as a snort escaped. He had forgotten she snorted like a piglet when she laughed, which surprised him because he had always adored it.

'Then there was your epic fight with that poor blanket. It was touch and go there for a while.' Another bubble of laughter escaped and filled the room. Only this one seemed to calm his temper rather than fire it. 'I had forgotten you had quite the temper, Owen.' She placed the bowl of stew on the table opposite the empty seat and picked up the second to serve herself. 'It is so nice to see something familiar.' Her smile this time touched her eyes and was like a balm to his soul. He had missed it. Missed them. 'Do you remember that afternoon you couldn't untangle the reins of my horse?'

Now there was a memory he hadn't visited for a while. She always rode in Hyde Park on his afternoons off. Her maid had been courting a soldier stationed in the barracks nearby and Lydia had been only too delighted to cajole her neglectful chaperon into abandoning her to visit with him so she could ride alone. Then the pair of them would meet on one of the quiet paths along the back of the Serpentine. They'd tie up her pony among the thicket of dense trees that lined it and sit and talk for an hour uninterrupted. Or kiss. There had been rather a lot of kissing in the weeks before he was snatched away.

'It had been raining.' Not that they had cared. 'And the leather expanded.' Welding the damn knot he'd tied shut tight.

'And you got so frustrated with it, you kicked the tree trunk...'

'And broke my little toe.' He found himself smiling back and sitting in the chair. 'You laughed your head off, as I recall.' There had been a great deal of snorting then, until he confessed he'd done himself a mischief and she had soothed and pampered his bruised ego while apologising profusely.

'In my defence, I had no idea you had broken a bone. I was laughing at the way you were carrying on. Much like just now. You do like to wave your arms about and howl at the moon...' Her smile suddenly turned wistful. 'But in those days your temper tantrums always blew themselves out very quickly. Is that still the case?'

'I am not waving my arms about now.' Because she had defused it, exactly as she always had when he became impatient with the world. 'I am sorry about...all that just now. I am usually better at controlling my temper nowadays.' None of this was her fault. She was here because her father was on the cusp of bankruptcy and she was selflessly bailing him out and Owen had selfishly moved heaven and earth to stop her marrying Kelvedon.

'These are peculiar times...for both of us. I dare say we shall both have a few tantrums till we find our feet.' Magnanimously, she served him some potatoes. 'It doesn't help that we are virtual strangers.'

'We never used to be.'

'No...' She stared down at her plate, then shrugged as she met his gaze again. 'But a decade has passed since then and you are not the same Owen Wolfe who used to meet me in Hyde Park any more than I am the same Lydia Barton.'

'It's Lydia Wolfe now.' And, Lord help him, he liked the sound of that.

'It is. For better or for worse we are stuck with one another…' She speared a potato with her fork and waved it at him like a flag. 'Something which might become a little easier if we call a truce.' He didn't want to spoil the moment by reminding her that he had tried that repeatedly since his return.

'A truce? When you are still furious because you think me a thief and I am still furious at you for believing it?'

Her tone became tart again. 'If you would only apologise, then perhaps…'

'I have nothing to apologise for, Lydia.' He watched her bristle, sighed because he knew she was about to argue and held up his palm. 'And neither can I prove my innocence categorically—although, believe me, not for want of trying. So we are at an impasse. Hardly the most solid of foundations for a truce. But even so, I do not have the energy to wage constant war with you.'

'Then perhaps we should agree to put the unfortunate past to one side…' Tellingly not behind them. Or to forgive and forget—not that he'd done anything to need forgiveness for. 'Never speak of it…' Because those seven stolen years were by the by as far as she was concerned. His just punishment for being so despicable. 'And try to make the best of things…such as they are.'

Owen was sorely tempted to kick the solid oak table leg. 'We would require an armistice, not a truce.' With a truce, you shook hands and moved on. This was more complicated. Messy and maddening.

'Then let us call it an armistice, then. A ceasefire. An agreement to end the war between us.'

That at least would keep things contained. And give

him some control back. 'How do you suggest we proceed? When there is so much bad blood between us?'

'Tentatively, calmly… And shall we also try politely?' She smiled again, mischief dancing in her lovely dark eyes. 'Let's start with a civilised discussion over a meal and then, in another decade or so, we might even learn to tolerate one another.'

Chapter Eight

I n a strange sort of way, seeing a glimpse of the Owen she remembered helped calm her nerves and for the first time in a fortnight there was a small square of stable ground beneath her feet.

He still had a temper. A temper which flared quickly over nothing, burned briefly incandescent and then just as quickly burned itself out. Bizarrely, it was one of the things she had always liked about him. Those spontaneous bouts of noise and bluster were as harmless as they were entertaining and for some reason, despite his unusual size and propensity to dominate the space when in the grip of an outburst, they had never intimidated her. Which was odd when one considered how much she had always feared her father's temper. But then Papa's had nearly always had dire consequences and brought out his callous side. The impact of his lingered while Owen's seemed to clear the air.

Last night, for the first time since he had returned, they had behaved a little like their old selves. Understandably, both were guarded. As Owen had rightly pointed out, there was too much of an ugly chasm between them to completely ignore. Each time Lydia thought of his betrayal, it broke her heart, so not talking about it was sensible.

That was one of the main reasons she had suggested an armistice. The other was pure self-preservation. Because the pathetic truth was she also couldn't think about his betrayal without wanting to deny it, too. A decade on and her silly heart still wanted to believe he wasn't a thief. Something which undoubtedly made her the biggest of fools but which she was damned if he would ever know.

But with the armistice freshly in place, they had found some common ground in their carefully chosen reminiscences over a very polite and civilised supper. It felt like a start, but went no way towards alleviating Lydia's stresses about her future as his wife and, the bed sharing aside, exactly what all that entailed.

She should have tackled the subject last night when he had been amiable rather than enjoy a brief hour of their not being at loggerheads. After the meal was done, he had swiftly declared a ridiculously early start. Tomorrow, he promised, would be exceedingly arduous because he had neglected his business long enough. Which necessitated a punishing travelling schedule that could not be helped.

However, now the first signs of dawn were pushing away the darkness and signalling tomorrow had indeed arrived, she was resigned to the fact sleep had evaded her. How exactly did one do so soundly when a man you happened to almost loathe slept but feet away separated by one thin and ill-fitting door? His presence alone sent her mind whirring.

And whirr it did all night, the numerous good and long-buried memories warring with the bad. The Owen she had thought she had known, the heart-wrenching truth and his new facade. Because his sudden bout of histrionics had also shown her the real Owen Wolfe was still there behind

all the impeccably tailored coats and shiny new gentlemanly manners.

His accent had slipped.

Not by much, because he had obviously worked hard
to polish those rough edges. Yet in the grip of his fury his
Ts had not been so pronounced, his vowels had been flatter, and for some reason that tiny detail bothered her the
more she considered it. It warned her he was every inch
the chameleon, his public face very different from his private one. Something which would not be so worrying if
she knew exactly which face he was wearing in front of
her. And had she ever?

Every time he shifted position in the night, Lydia heard
him. If she concentrated really hard, she was sure she could
also hear his breathing. Once or twice he had sighed, making her wonder what he was dreaming about. How did
he think? What did he feel? What mattered to him now
beyond the realms of his business? Did anything? And,
most importantly of all, where did she fit in to the picture?
How would they co-exist? Where would they live? Exactly
how much contact would they have on a daily basis? And
with so much still up in the air, was it any wonder sleep
evaded her?

Beyond the door she heard a thud, then a stream of muf-
fled expletives. Realising he was clearly up and keen to
get going, she decided to grab the bull by the horns. She
flung off the bedcovers and dashed to the door, pulling it
open intent on demanding answers, only to have the questions die in her throat.

Owen stood in the pale light of the window, the curtains still grasped in his hands as if he had only just tugged
them open, his eyes a little wide as he blinked at her over
his shoulder in the doorway. He was stripped to the waist
and barefoot. Her eyes drank in all those things as they

travelled the long, lean length of him, before they settled back on his ridiculously broad shoulders and the flock of intricately tattooed birds taking flight up his right arm from his elbow, over an impressive bicep and stopping a few inches shy of his neck.

'I'm sorry... I didn't mean to wake you.' He'd now turned to face her. His accent had slipped again, so she took his apology as fact, but conscious she was openly staring, forcibly dragged her gaze to meet his. 'I couldn't find my shirt in the dark and stubbed my damn toe on the sideboard...' His eyes followed hers to his naked chest again and he winced as he snatched the errant garment from the back of the chair. 'Sorry...' His head disappeared inside the fabric and briskly came out of the collar. 'I was going to wash down at the pump and then see to the horses. I really didn't mean to disturb you.'

Now that the distracting birds were covered up, Lydia at last found her voice.

'I was wide-awake anyway. I have never been good at sleeping in strange beds.' Especially when there was a strange man just feet away. A half-naked strange man. An unexpected and particularly distracting sight which was already seared on to her memory, replacing the feel of the younger Owen's chest beneath his shirt from all those years ago.

Except now it was fully grown. Bigger. Broader. The dusting of hair which arrowed down through his navel was also new. The tattoos most definitely were. Her fingers seemed to itch with the sudden need to explore both for comparison, so she tucked her hands into the capacious folds of her thick winter nightgown. 'Seeing as we are both up, why don't I save you a doubtless miserable visit to the pump and order some hot water so you can wash here?'

Bizarrely, her palm was sweating as she gestured behind her with her thumb. 'I could order some breakfast, too…seeing as it is going to be a long day.' To give herself something to do, she scurried to the bell pull and gave it a spirited tug. 'I wanted to talk to you anyway and over breakfast is probably going to be my only chance.'

Now that his shirt was back on, Owen had folded his arms over his chest, causing the muscles beneath to strain intriguingly against the soft linen. He had filled out. Practically everywhere. And, good gracious, did it suit him. 'What did you want to talk about?'

'Us.' His eyes widened. 'How everything is going to work… Back in London, I mean. The living arrangements…etcetera?'

Etcetera! That pathetic word covered a whole host of variables, none of which she could find the correct language for because now that the distracting birds were hidden, she was noticing other things she really would be better off not noticing. Like the way his tawny hair was delightfully rumpled from sleep or the manly shadow of morning stubble decorating his square jaw which also suited him. The old Owen had barely started growing a beard. The new one looked like he was fully capable of sprouting a vigorous one in a matter of days.

Thankfully, before she started babbling inanely to cover her awkwardness, the maid tapped at the door, giving Lydia the perfect excuse to turn away from his hypnotic eyes. She ordered food and hot water before he could argue, using the distraction to give herself a stiff talking, too.

This was no time to allow her foolish head to be turned by a mere flash of bare skin and a pleasingly broad pair of shoulders. He had always been handsome! Too handsome for his own good, so she needed to swiftly learn to control her pathetic reaction or else he would use it to his advantage. He had seen her staring. That had to be the first and last time she allowed him that liberty.

It was such a stern talking, too, she felt quietly confident she was over the worst as she closed the door, only to be hit with another wave of unwelcome desire when she turned to find him tucking in his shirt. Something which shouldn't have been the least bit attractive but was, largely because it highlighted his flat stomach. Then he bent over to pick up his boots and in so doing, drew her traitorous eyes to his taut behind and irritatingly muscular thighs. Was the wretch doing it on purpose?

Probably, but she would have to act nonplussed and therefore give him the benefit of the doubt.

'Where will I be living?' Her voice came out a tad too high-pitched.

'With me, I suppose.'

'You suppose?'

'I haven't given it much thought.'

'Then might I suggest you do? Seeing as I am now your wife...' which sounded uncomfortably proprietorial and possessive, making Lydia's face heat '...albeit in name only.'

'Thank you for clarifying that last part. I had *quite* forgotten it.' He couldn't hide his amusement at her stilted embarrassment. 'But you are right. We should discuss the living arrangements. For the time being my set of rooms makes the most sense.'

A set of rooms didn't sound anywhere near big enough now that she had seen those birds. 'And where is that?'

'At Libertas.'

'Your club?' She hadn't expected that answer. 'You expect me to live in a den of iniquity?'

He found that statement amusing and grinned. 'It's hardly a den of iniquity—but even if it was, the residences are completely self-contained and have their own entrances quite separate from the club.'

'There are *residences*?' Which suddenly sounded much more promising. 'As in plural?'

'Indeed. Two of them. Mine and Randolph's.'

'Oh.' She felt her shoulders slump. 'Are they spacious?'

'If by that you mean will you have your own bedchamber—then, yes. You could even have two if you wanted.' He was mocking her. 'We'll make sure the vacant one stands steadfastly between us as we sleep in case I am sent mad by the scent of your perfume and I go on the rampage.' He was enjoying her discomfort far too much.

'That is not what I meant and you know it. There is no need to resort to sarcasm when I am merely trying to get a picture of what I am going home to. That is hardly an unreasonable request. Especially as I am the one who has to endure all the upheaval. I thought we had agreed upon an armistice? A polite one.'

He rolled his eyes, but was still smiling. 'Very well. In the spirit of our *polite* armistice I shall resist the urge to resort to sarcasm. You will be going home to a very nice, if very sparse, set of rooms. There is a cavernous living room which is positively ringed with windows that let in the light, three bedrooms, all large enough to pace in when I inevitably irritate you, and a dining room which I was told by the builder who renovated the space is intimate— which I presume is the fancy society word for small. I wouldn't recommend you pace in there.'

His charm was winning her over and she felt her own lips curve into a reluctant smile. 'Would you care to clarify what *sparse* means?'

'It means I've had much better things to do this past year than decorate the place. Aside from my bedchamber, I have no furniture whatsoever.'

'None?'

'I believe that is what the term no furniture whatsoever means.'

Lydia felt her lips twitch at his purposely dour expression. 'That sounds dangerously like sarcasm, Owen—which we all know is the lowest form of humour.'

'What can I say?' Those broad shoulders shrugged as amusement broke through again. 'We all know that as a man I am undoubtedly of the lowest form—or should that be the lowliest—so it will *undoubtedly* be a hard habit to break. Even with your helpful chastisements.'

'If only your bedchamber is furnished, am I to sleep on the floor?'

'I am hoping Randolph has had the forethought to procure you a bed. Which I am sure he has. He's one for detail is Randolph. Surely you noticed that?'

She hadn't noticed that. Hardly a surprise when she had only met the man briefly while she had still been dumbstruck and reeling after accepting Owen's proposal. Because of that, she couldn't really recall much about his business partner. All she remembered clearly was being decidedly shocked to meet him. Firstly, because up until that moment she, like the rest of London, had assumed Owen was the sole owner of Libertas and, secondly, because Randolph was, for want of a better word, a dwarf.

'And if he hasn't?'

'Then you are welcome to sleep in mine.' He was flirting now, something he had always lapsed into with predictable regularity to deliberately set her off-kilter. A few weeks ago she had found it galling. This morning, and to her dismay, more than a tad thrilling.

Of their own accord, she felt her chin dip to gaze back at him through her lashes. 'I may very well take you up on that offer...' he wasn't the only one who could flirt on command and she was rewarded by the flash of unmistakable interest in those twinkling blue eyes '...seeing as I already know you are so comfortable on the floor.' His eyes narrowed and Lydia couldn't help but smile with triumph at the tiny victory. 'Or here is a better idea—why don't you have Randolph move into your sparse residence and I could live happily separate from you, and perfectly contentedly, in his?'

'I wouldn't suggest that idea to him! He might actually take you up on it.'

'And that would be a bad thing because...?'

'His wife and three children will be very put out.'

'Randolph is married?' She supposed that shouldn't really be such a surprise. He had been friendly towards her. Kind as well. He had plied her with tea, reassured her everything would turn out all right in the end and all while simultaneously planning the logistics of her elopement with Owen across the table.

'Indeed he is and for these past eight years. Although Heaven only knows how poor Gertie puts up with him as he is a menace.' This was accompanied by a subtle smile which told her plainly he was extremely fond of his friend. 'Something you will doubtless learn soon enough once we get back to town. I would be quite remiss in my duties as your husband—*albeit in name only*—if I didn't forewarn you. Randolph is a meddling, loud and thoroughly irritating force of nature. His offspring aren't much better, truth be told, but Gertie is lovely. I hope you will like her.'

An odd thing to say when Owen's original proposal had suggested they live almost entirely separate lives. 'I am sure I will.' The thought of another woman and children in the house made her feel better about it. Maybe she wouldn't be lonely after all. Or maybe she would. These were Owen's friends first and they might not take well to the woman who would never be able to get over the fact he was a shameless thief. And on the subject of his thieving...

'Can I ask a question, Owen?'

'Does it contravene the terms of our polite armistice, Lydia?'

'Maybe—but I need to know. How did you find the money to build Libertas?'

The flirty smile disappeared behind a stony mask. 'Did I steal it, you mean?'

'I just want to understand what sort of place I am going home to.' And what sort of man she was going home with.

For the longest time she thought he would refuse to answer, but then he raked a hand through his already mussed hair, wandered to the window to stare out of it and surprised her.

'Gambling was rife in Port Jackson—not that I was ever a gambler. I am not sure I'll ever understand what possesses a man to wager away his hard-earned money on a game of chance, but Randolph dragged me to a hell one day for something to do and as I sat around those gaming tables at night watching it all unfold, I found myself staring at the dealers and then the owner and saw my future. Because while fortunes are won and lost over cards or dice or reckless wagers—I couldn't help noticing the house *always* wins. So to cut a very long and difficult story short in order to adhere to the terms of our armistice, we started our own hell in the colony.' He turned then, his jaw jutting proudly as he stared her dead in the eye. 'An *honest* and entirely above-board hell—and a popular one as a result. Consequently, our fortunes rapidly grew and we saved practically every penny because we had plans for bigger and better things one day.'

'You made money as a convict? I didn't think...'

'That commerce could flourish over on the other side of the world? Or that I had it in me to be an entrepreneur?'

'Neither…' She flicked him an awkward glance, debating whether to ask what was on the tip of her tongue. 'I didn't think…you had that much freedom over there. I assumed all prisoners were…locked up.'

He laughed without humour and shook his head. 'There was no point locking us up, Lydia—we had nowhere else to go.'

'Was it…very bad there?' Because suddenly she wanted to hear the entire long story to better understand him now.

'That definitely contravenes the parameters of our armistice.' She heard the note of bitterness in his voice as he folded his arms once more and lent his weight on the sturdy windowsill. 'Because recounting it is guaranteed to make me angry. All you need to know is by day I worked at His Majesty's pleasure building roads or planting fields for no wages.' Which explained where he had acquired those intriguing muscles. 'And in our hell every night for myself. So to answer your initial question, Lydia, I earned every single penny that went into building Libertas—fair and square. And worked damned hard for it, too.'

She released the breath she had not realised she was holding because she believed him. 'Thank you for putting my mind at rest.'

He nodded, but continued to stare intently. 'I believe I am entitled to ask a personal question now, too.' She wanted to say no because the directness of his gaze was unsettling her and she feared he already knew too much already—but knew she couldn't.

'Go ahead.'

'Why did you never marry?' His gaze swept the length of her and she felt it everywhere. 'You must have been asked.'

'I was, but…' *My misguided foolish heart only ever wanted you.* 'I was waiting for the right man…' His head tilted. That insightful and hypnotic blue gaze stripping her bare as it searched for the truth. 'And he never came along in time.'

'Perhaps he did and…'

The arrival of the maid spared her from whatever else he intended to say, and Lydia was only too grateful to usher her in. Bizarrely, Owen seemed ridiculously grateful for the interruption, too, and rushed forward to relieve the girl of the two heavy steaming buckets she carried. This tiny gesture earned him a beaming, if bashful, smile from the maid which he returned so charmingly the poor thing blushed all the way to her toes before she bobbed a curtsy and dashed away.

'She seemed very taken with you.' The words popped out before Lydia could stop them.

'Don't be jealous… I'm a likeable chap.' The serious man of a moment ago was gone once again, replaced by the flirty rogue who had vexed her at too many social engagements over the past two years.

'I wasn't the least bit jealous.' Although deep down, and much to her chagrin, a minuscule part of her was. Jealous and flustered and feeling entirely exposed. His fault for asking her why she had waited. 'I was merely making an observation. You have a…knack with people. Which explains why you have done so well in business.' She was momentarily pleased with her quick and reasonable response. Then, because clearly her mouth had developed a mind of its own, more damning words tumbled out—waspish and unbidden. '*Especially* with the ladies.'

His bark of laughter galled. 'Is that your way of asking me *not* to flirt with them? Now that *we* are married…'

Lydia kicked herself for inadvertently giving him the

upper hand. 'I really couldn't care less who you flirt with, Owen.' She tried to sound bored as she looked down her nose at him. 'As long as it is not with me.'

He simply smiled in response as he effortlessly carried the buckets through the bedchamber door and poured one into the washbowl. All the while her stupid eyes watched him and the easily waylaid feminine part of her openly appreciated his form while she kept thinking about those dratted birds tattooed on his dratted gorgeous bicep.

As if he knew that, he took his sweet time in fetching his shaving equipment and a fresh shirt, before he casually sauntered back to the bedchamber and lingered at the door. 'If I curb the flirting, can I keep the sarcasm?'

'I really do not care either way.' Irritatingly waspish again when she was trying so hard to be nonchalant.

He nodded, his eyes dancing, looking more obnoxiously handsome than he ever had before. 'If you say so… *Wife.*'

Then he winked before he closed the door and, heaven help her, she found herself more than a little charmed as well as flustered as she stared back at the wood.

Chapter Nine

Owen was dead on his feet but still couldn't bring himself to go to bed. After that fateful night at the inn when he had lain awake for the duration, his body painfully aware of the temptation sleeping soundly in the next room, he had actively avoided resting anywhere close to Lydia. Something which had been relatively easy on the road, but which was practically impossible now they were freshly arrived back in London.

He had pleaded work as the reason he had abandoned her to what was now *their* set of rooms, an excuse he suspected he would have to use frequently in the coming days, weeks, months and years in order to remain relatively sane. Unless he set her up in her own household somewhere, which might be the only option open to him if he continued to lust after her with quite as much enthusiasm as he currently was.

He blamed their polite armistice, her perfume and that damned sensible nightdress she had tormented him in on their first official morning as man and wife. How such a capacious and practical garment tied all the way to the neck could send him over the edge was a mystery—but it had. Probably because he had known there was absolutely nothing lying beneath it and that dangerous knowledge, combined with the tousled curtain of dark hair hanging below her unbound breasts, had knocked him sideways. Yet another wholly unwelcome thunderbolt flying out of the blue when he really didn't need another reminder of the power she held over him.

How exactly was he supposed to sleep, or even function normally, a few scant yards from that?

Even now, the thought of her sleeping in the big bed Randolph had had the foresight to obtain was tormenting him. Lydia lying in the frothy and feminine bedcovers Gertie had probably had a hand in choosing, dark hair fanned over the pillow, those sooty lashes forming a beautiful and alluring crescent on her perfect cheeks. Over a week away from his business and a mountain of work was piled, waiting for him on his desk, and all Owen's brain could think about was her.

'You look like death warmed up.' To make his living hell complete, a yawning Randolph wandered in. Slugger must have awoken him to tell him Owen was home. 'Why aren't you in bed?'

'Too much to do.' For good measure, he grabbed the stack of correspondence he had been ignoring and began to sift through it.

'It's four in the morning!' Another thing he was only too painfully aware of. The last diehard patrons of Libertas had left long before they arrived back and the building was depressingly silent. 'And what the blazes were you doing travelling through the night? You're lucky you weren't accosted by footpads.'

'It seemed pointless staying in an inn when there were only twenty miles left.' Owen had mistakenly thought being on familiar territory would make things better. Another chronic misjudgement when he was usually so precise and measured in his decisions. Even Libertas felt odd now she was in it. Everything felt as though it was spiralling out of his control and he didn't have the first clue how to stop it. The roiling emotions which had led him to act so rashly were no less calm. If anything, they were worse. He couldn't think straight. Hadn't slept more than a fitful hour or two at a time in days and was desperately worried the situation was doomed to plunge ever deeper into chaos before it showed any signs of getting better.

His friend climbed into the chair opposite and shook his head. 'I didn't expect you till late tomorrow—at the earliest. In a hurry, were you? It couldn't have been much of a honeymoon travelling at that lick.'

Owen slanted him a warning look. Randolph knew full well this was supposed to be a business arrangement. His friend might not believe it and frankly who could blame him when Owen knew damn well it wasn't either, but that did not mean he was prepared to deviate from the flimsy lie. 'What have I missed?'

'A huge scandal in the papers. Reporters constantly knocking at the door. Rumour, speculation, endless gossip.' Randolph raised expressive eyebrows. 'And a massive leap in profits.'

'Good to hear… Have you paid Lydia's father?'

'Two days ago.'

Owen had known it was coming. Thought he had prepared himself for the consequences he himself had set in motion, but along came a whirl of fear regardless at the expected news.

Ten thousand hard-earned pounds. Gone.

Pouf!

Just like that.

'He didn't send a thank-you note.'

'There's a surprise.' Now he could add the uncertainty

which came from a severely depleted bank balance to the churning cauldron of emotions which threatened to engulf him. Thank goodness there had been an upturn of profits. Too many months feeling this exposed and vulnerable would likely finish him. 'Has news of the settlement leaked?'

'No. The last thing Fulbrook wants is for the world to know you had to bail him out of debt. Any more than he wants Kelvedon to learn he shamelessly double-crossed him.'

Not that he had shamelessly double-crossed him in the strictest sense. That suggested Fulbrook had a choice in the matter when Owen hadn't given him one. Unbeknownst to his friend, he'd used the mortgage deed as leverage—which he supposed was a polite term for blackmail—but there had been no way in hell he'd have allowed Lydia to marry that lecher.

'And how is the odious Marquess?'

Randolph grinned. 'The Marquess of Kelvedon is spitting feathers. Not only did his beautiful fiancée run off and leave him in the lurch, but somebody forgot to tell *The Times* the wedding was off and the joyous news of his nuptials was printed the day after the scandalous news of your elopement leaked. It is widely reported he wants to seek satisfaction on the duelling field—although he is still ensconced at his estate and will probably stay there until the need to polish his pistols diminishes with time.'

'We expected as much. It's all bluster to save face. What has the Earl of Fulbrook had to say?'

'Nothing. Neither has her brother. Both are lying low till the dust settles.'

'And how is the dust settling?' Because that was the crux of the matter. If society turned against him, they would turn against Libertas and everything the pair of them had worked, suffered and sacrificed for would crumble around their ears. For a man who didn't gamble, he had certainly wagered everything including his shirt on this. His best friend's shirt, too.

'Very well. Exactly as I predicted.' Randolph gestured to the stack of letters beneath Owen's hand. 'Most of those are invitations. You and the lovely Lady Lydia are suddenly in very high demand. The talk of the town. The modern-day Romeo and Juliet—except without the tragic ending.' The slow grin stretched from ear to ear. 'You've come out well, Owen. Much better than expected, in fact. You are being lauded a noble hero.' Largely, he wouldn't doubt, because of Randolph's carefully leaked embellishments. His friend's talent for spinning things to their advantage was legendary.

'Then my mission was accomplished.'

His friend huffed out a withering sigh. 'Of course it was... That's why you're hiding down here, needing matchsticks to prop open your eyes and staring into space.'

'I told you I have...'

'Things to do. *Yes*... I heard that pathetic excuse, yet we both know you are down here hiding. From the woman of your dreams, no less... The *one* that got away... The *one* you could never forget... The *one* you could not bear to be in the slimy arms of another...'

Owen felt his temper bubble despite the accusation worryingly being spot on. He had done a lot of thinking on the road. And all the introspection had made him realise two inescapable and undeniable things. He had married Lydia because he wanted her—always had, always would—but he really didn't want her like this.

Not still hating him and distrusting him.

She wanted to put the past aside in a locked box and pretend it didn't exist. But he had lived it and wanted, if not retribution, certainly recognition that he was innocent, and redemption. Especially from her. Except he had no earthly idea how to get it now all the potential avenues to proving his innocence had gone stone cold. 'It's not like that!'

'It could be…' Randolph ignored his murderous scowl. 'It all depends on how you play it. Perhaps it's time for a bit of wooing…'

'Absolutely not!' The flirting was killing him. The only way they seemed to be able to cope with the all great unsaid, certainly the only way Owen could cope with any time spent in her presence, was to behave in a light and superficially sparring fashion. Which inevitably lent itself naturally to flirting despite giving him the upper hand. At least that was how he justified the constant need to flirt with her. Until he had found a satisfactory way of controlling the rest of the heaving mess he had irrationally created, that was the story he could cope with in his mind and he was stubbornly determined to stick to it.

'I fully intend to keep my relationship with her on a strictly business footing!' Why, for the life of him, could he not suddenly seem to finish a sentence without raising his voice? Clearly he had a lot of pent-up rage regarding Lydia, alongside all the lust, which he couldn't release in front of her because of their polite and civil, frustratingly futile and flirting armistice.

'Then I suppose the alternative is to stay here indefinitely, camp out in your office like a coward and avoid her until you are both old and grey and one of you gives up the ghost, turns up their toes and dies.'

It really wasn't much of a plan when Owen heard it spoken aloud, but in the absence of a better one, it would have to do until his addled mind could function well enough to conjure up a viable alternative. Until that miracle occurred, he was trapped inside a racing carriage being dragged by a team of horses without any reins. Lost in the outback without water. Strapped to a table in a room full of tiger snakes…

'Then if you don't mind, I shall leave you to it.' His friend slithered off the chair and shook his head pityingly. 'I have a lovely warm wife to snuggle up to and while it is still the middle of the night, I fully intend to do some snuggling. Enjoy your hard desk, my friend. And your moral high ground. I expect both will be cold comfort.'

He waved his hand and walked away. But Randolph being Randolph, he couldn't resist one last dig to completely ruin Owen's night. 'Seeing as you're *in hiding*, shall I send your breakfast here? Only Gertie is planning a welcome breakfast first thing for your lovely new wife, seeing as your sorry, spartan excuse for a home leaves a great deal to be desired and the poor thing has absolutely nothing to sit on—let alone eat at. But don't worry…' He gave another theatrical wave. 'I'll make excuses for you. Besides, with you absent, it gives us plenty of opportunity to get to know her better. We are both very intrigued… about the pair of you. Then as well as now. You'll probably feel your ears burning…'

Knowing silence was the best and safest option, he let his meddling partner leave before he groaned aloud and dropped his forehead to the desk.

Lydia stood in the middle of the cavernous living room and spun in a slow circle. Owen hadn't lied. What it lacked in furniture it certainly made up for in windows. The sunrise over Mayfair was spectacular. She knew that emphatically as she had watched it from its inception when she had never been one for early mornings. Unfortunately, since her world had turned upside down, she had seen far too many of them—but this was the first she had had to suffer without the restorative properties of a good cup of tea. She had no earthly idea if she had the use of servants or needed to make it herself.

'You're up, then?'

Her new husband strode in carrying two heavy-looking dining chairs and looking annoyingly as fresh as a daisy in a clean suit of impeccably tailored clothes, smelling sinfully of the spicy cologne he favoured. The sight instantly galled because she felt, and no doubt looked, a shocking mess. With no apparent maid to help her, she'd had to do her own hair this morning and as hairdressing was really not her forte, the simple, austere knot was lacklustre at best against his golden handsomeness.

Then there was her gown, of course, which was the least crushed from their arduous journey to and from Scotland. She had only packed enough for the trip, assuming foolishly she would have her entire wardrobe at her disposal upon her return. But while she had an enormous new wardrobe in her huge new bedroom, it was as depressingly empty as the living room. Her father could have at least arranged for her things to be sent here. She had selflessly wrenched him out of crippling debt, after all.

'I've brought chairs.'

'So I see. How positively homely. A miraculous transformation.'

He grinned in response and deposited them in front of the fireplace. 'I thought you said sarcasm is the lowest form of humour.'

'Only when it comes from you. From me it isn't sarcasm, it's well-timed and witty pathos.'

'I'm glad to see the double standard is alive and well and residing in my own living room.'

'Alongside two uncomfortable and impractical chairs, I see.'

One of which he had just sat on. 'Sit with me, *Wife*—' He smiled as she bristled, which had doubtless been his goal all along, and patted the other seat. 'We have things to civilly and politely discuss this fine morning.'

'As I haven't had my tea yet, I can promise neither.'

'It hasn't escaped me you are grouchy in the mornings.' He folded his arms across his chest and stretched his long legs out in front of him, making himself comfortable while she sat stiffly upright in hers, affronted at the accurate observation. 'Hence I have already taken the liberty of ordering you tea. Slugger should be bringing it up at any moment, so try to remain civil in the interim.'

Slugger, she now knew, was the big brute with ink tears etched into his cheeks. 'He's not your typical butler.'

'That's because he's not a butler at all. He's more of an assistant. A jack of all trades. One who happens to also be very good at ejecting rowdy aristocrats from the club with the minimum of fuss when they get too boisterous as well as gently pouring the inebriated ones into their carriages when they are too deep in their cups to be able to walk straight. He looks more terrifying than he is. In truth, he's not terrifying at all once you get to know him. Slugger is the archetypal gentle giant and a soulful, suffering artist.'

'And it was at his easel he earned the delicate name of Slugger, I presume?'

'No.' When he held back a grin, he looked too much like the mischievous stable boy she had fallen in love with. 'He earned that in the ring, of course…where he remained undefeated until he retired from the sport.'

'Only you would have a boxer for a butler.'

'He wasn't so much a pugilist in the traditional sense, more a no-rules, bare-knuckle, spit-and-sawdust sort who happened to paint on the side. Very well, as it happens. In fact, three-quarters of the artwork dotted around this building comes from his talented brush. He is particularly good at copying the old masters, although I've always preferred his original compositions.'

'And a fellow convict, no doubt?' Lydia made sure she looked straight down her nose, only for him to grin unoffended.

'Half of Libertas is made up of fellow convicts and I'd trust each and every one of them with my life. And certainly over *all* of your lot.' He made a great show of looking down his nose, too, those blue eyes twinkling and charming her when she had been so determined to endeavour not to be charmed once again. 'But I didn't come here to discuss Slugger or art or chairs or your disagreeable morning moods. I came here to ask your opinion on something, actually.'

Now there was a novel idea. A man seeking a woman's opinion. 'Really?'

'We've received all these.' From somewhere inside his coat he produced a stack of invitations. 'In view of the delicious scandal we have caused, I wondered which of these we should accept?'

'From a business point of view?' She supposed it was inevitable her new husband would want a quick return on his investment, so she really shouldn't allow herself to be upset by it. It was, after all, what she had agreed to.

'Partly... But I am also aware these are *your* people, Lydia, and I don't want to make a mistake and unintentionally alienate them from you. I want your friends to remain your friends. In my experience, the world is always a nicer place with friends on your side. Nor do I want to inadvertently throw you into a pit of vipers. There seem to be a lot of those out there.' He gestured absently through the window towards the city. 'And most of them seem to also live in Mayfair.'

'That's actually very thoughtful.' Touching, even. 'There are certain individuals I would like to avoid—for a little while at least. Although I suppose everyone wants an opportunity to gawp and stare at us now that we are the latest scandal.'

'Then let them. What's the worst that can happen?'

'Easy for you to say. You are used to being a scandal. This is my first time. I don't even know what people have been saying about me.'

'Randolph saved all the newspapers. Read them if you think they matter. From personal experience I think there is a lot to be said for blind ignorance. If I don't know someone has been defamatory or told a bare-faced lie, I don't care about it. It's much easier to be civilised when you are not spitting nails.'

'Am I to take that to mean not all the newspaper reports are favourable, then?' She'd thought she was braced for the scandal. Now that lofty, pride-fuelled bravado was waning.

'The Marquess of Kelvedon has some supporters.' Hardly a surprise when he was so well connected. 'But you have more.'

'Has my father said anything?' She wished she didn't care, but couldn't help herself. In view of all she had sacrificed, she hoped he would at least defend her.

'Not to the press. I expressly forbade him from saying anything derogatory in public as part of the agreement.' Another surprisingly thoughtful thing—unless it hadn't been for her benefit at all, but his. 'But he hasn't been able to stop himself from voicing his disapproval to a few, as you would expect from a man eager to keep Kelvedon on side, and those people have passed his words over to reporters.'

'Who have doubtless twisted them to make us look bad.' Of course he wouldn't defend her. How foolish of her to

have hoped her sire might suddenly surprise her when he
hadn't even had the decency to send her belongings over.

Owen shrugged, then sighed, and for once she believed
the sympathy she saw darkening his lying eyes. 'Sticks and
stones… But we can postpone our first public outing for
another few weeks if you're not up for it. There's no hurry.'

'Would that make it any easier?'

'Probably not.'

'Then we might as well get it over with. I presume the
press have been told we are madly in love?'

He seemed suddenly embarrassed and uncomfortable
in his own skin. 'I left that part to Randolph.'

She smiled then. She couldn't help it while he was being
so charming. 'I shall take that as an affirmation then, as
from what you have told me about him, I doubt Randolph
could contain himself. I dread to think what far-fetched
romance he has added to the tale.'

'He annoyingly leans towards the theatrical. I blame
too many years on the stage.'

'Randolph was an actor?'

'He likes to think he was. He spent his formative years
in a travelling museum of curiosities where I suspect he
was the loudest exhibit.'

'That's…dreadful.'

'Maybe for some, but typically Randolph adored it. He
enjoys nothing better than being the centre of attention.'

'Unlike me. I can think of nothing worse. Thank goodness I am not at the centre of an enormous scandal.' She
tried to smile and watched his handsome face fall.

'I meant it, Lydia…you don't have to accept any of these
invitations if you do not feel ready.'

'I am not going to cower and hide, Owen.'

'Then I shall hand these over to you.' He held out the
invitations as the shadow of the aptly named Slugger sud-

denly loomed large on the floor. 'For you to peruse at your leisure later. Now, though, you must have a fortifying cup of tea to prepare you for today's most terrible ordeal.'

The brute looked confused as he came in. 'Where shall I put this?' To be fair to him, there was no table or sideboard, so she sympathised with the man's plight.

'I suppose the floor will have to do. Until my delightful wife decorates the place.' Owen cheerfully relieved him of the burden and placed it at Lydia's feet. 'Assuming you want to decorate the place, that is. If not, I can arrange…'

'No… I should like to decorate.' Not that she had ever bought a single stick of furniture before. There had been no need. Although the idea of building a home from scratch appealed.

'Thank the Lord!' Owen joined the tea things on the floor and began assembling cups on saucers as if preparing tea on the floor was the most natural thing for the master of the house to be doing. 'I'm glad you said that. It's one less job for me. Randolph keeps a list of reputable and reliable tradesmen and merchants. Use them and get them to send me the bills.'

'I shall collect some catalogues first for you to…' He held up his hand, frowning.

'Just the bills, Lydia. I am stretched to capacity as it is with Libertas—I simply do not have the time. Unless you can magic some additional hours to each day, I shall have to trust your judgement implicitly.'

'Why?' Because she was stunned he did not want a say in it all. Her father insisted on his say in everything, from the weekly menu choices to the necklines and colours of her gowns, and what he said went regardless of anybody else's opinions on the matter. 'I might do it completely against your taste.'

'As I have never owned a living room before and will rarely have use for it, surely it should be to your taste?'

A polite way of informing her it would be her room because he really did intend to avoid her. The harsh realities of their marriage of convenience, which she should have been prepared for, but oddly wasn't. Her new home seemed destined to be as lonely as her old one. Not that she would let him witness her disappointment.

'Do you at least have a budget in mind?'

'As budgets are notoriously problematic, I'd say you need to use your discretion. Invariably, from the experience of setting up downstairs, things inevitably cost twice as much as you originally anticipated.' He handed her a cup of tea and then wielded the ridiculously tiny silver tongs in his big hands like snapping jaws. 'Sugar?'

'No, thank you, and that advice is not the least bit helpful.'

He shrugged and loaded his own cup with three lumps of sugar, then for good measure, added a fourth. 'Then here is some sage advice that is. Never take the first price. Or the second, for that matter. And don't be afraid to walk away. That is the ultimate negotiating tool as no merchant or trade worth his salt wants you to take your business elsewhere.'

'That actually *is* good advice.' Advice her father would probably benefit from, but would never dream of listening to. 'Thank you.'

'I wouldn't be so quick to thank me—I still haven't told you about this morning's ordeal.'

'Decorating your empty, sparse home is not the ordeal?'

'Not even close.' He exhaled loudly. 'I had Slugger make the tea strong and I shall apologise profusely in advance for the horror I am about to subject you to—because, my *dear wife*, we are about to have breakfast with Randolph.'

Chapter Ten

Randolph Stubbs magically appeared on the dot of eight, seemingly out of nowhere, and grinned before kissing her hand.

'*My lady*… Welcome to your new home.' Would this strange place ever feel like home? She sincerely doubted it, but smiled anyway. It was what it was and she would try to make the best of it for the sake of her own sanity. 'I hope you will be very happy here.'

'Thank you. I am sure I will.' Hoped more like. Which she hoped wasn't doomed to be futile.

'My wife and I are excited to be breakfasting with you. Besides…' he cast a withering glance at the two forlorn chairs she and Owen were sat on '…we also thought you might appreciate being able to sit in comfort.'

The kind invitation on her first morning in this strange place touched her. 'That would be lovely, Mr Stubbs.'

'Oh, good gracious!' He waved his hands in the air. 'We have no airs and graces here! Everybody calls me Randolph and so must you. Especially as we are now family.'

'Family? I wasn't aware you and Owen were family.' She had always believed Owen had no family, unless that detail was another one of his many lies. Instead of offering his arm, which in fairness she would have had to bend double to take, Randolph took her hand and tugged her quickly towards the open door and along the airy landing towards the opposite side of the house.

'While not technically blood brothers, we are as good as brothers here…' He thumped his small chest dramatically. 'And that is where it counts.'

'What he means is…' the sound of Owen's deep voice directly behind sent a tingle down her spine as he fell into step behind them '…he latched on to me a decade ago and, despite trying my damnedest to be rid of him, he remains a constant thorn in my side.'

'I thought you had work to do?' Randolph winked at her. 'Obviously, you are welcome to break your fast with us *if* you must—but feel in no way obligated, Owen. We can manage well enough on our own. Or are you worried Gertie and I might gossip about you in your absence?'

'I was more worried for poor Lydia's sanity. I wouldn't leave my worst enemy to the pair of you all alone. I hope you are braced for an ordeal, *Wife*.' She was convinced Owen suddenly now used that endearment to vex her. 'Remember, I warned you he is a menace to society.'

'We are the perfect partnership,' said Randolph, completely ignoring the insult, holding her hand aloft in his fingers as if she were a duchess. 'I provide the brains, the ideas, the vision, the phenomenal good looks and he…' He gestured behind with one stubby thumb and shrugged. 'Well…to be honest, I am not entirely sure what Owen adds to anything. But my wife adores him and the children do not seem to mind him either.'

'I am looking forward to meeting them, Mr Stubbs.'

'It's Randolph, remember—and so are they! Gertie, especially, is beside herself with excitement at finally meeting you. We so wanted to attend the wedding, but *Mr*

Spoilsport here would have none of it. He can be very disagreeable sometimes. Have you noticed that, my lady?'

'It's Lydia.' She couldn't resist shooting the man in
question a glance over her shoulder before dropping her
voice to a stage whisper to his friend. 'And, yes—I have
noticed. He has quite the temper.'

'Indeed he does—and over the daftest of things, too,
Lydia.' Randolph dropped her hand to open a door. 'Cravats in particular vex him immensely.'

'As do door latches and innkeepers.'

'I am here, you know.' Again, that voice did odd things
to her insides. Tiny goose pimples sprang to attention
around her neck which she sincerely hoped he couldn't see.

'It's his fingers,' said Randolph, taking her hand again.
'He has hands the size of shovels, so I suppose it's hardly
any wonder they struggle with delicate tasks.'

They could be achingly gentle, too, she remembered,
and immediately felt off-kilter as her body also remembered the heady power of just his touch.

They suddenly came to another door which Randolph
threw open. 'They are here!' Then he stepped to one side,
dragging her with him, a split second before three children stampeded past.

'Uncle Owen!'

One was the usual size of a girl of about seven or eight.
The other two, a younger boy and another blonde-haired
younger still girl, were shaped like their father. All three
threw themselves at Owen who engulfed them in a hug,
before they clambered up his legs and he half-carried
them, half-dragged them. The sight of him smothered in
giggling children was disarming, especially because he
clearly adored them. As he squeezed past her on the landing dragging his friend's boisterous offspring, a beaming
woman appeared.

'Well, aren't you a pretty thing!'

She was a few inches taller than Lydia, more generous in both hips and bust, with bouncing blonde ringlets and a lovely, welcoming smile. She was also, if Lydia was any judge, about to give birth to another boisterous offspring at any given moment.

'My husband said you were a beauty!' Gertie Stubbs enveloped her in a perfumed embrace. 'I am so looking forward to having another woman in this house filled with infuriating men.' Her accent wasn't the least bit genteel and to her credit she made no attempt to make it so. 'But listen to me carrying on! Where are my manners? Breakfast is almost ready, but in the meantime you will need tea.'

As if the heels of her boots had suddenly sprung wheels, Lydia found herself manoeuvred into a cosy sitting room and into a comfortable chair near the roaring fire. She hadn't felt her shawl leave her body, but saw Randolph spirit it out while his wife pushed a steaming cup of tea into her hand and their children continued to climb noisily over Owen on an equally comfortable-looking sofa opposite.

'Get off him! Let the poor man breathe!' Gertie shooed her brood away, then hoisted him up before she beamed at him, too, and hugged him tightly. 'We've missed you, Owen.'

'I've missed you, too.' Instead of entirely pulling away, he continued to hold Gertie by the shoulders as his eyes dropped to her protruding belly. 'No sign of the latest monster, then?'

'As if I would dare go into labour without you here.' Gertie gently caressed her own stomach before glancing affectionately at her husband, love shining in her eyes. 'Who would deal with Randolph? You know he gets in a frightful state every single time I go into labour... Bless him. Besides, I knew you wouldn't want to miss the big event either, so I've had words with the baby and we both agreed to wait till you got back.' She dipped her head and spoke directly to her belly. 'You can come out now, darling. The cavalry is back.'

'Don't be in a hurry, little one.' Lydia was more than a little shocked and strangely moved to see her husband's hand affectionately pat the bump as he spoke to it. 'I've probably got a mountain of catastrophes to sort out after leaving Libertas in your father's *incapable* hands for so long. Give me at least a week to fix it first.' Then he kissed Gertie noisily on the top of the head. 'Preferably two.'

Such genuine and exuberant affection and easy camaraderie was not something Lydia was used to either witnessing or experiencing. The people of her acquaintance were never publicly affectionate. It simply wasn't done. Obviously, she cared for her brother, but she and Justin never shared more than a polite peck on the cheek now that they were adults and her father was as cold as a dead fish. One packed to the gills in ice and frozen solid. Her mother had been a little more demonstrative in private, but she had died shortly after Lydia turned seventeen and there had been precious little since. She hadn't realised she missed it—but seeing it now right in front of her made her feel envious of the bond Owen had with his adopted family.

Because staring at the touching scene felt voyeuristic, she stared at her tea instead, until she felt the weight of a small pair of eyes on her as Randolph's eldest daughter edged ever closer.

'Are you my new auntie?'

Owen held his breath as he awaited Lydia's answer. For her sake, he wanted her to be part of his effusive and irrepressible adopted family. She was going to feel very isolated if she wasn't and the last thing he wanted was for Gertie to ever feel awkward.

'I am indeed.' She beamed at the child. 'Your Auntie Lydia. And you are…?'

'Lottie,' said her mother with an indulgent smile. 'And that one there is Harry and the littlest is Eliza.'

'I am very pleased to make your acquaintances, Lottie, Harry and Eliza.' As she smiled at them, the shyer two came forward and hovered behind their sister while they debated whether or not to be brave.

'Can you read, Auntie Lydia?'

'I can.' She reached her hand out and brushed a wayward curl out of Lottie's eyes, which warmed Owen's heart, before taking the proffered picture book. 'Can you?'

'Very well. Papa says I am a child genius.'

Instead of laughing at the child or scoffing at her claim, Lydia nodded, smiling. 'I can tell that already. This looks like a very complicated book for a young lady of your age. Certainly a much more advanced and weighty tome than I was capable of reading at eight.'

'I am still only seven.'

'Only seven? Gracious! You must be a very clever and grown-up young lady indeed. Exactly as I suspected. But not so grown up as to not enjoy being read to, I hope? We aunties like to read to our nieces and nephews, you know. Alongside spoiling them rotten, of course.'

And all at once Owen felt ashamed of himself for momentarily doubting her when it had been her friendliness and lack of aristocratic disdain which had drawn him to her so completely all those years ago. Lydia had been the only family member at the Barton house who not only remembered the servants' names, but the people behind them.

'Can you read to us now?' All three stared up expectantly.

'Let the poor dear have her breakfast first, children.' Gertie spirited them away. 'And then perhaps you can have a story.'

With perfect timing, Slugger appeared at the door with his customary scowl. 'Food's in. Best get it down you before it goes cold.'

As was typical, breakfast was a chaotic affair. The children always ate their first meal of the day with the adults, which inevitably meant more mess and noise than his new wife was used to. Although to her credit, she took it all in her stride and in remarkably good spirits, even cutting up Harry's sausage for him while his mother saw to Eliza and Randolph waxed lyrical, enjoying playing the host and making everyone laugh—usually at Owen's expense.

Once the meal was done, Gertie insisted on prolonging his agony by having another cup of tea in the living room so they could discuss the best furniture merchants for Lydia to visit before she embarked upon the decorating. A task which had been a hasty stroke of genius on his part. He was ridiculously relieved to have given her something substantial to occupy herself with while he worked out how they could politely co-exist without him descending into lunacy and inevitably being committed to Bedlam where he probably belonged.

'The pair of you must still be exhausted.' Gertie was pouring tea out of the best teapot. 'Slugger said you arrived in the small hours.'

'It was nearly three.' Lydia took the cup and slanted Owen a chastising glance over the rim. 'And we had started out at barely eight that morning.'

'Oh, Owen!' Gertie was appalled. 'What were you thinking? Your poor wife must have been in agony after all that time in the carriage.'

'It's a very comfortable carriage.' The best defence he could think of without admitting he couldn't bear the thought of another night at an inn. 'I'll wager her suffering was nothing compared to mine. It rained all the way home and I was soaked to the skin.'

'You could have ridden in the carriage.' Lydia couldn't resist the dig. 'I repeatedly suggested it.'

'Somebody had to keep an eye out for footpads.'

Gertie rolled her eyes at the flimsy excuse. 'You wouldn't have needed to keep an eye out for them if you'd avoided travelling at night in the first place! Where was your common sense? And you did it in a downpour to boot, you silly man. You're lucky you haven't caught your death of cold!'

'Or more likely pneumonia, Gertie.' Lydia was clearly enjoying her new ally. 'It rained solidly for three days and it was freezing, yet he stubbornly sat in the saddle for all of it.'

'It would take more than a drop of rain to beat me. I have the constitution of an ox.'

'That he does.' For the first time this morning, Randolph came to his defence. 'Owen is never ill. Besides, Lydia, hell would have to freeze over before *he* ever rode in a carriage. He hates confined spaces.'

Owen was going to strangle his friend! In case Randolph felt the urge to embellish, he shot him a subtle warning look, not at all happy with the uncomfortable turn the conversation had suddenly taken.

'He does?'

'He's been funny about them since *The Portland*.'

'The Portland?'

'The prison hulk I met him on.' Owen was now shooting daggers at his oblivious friend. So was his wife. But Randolph neglected to notice either in his eagerness to tell another convoluted story to the suddenly rapt Lydia. 'We spent eight months on the thing before we were shipped off. Dreadful place it was—and probably still is. It's still anchored in the Thames by Woolwich.' Randolph shuddered and Lydia blinked back at him, appalled.

Owen, on the other hand, felt his heart begin to race.

'No matter what time of the day, it was always dark and constantly damp. Rats everywhere. Especially at night. The blighters would walk all over you as you lay in your bed.' Their sharp-pinned claws would scratch the skin, the chains around his ankles preventing him from kicking them off. 'And those bunks were a disgrace...' Like a coffin. The lid nailed in place. Unable to escape for hours on end. 'I frankly struggled with the size of them! Poor Owen is nearly twice my height and probably thrice my width. You just can't chain a man of six foot three to a bunk that's barely five foot ten! It's inhuman!'

Lydia's eyes sought Owen's—he could feel them boring into the top of his head as he resolutely stared into his cup and tried not to appear thoroughly traumatised by the unwelcome memories which were being dredged up.

'Owen hated the chains...'

Because he couldn't breathe. Couldn't move. The stagnant air had choked him then, just as it was choking him now. The constant rocking of the hulk had made him sick. And the chains had robbed him of all power. Rendered him helpless and entirely at the mercy of others.

'Randolph, *dearest*...' Gertie must have seen his discomfort because she was shooting her blabber-mouthed husband daggers. 'Don't you and Owen have *work* to do?'

Chapter Eleven

After Owen and Randolph hastily deserted them straight after breakfast, Gertie had taken the trouble to show her around her new home and introduce her to the staff who worked there. That, and more tea, had killed at least two hours, but as her lovely new friend had three lively children to contend with and was heavily pregnant with another, it did not seem fair to occupy all her time, especially as Gertie had insisted she eat all her meals with them at least until Lydia bought a table.

Seeing as the carriage was standing idle, and Gertie had given her a list of furniture merchants to visit, she had commandeered it to begin her shopping. Only this time without the single lady's requisite chaperon—which felt both liberating and daunting in equal measure. Liberating, because she had never had such freedom before, and daunting, because of the enormous scandal waiting for her outside.

As all the recommended merchants were in Cheapside, she was spared the ordeal of the familiar society haunts of Bond Street and St James's, and spent a fascinating and blissfully anonymous few hours leafing through catalogues and discussing possibilities. Yet as interesting and exciting as it was to discuss the particulars of wallpapers, brocade sofas and curtain fabrics for her very own living room, her mind kept wandering back to this morning, trying and failing to put the image of the eighteen-year-old boy she had once thought the sun rose and set with, clapped in irons and covered with rats, out of her thoughts. A near-impossible task now it was seared indelibly on to her mind.

She had read about the hulks.

Everyone had.

They were notorious and a complete national scandal considered by almost everyone to be horrifically inhumane. To think of Owen stuck on one for eight whole months, yards away from the city he had always called home, didn't bear thinking about.

But he had lived it. Survived it. What strength had that taken?

More than she possessed that was for sure. Especially as she had spent most of the afternoon between merchants diligently hiding from anyone who might possibly recognise her inside the carriage, when she could have easily walked the short distances, pathetically trying to avoid the scandal.

Not for the first time during her impromptu little outing, she found her attention drawn to the silk-lined walls of his carriage and wondering about the conditions he had suffered. Understandably, perhaps, she had focused on her outrage at his crimes for years, purposefully blotting out all thoughts about where he was and what he might be doing. He hadn't hanged for them. That was what she consoled herself with in those grim early days when her heart had keenly mourned him. Something she had been dreading could have happened when they had caught him red-handed.

The utter relief of the verdict after the turbulent lead-up

and ordeal of the trial had left her a slumped and weeping mess on her bedchamber floor moments after her outraged father had returned from the courthouse. He had been furious at the leniency shown. She had been both ridiculously grateful and disgusted at herself for still caring when Owen clearly hadn't cared enough about her to do what he had done.

After that, she had vowed to harden her heart and refused to entertain any of the lingering and niggling concerns about his welfare, reminding herself he had made his bed. If he hadn't stolen her mother's jewellery, then he would not have been transported. It hadn't worked, of course, and she had still worried about him and yearned for him regardless, right up until the day he had turned up in Mayfair again like a bad penny.

Once she had got over the shock of that reunion, when once again time shuddered to a grinding halt simply because he was there, she had hardened her foolish heart to focus on loathing him properly as she was supposed to.

But now, burdened with the fresh and unsettling knowledge of him languishing shackled and hopeless in a fetid, vermin-infested hulk for eight months, she could not help but wonder what else he had endured in the seven interminable years he had been away. What was the long and difficult story Owen had neglected to tell her? What had happened on the hulk to make him fear confined spaces? And did those horrendous conditions continue during the voyage and beyond?

All she knew about the penal colonies at the ends of the earth were what the newspapers told her. That it was a barren and desolate place which nobody in their right mind would wish to inhabit, which in turn made it the perfect place to send the very dregs of society to pay for their heinous crimes through hard work. However, if the hulks were the precursor to a worse fate, or merely a taste of what the future of a transported convict had to endure, then she suspected Owen might well have mourned being spared the hangman in those seven years away.

Which didn't bear thinking about. Yet she couldn't seem to stop.

'We're here, my lady.' The coachman's shout dragged her back to the present and she tentatively pulled back the comforting veil of the carriage curtain in time to see Berkeley Square as they turned into it.

Thankfully, he pulled up directly outside, which meant she only had to navigate a few feet of pavement and four white steps before she could disappear behind the safety of her father's front door. She did both briskly, staring straight ahead in case a neighbour saw her and wanted to engage in conversation, and felt her tense muscles relax when her knock was answered promptly by the same butler who had been with the family for all the years Lydia had been alive.

'Hello, Maybury. How are you?'

His usual cheerful smile was gone, replaced by strangely darting eyes which did not want to meet hers and a distinctly ashen face. Both made her nervous. 'I am…well, my lady. You?'

'Well, too.' At this point, she would have usually continued the pleasantries inside while he relieved her of her bonnet, gloves and coat, but Maybury was yet to step aside.

'I have come to visit my father.' That she had to clarify her intention was a worry—one which set her pulse jumping as unease settled like too much porridge in her tummy.

'I shall see if he is in, my lady.' He tried to shut the door on her and she only just managed to stop it with her foot.

In? What was that about?

'We both know he hasn't left the house in months, Maybury.' His heart was too weak and his chest too bad. 'What is going on?'

The darting eyes began to blink rapidly before they dropped to a spot on the step before her and his shoulders slumped. 'We are under strict instructions to announce you, my lady…' When his gaze finally found the courage to lift to hers, it was filled with regret. 'It is more than my job's worth to…'

Lydia held up her hand, fighting for calm herself, but keen not to create more of a scene than she was conscious was already being created. She did not need to see the curtains twitch all around the square to know they were. Such delicious gossip was the lifeblood of Mayfair.

'I understand, Maybury.' Her father was a harsh and unforgiving employer. Always had been. One day staff were there, the next gone and usually with absolutely no explanation. The butler was one of the few who had stuck it out beyond a year and doubtless the only one who had remained for over five. Heaven only knew where he drew his resilience from. 'I am nought but a visitor now and, as such, you are quite right to follow the correct protocols. I shall wait.'

'Very good, my lady.' His relief was palpable as he gently closed the door.

Stood all alone on the steps, she momentarily considered rummaging in her reticule for a handkerchief to give herself something to do which might hint to the nosy neighbours she was nonplussed, before she abandoned the idea. Nobody would be fooled by it and if Papa was intent on sending them a message, then she would hold her head high while he did it. Especially as she had done absolutely nothing wrong.

One painful minute ticked by, followed by two more. Out of the corners of her eyes, she could tell more than a few people had suddenly felt the overwhelming need for some fresh air and were taking a hasty walk, yet still she stared resolutely straight ahead. The temptation to dive back into the sanctuary of Owen's shiny carriage was overwhelming and she was on the cusp of giving in to that urge when the front door finally opened again. Only this time, there was no sign of Maybury. It was Justin who had come to greet her. And by the sight of his attire, the buttoned greatcoat, the tall beaver hat and his favourite ivory-tipped walking cane, they weren't staying.

'Sorry to have kept you waiting.' His smile was feeble as he bent to kiss her cheek. 'Shall we?' He offered her his arm and, to save face and give credence to the charade, she took it and allowed him to lead her back to her conveyance and follow her inside—but not before he instructed her driver to take them to Hyde Park.

The coach jerked forward and they sat opposite one another smiling as if nothing whatsoever was wrong until it left Berkeley Square.

'What is going on?'

Her brother's face was pale, his expression distraught. 'Our father has decided to disown you.'

'What do you mean disown me?' The very idea was preposterous. 'Why would he do that?'

'Because you married beneath you. Because you eloped and embarrassed him in front of Kelvedon. Because you married Wolfe...'

'All three at his express instruction!'

'I know, poppet.' He took her hand and shook his head, huffing out an exasperated breath. 'I've tried to reason with him. Lord knows I've tried to reason with him—but you know Papa. He's a callous bastard who only cares about himself!'

'But I've paid his debts. Saved him from eviction...'

Her head began to spin at the blatant unfairness of it all. 'I married my enemy for him! And now I am to be disowned for simply doing my duty?'

'I'm sure it won't last long. You know Father…he's all about saving face and putting on a front. As he sees it, if he had flung open the door to you and welcomed you with open arms, it might be construed as forgiveness…'

'I have nothing to be forgiven for! *Nothing!*'

Always the frustrating fence sitter, her brother's tone was placating. 'I know that, too, poppet. But Wolfe expressly forbade him from rubbishing you publicly and had it written into the contracts, so in our father's head, cutting you out of his life and leaving you stood on the doorstep clearly sends everyone the same message.'

'Heaven forbid he insults the Marquess of Kelvedon!'

'Perhaps he needs a little more time… In fact, I am sure all he needs is a little more time. You know how he likes to control things and you caught him unawares just now. He wasn't expecting you today. None of us were. To be fair, we didn't even know you were back from Scotland.'

'To be *fair*? What did you expect? That I would stay there for ever?' Sometimes his lack of thought mirrored their self-absorbed father's.

'Of course not… But you sent no message.'

'I wasn't aware I needed to send word to be allowed home!'

He reached for her hand and squeezed it. 'I know it's no excuse for his behaviour, but things haven't been easy since you left.'

'You don't say. Try marrying a complete stranger!' An outright lie, but certainly the truth as far as her brother was concerned. Owen might not be a stranger, not in the biblical sense either, but he was certainly no longer her friend either. Not that Justin had ever known she had once befriended then fallen in love with a servant. She had planned on telling her menfolk when she was old enough to marry Owen without their permission, when they were not in any position to stop her choosing her own mate even if it meant certain banishment. At sixteen, she had been prepared to sacrifice everything for him and probably would have if he hadn't resorted to what he did. After he was arrested, and with her mother so ill and so distraught at his treachery, admitting she had been complicit in bringing a thief into the house was out of the question. 'Things haven't been easy for me either, Justin!'

He acknowledged it with a curt nod. 'The Marquess took your elopement badly and blamed us for not keeping a closer eye on you. Because of his strong connection to the government and his loyal friends in the Lords, Father has been worried about the repercussions. The last thing we want is to fall foul of those men.'

'But I am his daughter. I suppose that counts for nothing in view of Lord Kelvedon's *superior* connections. Better to fall out with me than an old lecher who couldn't pay the asking price!'

'You know how the *ton* works, poppet.' He patted her hand as if she did not and she was sorely tempted to slap it away. 'We are not yet in a financial position to alienate our allies. Then there is the press—who have been an absolute nightmare and have printed such vitriolic lies, the family has not come out of things well.'

'By that, you mean the press have had more sympathy for me and Owen than Papa and the awful Marquess.' Lydia had gone against her new husband's advice and had read every story in Gertie's comfortable parlour. While the reports of their purported 'secret love' were the stuff of fairy tales, not many had expressed their outright outrage at the elopement. Largely because Randolph had successfully turned Owen into St George and Kelvedon into the dragon. 'In which case, Father's perceived loyalty is now misplaced.'

'He's not going to change his mind today, Lydia. If we push him too far, too soon, he might never change his mind at all. Give it a few weeks...'

'*Weeks?* Or months?'

Through the confusion came acceptance and the realisation that, while she was devastated, she wasn't at all surprised by what had just occurred. It had been stupid to expect gratitude for her great sacrifice when her father had never thanked a soul in his life for anything as far as she was aware. All he had ever cared about was himself and his elevated position within the ranks of society.

She also knew he would happily leave her floundering in purgatory for as long as it took to completely and convincingly dissociate himself from her scandalous behaviour—never mind that it had been at his unbending insistence. She had done her duty and now she was no longer his problem. Always the inconvenience. A daughter instead of the spare he had so desperately wanted. Yet without her, dear Papa would currently be doomed and publicly shamed in court and his entire flimsy charade would have collapsed in a far bigger scandal than the one she had been ordered to cause. And to rub salt in the wound, he had the gall to publicly shame her! It beggared belief.

'He hasn't even sent my things, Justin!' Anger at the injustice swiftly replaced the hurt. 'Or am I to be left with just the clothes on my back? Does he also expect Owen to now pay for an entire new wardrobe as well as all the other frivolous debts he bailed our father out of?'

'I shall try to get your things sent to you.'

'*Try?*' Today she had no patience for her brother's particular brand of cautious diplomacy. 'You'll do more than "try", Justin! You *owe* me!' She had only agreed to sell herself in the first place to save her ineffectual elder sibling. 'You *both* owe me! Treating me like this is outrageous.' She was braced for the scandal—not a pillorying from her nearest and dearest.

'You are right.' Instantly, he was contrite. 'Of course you're right… You should have your things…' He dropped her hand as the carriage slowed and the entrance to the park loomed. 'I *will* have them packed today. I promise. Regardless of what Papa has to say about it.' As soon as the wheels stopped, he had the latch open. 'I'll have it all sent to Wolfe's club…unless you'd like it to go somewhere else?' He didn't even know where she lived. Did he not care or was she reading too much into things because she was angry?

'Send it all to Libertas.' And suddenly she was eager to get back there, too. 'Owen and I have a set of rooms on the top floor.' Which she had hoped her brother would visit her in. 'It has a private entrance in the back which is concealed from the main road and quite separate from the club.' She added that as a test, to see if he would ask anything about it or show some interest in her new living arrangements or life or at least give her hope he still wanted to be part of it.

'Splendid.' He squeezed her hand, clearly keen to be off. 'This will all blow over, poppet. I promise. Then everything will be back to normal once again. You'll see.'

Normal? For him, perhaps, but not her. But there seemed no point in voicing that when he was already staring down the road and wishing he was gone.

'And in the meantime?'

'We will work something out.'

Lydia nodded as he closed the door, then practically sprinted back in the direction they had come without as much as a backward glance, feeling more alone than she ever had in her life. While she sympathised with Justin—he held hardly any more sway over her father than she ever had—she couldn't help but feel wounded by his thoughtlessness, too. He was blithely abandoning her to her fate and expecting her to cope with it all alone. It was most unlike him when they had always been so close. Although now she was a married woman, and in view of who she was married to, she supposed that did make things difficult—and Justin had never been good with anything difficult.

'I am fine…thank you for asking.'

Her sigh misted the carriage window as she watched him disappear down Piccadilly.

'And you and *dear* Papa are welcome.'

Chapter Twelve

Gertie had put a flea in Owen's ear. A big and bothersome flea which had been accompanied by a great amount of prodding, eye-rolling and one totally uncalled-for cuff around the ears when she had caught him eating dinner all alone in his office. He was, apparently, a thoughtless, heartless, spineless fool who should be thoroughly ashamed of himself.

He had taken his punishment like a man and nodded belligerently, not mentioning the fact that he already agreed with her unflattering summation and was heartily ashamed of himself anyway. Lydia had lived under his roof for two entire days and, apart from one uncomfortable breakfast, he had so far deftly avoided her for the duration.

However, as much as it pained him, he had to concede Gertie made a valid point. This couldn't be easy on Lydia and it was his role as her husband—a role which still felt like the most ill-fitting pair of boots—to ease her adjustment into his world before he completely abandoned her to it. Especially if she was as miserable as the interfering Gertie had been at such great pains to imply.

It was time to be that bigger man.

He paused outside the door to the living room, briefly

considered whether he should knock and then took a deep breath when he decided against it before actually opening the thing. The room beyond was empty of both Lydia and any furniture, bar the one comfortable armchair Gertie had lent her placed dejectedly in front of the fire which provided the only light.

'Hello?' His voice echoed in the barren space. 'Lydia?'

'I'm here.' Her voice came from behind, making him turn, only to see her sat in the corner hugging a cup of tea, looking so lost and alone it made his chest ache.

'What are you doing on the floor?'

'I thought, for a change, I'd stare at a different wall while I wait for the furniture to arrive. There are only so many hours in a day a lady can shop, especially when the shops have the annoying habit of closing for the evening. Did you get the bills, by the way?' Her voice was flat. Despondent. 'I hope I haven't spent too much. Only you've been so busy we haven't had time to discuss them—so if they are you only have yourself to blame.'

'Was that a dig?'

Her dark eyes finally left her teacup and fixed on his molten ones and he breathed a sigh of relief to see her spirit was nowhere near broken no matter how much Gertie had hinted it was. 'How incredibly perceptive of you to have noticed.'

He was in no doubt he probably deserved that. 'I've been a bit remiss, haven't I?'

'Just a bit.'

'I suppose we should talk… Discuss a few things properly.'

He would hold out an olive branch and try to make amends. As Gertie quite rightly also said, they were stuck in the same leaky rowing boat. If they did not find a way to coexist peacefully, they were both doomed to sink. He really couldn't hide in the office for ever. He'd sat in it so long, the walls were beginning to close in and he had no outstanding work left to do to occupy the time. In desperation, he'd even resorted to dusting off all the futile investigation notes he and Randolph had meticulously made when they had tried and failed to find concrete proof of his innocence. A veritable hornet's nest of dead ends and disappointments which wouldn't go any way towards improving his state of mind.

'Maybe I should order some more tea first? And some cake. You look as though you need a bit of cheering up.'

'What a splendid idea. You order some tea and while it is brewing we can fight over that single chair over there. Although I must warn you, Owen, as I fetched that chair and have sat in this barren room all alone in it these past two interminable days, I'll fight you to the death for it!'

'I already surrender any claim and will sit on the floor as penance.' He held out his hand to help her up and instantly regretted it as she took it. There was something about her touch which awoke all his nerve endings and gave his body ideas. The second he had hauled her upright, and only too aware of how natural it felt to pull her into his arms, he severed all contact and tried to pretend he was blithely unaffected, even though he was.

Supremely affected.

An unfortunate state made worse by the scintillating waft of her signature perfume and the single dark tendril of hair which had escaped its pins and bounced alluringly next to her cheek.

'I'll even commandeer a whole lamp from somewhere if you'll stop scowling at me.'

It wasn't as much of a scowl as a pout, reminding him of the way she looked before she used to raise herself on tiptoes to kiss him goodnight and he reluctantly took him-

.self back to the stable block, all those years ago, to relive the kiss for hours. To torture him, one often-visited memory suddenly jumped to the fore again, of the pair of them one lazy spring afternoon in Hyde Park. They had been rolling around among the trees in their favourite hiding place. She had leaves in her hair and was giggling against his mouth until she stopped giggling and dragged his lips back for another kiss.

Back then, Lydia had loved kissing. And while their trysts had always stayed on the right side of innocent, the feel of her pert breasts flattened against his chest that afternoon had made his unschooled body rampant. But then again, back then, the merest glance at her bosom had done much the same. Those breasts were distractingly fuller nowadays and his body certainly wouldn't mind feeling them pressed against his chest. Or releasing them from her gown and filling his hands with them…

'I am not sure I am quite finished scowling at you.'

It took all his strength not to allow his eyes to drop to her bosom now. 'What happened to our polite armistice?'

'It ceased being polite when you abandoned me to my own devices yesterday morning and failed to return. You didn't even show me around, Owen! You brought me to a strange place, filled with strange people, and deserted me at the first opportunity. That was very poor form.'

'It was.'

'Most ungentlemanly.' Her delightful nose poked in the air. 'Not that *you* have the first clue how to be a gentleman, of course—but as it is the facade you wish to portray to the world it wouldn't hurt you to practise it here, too. At least until I am settled and have a table to place my tea upon.'

'You are absolutely right… Most ungentlemanly. I cannot deny it.' As much as he was enjoying sparring with her, sparring always led to flirting and he wasn't entirely sure he could cope with that in his current state. 'I have no defence of that other than to tell you the truth.'

'Which is?'

'That I am as overwhelmed and confused by our new situation as you are.'

'You are?'

'I am. I have no clue how to behave.' For two days he had felt like a man trapped in a cave with a nest of funnel web spiders, waiting for the inevitable bite, but never knowing quite when it would come. 'I know I said we would avoid each other, but that is not proving to be very practical. There are only so many hours a man can bury himself in work.'

He missed his bed. And her, God help him, which bizarrely was the single biggest reason he'd been hiding. Having her right under his nose was churning up too much of the past. He didn't want to want her, but that did not seem to stop it happening regardless. And as much as he was sorely tempted to act upon it, how could he when she still believed him to be a thief? Their polite armistice wouldn't hold for very long when they couldn't completely bury the hatchet.

'At least you have things to do.' Her tone was wistful. 'I cannot even read a book because there aren't any. Gertie has been a godsend—but I cannot foist myself on her all the time. I've shopped all of Cheapside with impunity, but fear if I purchase any more furniture, there will be no space left to put it when it finally arrives. I would love to visit Bond Street or perhaps call upon my old friends and acquaintances, but…' She shook her head and wandered towards the window, staring out at the night sky cloaking Mayfair, all traces of the previous bravado gone as she rested one dejected hand flat against the glass. 'But it turns out I am a coward at heart, Owen, and do not feel able to face the world properly until we have faced the scandal together. I need to see the lay of the land.'

A husband was meant to stand by his wife. Especially in hours of need. While wallowing in his own self-pity he hadn't considered that either. 'Then we should go out. As soon as possible. Get that part over with so you don't feel so hemmed in.' And perhaps, once she was ensconced safely back into society she wouldn't be constantly underfoot and he would be able to naturally avoid her rather than hiding. 'Did you have a chance to look over all the invitations I gave to you?'

'Of course.' She shot him an exasperated glance over her shoulder. 'Twice, in fact. It's not as if I had anything more pressing to do.' She gestured to the piles neatly arranged on the mantelpiece with a nod. 'Due to sheer boredom, they have been organised into three distinct categories—definitely, maybe and not in a month of Sundays. I've even sorted them in date order.'

'Well, that's a good start.' He grabbed the first bundle and skimmed the details of the invitation on the top. 'Lady Bulphan's...tomorrow. She's a nice old dear. I would certainly be up for that.'

'I can't.' She was back to staring out of the window and sounding sad. 'Not tomorrow.'

'If it's still too soon for you, Lydia, I absolutely understand...'

'It's not too soon, Owen. I think the longer we leave it, the worse it will be. It's just tomorrow is...' He saw her shoulders stiffen before she turned around. 'Merely impossible at the moment. And, much as it pains me to have to admit it, for the stupidest and most shallow of reasons...' She huffed out a breath and stared at a spot somewhere over his left shoulder rather than at him. 'You see, I have absolutely nothing to wear.'

It was obvious she was embarrassed to have even ut-

tered this statement, but attempted to cover it with an imperious flick of her wrist. 'My father, in his infinite and
twisted wisdom, has decided to disown me for having the
audacity to marry you.' She gave him a exasperated shrug
when his mouth fell open. 'And, in the process, has neglected to send over any of my things. Either that or he is
holding it all hostage… Who knows?' Another irritated
flick of the wrist which did not fool him in the slightest.
'All I have are the travelling clothes I packed for Scotland
and not one of those gowns are even slightly suitable for an
evening soirée at Lady Bulphan's. Even an intimate one.'
She tried to make it sound flippant and matter-of-fact,
but he could see she was hurting. Clearly he had missed
something very important while he had been holed up in
the office, pretending to be busy. Something not even the
intuitive Gertie had discovered.

'What do you mean he's disowned you?' The anger was
so swift and fast he didn't have time to mask it. 'How can
he do that when you got him out of debt?'

'Clearly you do not know my father very well, Owen.
Getting him out of debt was merely my duty. Saving face
among the *ton* overrides all else.'

'Where did you read this? Which scandal rag had the
nerve to print it?' Because Owen was going to take the
damning evidence to Fulbrook and demand his ten thousand back for breach of contract! 'I have a signed document—bearing *his* signature—which expressly forbids him
from libelling or slandering you in any way!' The damn
signature was barely dry, too! The lying, conniving, duplicitous snake! He was going to ram it down the vindictive old fool's neck.

'I didn't read it. He's not that stupid. My brother told
me.'

'He came here?' Another titbit he was furious to learn
when he had given all the staff express instructions to

keep an eye out for Lydia's family on the off chance they decided to darken his door. Not that he had intended to stop them darkening it—merely keep a close eye on them if they did. He didn't trust them. Hardly a surprise, really, when they'd had him hauled away in chains.

'No.' There was a hint of disappointment in her voice. 'He never came here. I *foolishly* went there yesterday and was left standing on the doorstep.' The proud bravado cracked a little then. 'It was, as I am sure you can imagine, awful.'

'Oh, Lydia…' He wanted to hold her. Go to her, gather her up into his arms and kiss it all better. Instead, he gripped the back of the chair in case he did.

'I was made a spectacle of so my father could keep in well with Kelvedon and his cronies—and undoubtedly to thumb his nose at you and your clever legal document. Something which I am kicking myself for not considering beforehand—because my father is predictably petty, especially when it comes to getting his own way, and I should have known he would find a way to have the last word now that he has the money.' She shrugged as if it were of no matter, when it obviously was, and his heart wept for her. 'The neighbours certainly enjoyed it.' Her bottom lip trembled slightly before she bit down on it ruthlessly to stop it. 'I am livid, Owen.'

Maybe she was, but above all else she was upset. She had never been very good at hiding her true emotions and the firelight shimmering off the unshed tears in her dark eyes proved his undoing. Of their own accord, his feet took him to her and his hands caressed her arms tenderly before he realised what he was doing and clamped the errant things behind his back. 'Oh, Lydia… I am so sorry. I was trying to protect you with the contracts—I had no idea he would use it against you.'

'This isn't your fault.' Her palm briefly flattened against the front of his waistcoat before she stared at it in bemusement, then took a hefty step back. 'As much as we both know I would like to blame you, it is entirely mine. I went there of my own accord and unannounced, assuming he would go against type and behave like a decent human being, and stupidly handed him the opportunity to humiliate me on a platter. Then I was daft enough to beg for my things, which in turn gave him the power to deny them. My father would have loved both. He likes nothing more than to have the upper hand and to humiliate people. He's a bully at heart. A petty-minded, vindictive, dictatorial… Owen? Where are you going?'

It had been the word *power* which had set him off. Or perhaps it had been *upper hand*, *humiliate* or *bully*. All four had the potency to unleash his rage. All four demanded immediate retribution.

'*Owen?*'

He could hear her confusion from the landing as he tore down the stairs, then the red mist descended over his eyes and he heard nothing more than the heated blood pounding in his ears as he stalked towards the door with his fists clenched.

Chapter Thirteen

The first laden coach arrived at dawn the next morning. By eight, Lydia was surrounded by a sea of hastily packed trunks and boxes strewn haphazardly in the hallway, containing every last stitch of clothing she owned. Clearly Owen had worked a miracle with her stubborn father, although heaven only knew how as he had yet to make an appearance. He had apparently disappeared first thing in another temper, according to Slugger, but nobody knew where he had gone or why. But as Randolph had just informed her he was finally holed up in his office again, she was determined to find out and sick of waiting for the opportunity.

Lydia turned away twice before she found the courage to knock on his door. She had always considered his office sacrosanct and he had never given her cause to think otherwise. However, whether he wanted her there or not, and no matter how awkward she felt by encroaching on his private and personal space, she genuinely needed to thank him for coming to her aid.

He answered her second knock with a distracted enter, so she did just that and found him hunched over the desk, his chin resting on one hand while the other held the quill which scratched as he wrote.

He was also coatless.

Meaning she was treated to the sight of the tight cream silk of the back of his waistcoat stretched taut over his impressive broad shoulders while the soft linen sleeves draped the muscles in his arms as they moved. Her thoughts instantly drifted to the all-too-brief sight of his golden skin, and more specifically the flock of birds etched into it, and all at once, she felt hot as well as awkward.

He finished what he was writing and glanced up, then appeared thoroughly stunned to be confronted with her.

'Hello, Owen.'

'Hello…' He quickly slipped the sheet of paper he had been writing on beneath a ledger and laid down his pen, looking every inch as uncomfortable about her intrusion as she felt. 'Is everything all right?'

'I came to thank you for liberating my things.' Suddenly she had no earthly idea what to do with her hands, which seemed to want to twiddle with her hair, and instantly regretted not bringing him a cup of tea to give them some purpose despite that being a very wifely thing to do. 'It was noble of you to confront my father and call him out about his petty behaviour on my behalf.'

'It was no trouble.'

'As my father is nothing but troublesome, I suspect it probably was.' She pulled out the chair opposite him and perched on it. He hadn't invited her to sit—but standing was making her self-conscious and she wanted some answers. 'How did you manage it?'

'I reasoned with him.' Clearly getting any conversation out of him this morning was going to be like squeezing blood from a stone.

'Impossible.' She found herself smiling at his implausible explanation. 'My father cannot be reasoned with. And you left in such a temper, I doubt you were capable of being reasonable either. There must have been quite the to-do because he wouldn't have relented otherwise'

'It was a bit more than a *to-do*, I'm afraid.' He winced, looking delightfully wary. 'You know me…and my temper… I fear I went too far.'

Clearly he thought she was going to be angry at him for that, when nothing could be further from the truth. She was supremely grateful and inordinately proud of him in equal measure. Nobody had ever fought her corner with quite so much dedication and determination, and absolutely nobody—not even her brother—had ever got her father to see reason. Not once in all her six and twenty years had he ever overturned a decision after he had made it—no matter how wrong he was.

'As I'm not feeling particularly charitable towards him after he left me stood on the doorstep, I dare say he deserved it.'

He winced. 'I *might* have caused a bit of a scene on that same doorstep.'

'You don't say.'

'I might *also* have threatened to rip the front door down with my bare hands if your lily-livered sire continued his cowardly refusal to grant me an audience.'

'Lily-livered?'

His pained expression was completely disarming. 'It was one of a stream of colourful adjectives I *might* have used in the heat of the moment.'

Instantly, she pictured him shouting blue murder and flinging his arms about as he had that evening at the inn and felt laughter bubble. 'I should imagine the neighbours greatly enjoyed that.'

He smiled for the first time and it was devastating. 'I

think they did. I was in full flow by then and drawing quite a crowd.'

'And that was all it took? A noisy scene on the doorstep for him to wave the white flag of defeat?' Had she known that, she might have been brave enough to do it herself, even though it went against years of genteel breeding and doing as she was told.

He shook his head then raked a hand through his hair, clearly considering the best way to answer which might lessen the blow. But he needn't have bothered. It might well be petty, but the thought of her stubborn and pompous father cowering in front of a furious Owen, magnificently incandescent with rage, was too glorious to discard.

'Once I was inside, I *might* have threatened to accidentally drop my copy of the settlement document and my extensive list of the Barton family debts on the doorstep of the *Morning Chronicle* and allow them to publish them with impunity.'

'I am sure that went down well.' Her father was used to his word being final. A challenge like that would have given him an apoplexy.

'He threatened to sue me if I did. For libel of all things. And then had the audacity to remind me of my place and his *superior* connections.'

Two things guaranteed to rile Owen to his core. 'To which you doubtless told him to do his worst.' She could picture it. Owen defiantly standing tall, impressive shoulders pulled back. Perfect jaw lifted as he stared her father straight in the eye.

'I might have called his bluff.' He winced again. 'Actually, I'm certain I did go too far. You see… The thing is…' He huffed out an irritated cross between a huff and a grunt, his features scrunched in consternation. 'Because I was angry…' He was so blatantly annoyed at himself,

Lydia gave in to the urge to reach for his hand across the desk. It was big and strong and comfortingly warm. 'I might have used...'

She touched his arm. It was gloriously solid. 'Whatever you did, I am sure he deserved it, Owen. All of it and more. My father is not a nice man. In truth, I've never particularly liked him.' It felt cathartic to finally say that out loud and not fear the retribution. 'In fact... I am glad somebody finally put him in his place because I cannot stand him.'

'Yet you married me to save him from ruin.'

'It wasn't him I was saving. It was my brother, the tenants and servants, the pensions...' Which all sounded far too noble and selfless when it wasn't entirely true. 'And myself, of course. I couldn't bear the thought of for ever with Kelvedon.'

'You preferred a thief over a lecher?' Lydia couldn't decipher the intense emotion suddenly swirling in his intense, unnerving gaze.

'Better the devil you know.'

Which she realised was an outright lie as soon as she said it and before she saw the flash of disappointment on his face. Maybe there had been some truth in it when she had first accepted his out-of-the-blue proposal, but even then, there had been so much about Owen that appealed more. Now she was supremely grateful she had ignored her brother's advice and listened to her heart and not her head. In the short time they had been married, it was obvious a great deal of the old Owen still remained. He was kind and noble. Thoughtful. Gentle. Loyal to the core. Regardless of the informality of Libertas, his staff adored him. That spoke volumes in itself. And deep down, beneath all the murky, unpalatable and disappointing aspects of their relationship, she instinctively felt she could trust him once again. She also realised she still liked him—very much—warts and all.

'You still think me a devil?' He stared down at where her palm covered his so intently before politely extricating it, doing his best to disguise his obvious disappointment behind a bland expression which failed to reach his expressive eyes.

'No... I didn't mean that the way it sounded.'

'Then what did you mean?'

'I realise things are complicated and very probably insurmountable between us—but I married you because I still believe you are a fundamentally decent man...and I knew he wasn't.'

'Fundamentally decent?'

'It's a start.'

'To what?'

She shrugged, a little shaken by the stark honesty which had suddenly materialised out of nowhere between them, but which also felt necessary. 'I have no earthly idea... Do you?'

Their eyes locked. Then held. And for a moment she saw as clear as day the old Owen completely in those fathomless blue depths. The one she had fallen head over heels in love with. But then, his flicked away, he shook his head and when they returned the old Owen was gone. 'This is uncharted territory for both of us, *Wife*, and until we can find the map, I suppose a start will have to do.'

Chapter Fourteen

They were going to Lady Bulphan's at Lydia's suggestion, now that she finally had all her things and because, undoubtedly, she felt beholden to him for facilitating that. She was boldly taking his advice to face the scandal head on, but while he applauded it wholeheartedly and knew it was absolutely the best way to tackle things, now that the time had undeniably come, he wasn't entirely sure he was ready.

Since she had laid siege to his office earlier, Owen had been at sixes and sevens. Firstly, he hadn't expected her so had not been the least bit prepared and secondly she had held his hand.

Something so pathetically tame and innocent had rendered him a complete mess since. For once it wasn't the uncontrollable lust which was plaguing him, although that had been near constant since their wedding, it had been something else. Something emotional, spiritual and so inexplicably elemental he couldn't begin to put it into words, let alone rationalise other than it had felt right. There had been no thunderbolts. No shifting axis. Certainly no new understanding of the woman he had married. It was more akin to the comforting warmth of a warm feather eiderdown on a chilly night and he had never experienced anything like it in his life.

And then she had admitted, after he had unsubtly prodded, that she thought him fundamentally decent. Which was unsettling. So unsettling he had avoided her for the rest of the day while he attempted to unravel what it meant.

He couldn't avoid her tonight, though. There would be no sanctuary he could flee to when he didn't trust himself around her. No Randolph or Gertie to act as chaperons. They would be in one another's company for hours playing the happy couple for a rapt audience, Lydia by his side or on his arm—and he already knew that would be pure torture because one simple, innocent touch on his damned hand had wreaked havoc with his senses.

And if all that wasn't bad enough, he would have to sit imprisoned in a blasted carriage with her, because that was what the aristocracy did when they went somewhere fancy less than a mile down the road. Already his heart was hammering nineteen to the dozen at the prospect.

Irritated, he tossed the penultimate starched cravat to join the three he had already ruined and realised he would need to seek out Randolph, despite flatly refusing his offer of help only minutes ago, and shamefacedly admit a damn necktie had bested him again. His wily friend would know, without any room for doubt, it was because of her.

He snatched up the last one and flung open his bedchamber door and was confronted with her looking so damn beautiful standing in the glow of the fireplace he momentarily forgot to breathe.

'You look very smart, Owen.'

'You…are wearing red.'

Her smile faltered. 'Do you not like it?'

Not like it? It would be a blasted miracle if his eyes

weren't protruding from his head on stalks! As it was, he had to grit his teeth.

'Should I change?'

Yes! Hours of her wearing that while hanging on his arm would likely be the death of him.

'Of course not.' His voice came out strangled and he was forced to clear his throat. 'You look lovely.' An understatement. She looked ravishing. 'I've just…never seen you in red before.'

She always wore pale colours. Safe colours. The gowns were always pretty—but conservative. This one was anything but. It wasn't fussy, yet the plainness of the scarlet watered silk broken by only a gossamer veil of gauze over the bodice was a statement. The low square neckline was, for want of a better word, spectacular. Enough that all the blood in his body decided to pool hot in his groin.

'That's because I have never worn red before.' She smoothed the seductive concoction self-consciously. 'Papa disapproved of bold colours and would never allow me to wear them, so heaven only knows what possessed me to allow the modiste to talk me into this.

'But Gertie found it in my trunk and insisted this was the gown I should wear for our debut.' At least he now knew who to strangle later—if he survived the night. 'She was adamant the wife of London's most exclusive gentleman's club would make a splash.' Lydia offered a tenuous smile, clearly seeking reassurance. 'Only I am concerned I might be making *too* much of a splash…' her hands flapped awkwardly in the vicinity of her impressive décolleté, drawing his eyes there and giving his body wholly inappropriate ideas '…because she thought the cut too sedate and altered it a bit.'

Pregnant or not, Gertie was going to die.

'You look stunning, Lydia.' Even her hairstyle was

designed to send him mad. And most definitely Gertie's handiwork again, no doubt. Instead of the demurely arranged knot and subtle ringlets he was used to seeing her in, it was now an artful tumble of loose curls which his fingers itched to plunge into.

She beamed at the compliment before her gaze drifted to the starched bit of linen he was clinging on to for grim death, and she giggled, amused. He felt that damn giggle everywhere like a caress. 'Were you in such high dudgeon just now because you are struggling to tie your cravat again?'

His ineptness made him feel like a tongue-tied stable boy. 'Randolph is always better at a fancy knot than I.'

'I could do it.' She shrugged her perfect and completely exposed alabaster shoulders. 'If I say so myself—I have quite a way with cravats. My brother always preferred my knots over his valet's.' She reached out her hand to take it, and he momentarily considered running for the hills before he reluctantly relinquished it and wished he were dead.

While he stood as still as a statue, engulfed in a sultry sea of jasmine, and fully and painfully aroused beneath his coat, she looped the linen around his neck. 'What sort of a knot do you want?'

He couldn't think of a single knot. All their stupidly pretentious names had escaped him. 'Whichever you think is best.'

She stepped back for a moment, tapping her lips in thought as she studied him, drawing his eyes there now, too, and reminding his needy body how much those lips enjoyed being kissed.

'To be frank—I think you should always avoid the fussy. With your height and breadth and handsome face...' Her teeth suddenly decided to worry her bottom lip, drawing the plump skin so achingly slow beneath it he almost groaned aloud. 'In fact...' she offered him a shy and almost tentative smile which he could not begin to decipher '...the more I think upon it, I believe a simple cascade would suit best.'

Owen managed to nod and then held his breath again while her fingers went to work, trying and failing to ignore each accidental brush of his neck and the scant few inches of charged air between them.

Or at least it was charged for him. She was so engrossed in the knot she was obviously not similarly afflicted.

She gazed up into his eyes and all at once he remembered how she used to gaze up at him, back when he wouldn't have hesitated to dip his head and taste her mouth, wondering if she still possessed that earthy passion which had always tipped him over the edge. 'Do you have a stick pin?'

Another curt nod before he held out his other hand and uncurled his clenched fist, mortified to see he'd clenched the damn thing so hard the ostentatious sapphire Randolph had talked him into wearing had made a deep indent into his palm. He held back the wince this time—just—hoping she wouldn't notice the damning evidence of how completely she affected him without even trying.

'Blue...like your eyes.'

Which had been why his meddling friend had insisted he wear it. To match his equally blue patterned-silk waistcoat. The tailor had called it periwinkle, which was a ridiculous shade for a grown man to be wearing. Owen never should have agreed to it. He probably looked like a blasted dandy! One who was trying too hard to impress a certain lady with his refined gentlemanly tastes, who only thought him fundamentally decent, but whom he suspected he still adored.

'Randolph picked it.' Seeing as she was already in the

process of arranging the jewel in the folds, he stared up at the ceiling rather than stare directly down her cleavage, wishing he had worn black or beige. Dull colours which would help him blend into the wallpaper seeing as the ground was resolutely refusing to open and swallow him in his hour of need. 'Should *I* change?'

'No... Blue suits you. You look...very dashing.' Her fingers left his neck to smooth his lapels before she finally stepped back, looking every inch as awkward about what had just transpired as he did. Had she sensed he was practically aflame with desire? He certainly hoped not.

'Isn't it funny the pair of us took separate sartorial advice from Mr and Mrs Stubbs?' Her index finger played with a loose tendril against her neck. She had such a sensitive neck. And ears. She used to sigh when his teeth nibbled them. 'Nerves always make me doubt myself and I cannot deny I am anxious about our first public appearance.'

'Just look them dead in the eye and smile unapologetically.' The firelight was picking out the copper in her hair and throwing enticing shadows on her skin. Owen couldn't seem to stop gazing at her or ignore the loud voice in his head which was suddenly insisting they forget all about Lady Bulphan's soirée to stay home and get reacquainted. 'If you appear as if you happily belong there, nobody will question it.'

'Is that *your* secret, Owen? Bravado?'

Yes.

Obviously.

The public face of the new Owen Wolfe was a complete fabrication. A battle-ready suit of armour which he could don at will. Except around her apparently. Around her it was as flimsy as a cobweb.

He ignored her question to glance at his pocket watch.

'We should go.' It came out more bark than observation. 'By my reckoning all the other guests should be there now.'

It had been his idea they be a little more fashionably late, reasoning they'd get all the gawping and whispers over and done with in one fell swoop rather than dribs and drabs—but that, too, was making him nervous. Especially if he appeared as overwhelmed with his stunning new wife as he was right now. The gauche stable lad rather than the successful businessman. Fundamentally decent, but desperate to be more.

Lydia nodded and grabbed the heavy velvet cape he had not noticed draped over the chair. 'Yes... I suppose we should.'

She left the room first and they descended the three flights of stairs in total silence. Waiting for them in the hallway was a grinning Randolph and Gertie and a less frowning Slugger than usual.

'Oh, my!' Gertie's hands cupped her heart. 'Don't you both look wonderful! Like a princess and her handsome prince.' He would strangle the witch for that comment later, too. The last thing he needed was Gertie's well-intentioned matchmaking on top of her successful attempt at turning his wife into a lethal seductress.

It was Slugger who stepped forward to help Lydia on with her cape, and Owen felt stupid at not having the wherewithal to have offered. But as he felt as though he was stood on the edge of the crater of an erupting volcano, his mind resolutely refused to work properly. Randolph gestured to the open door, sweeping into a courtly bow. 'Your carriage awaits, Your Royal Highnesses.'

'Carriage?' She turned to him, concerned, and Owen felt two inches tall.

'How else are we supposed to get to Lady Bulphan's?' He would brazen this out. If it was the last thing he did, he would muster every last drop of bravado to act convincingly nonplussed about the locked box on wheels encasing him and the jasmine-scented enchantress who was scrambling his wits.

Owen stalked in the direction of the mews, expecting her to follow, but she hesitated on the frosty cobbles, then gazed up at the stars and her sigh turned to wispy clouds in the frozen air.

'As it is such a lovely night and as I am in no great hurry to be a public spectacle, would you mind if we walked? We are less than five minutes away...'

She was rescuing him. He was simultaneously humbled, grateful and thoroughly touched at the gesture. 'I suppose I wouldn't mind the walk.'

'Good...because we need to talk about wallpaper.'

'We do?' Because it seemed expected, and suddenly felt entirely natural, he held out his arm and she took it.

'I was thinking stripes—unless you prefer a pattern?'

'I like stripes.' And bizarrely some of his nerves lessened as they strolled companionably together into the night.

Chapter Fifteen

'Make no bones about it—being invited to stay at Aveley Castle is quite the coup, Owen. And just before Christmas, too! The Aveley Christmas soirée is legendary. Very intimate and very exclusive. They never invite more than twenty people, so to be one of them is beyond impressive. My father would have given his eye teeth for such an invitation.' It was past midnight and they were walking home from a sumptuous dinner at the Renshaws in Grosvenor Square. 'The Duke must be very taken with you…or is it the Duchess you have so thoroughly charmed?'

Life had settled into its own rhythm over the past two weeks and Lydia found herself surprisingly comfortable with many aspects of it. She had made great friends with Gertie, which had been lovely, adored helping her with the children and found Libertas feeling more and more like home. One by one, the individual pieces of furniture, curtains and rugs she had meticulously chosen began to arrive and the barren living room was now a cosy oasis—albeit one her husband rarely stopped in for long.

After their first public appearance, which had gone far better than she could have possibly imagined, they received a flurry of invitations to different events and she and Owen had gone out as a couple at least twice a week since. As he had predicted, the romantic fairy tale, which the newspapers had helped embellish, ensured they were largely accepted wherever they went. While she was in no doubt this was probably more to do with the appetite for gossip than her former standing in society, in the main most were polite at least and some went out of their way to be friendly. A few turned their noses up and she didn't feel ready to call upon acquaintances again yet, but all in all the dust had settled and most of the initial scandal seemed to have passed.

That was such a relief. It was nice to feel able to venture out in the world again, especially as she no longer needed to worry about chaperons or asking her controlling father's permission. As a married woman, she had more freedom and independence than she'd ever had and was grateful her new husband was nothing like her father.

It was nicer still slowly rediscovering aspects of her friendship with Owen on these quiet evening strolls when it was just the two of them. She hadn't realised quite how much she had missed it and found herself wishing they spent more time together at home. But he religiously maintained his distance from her there unless Gertie and Randolph were around—or they happened to be en route to or from a social engagement like tonight.

'As I am sure you are well aware, *Wife*...' He slanted her a mischievous glance. 'I have such a way with the ladies, it is obviously the Duchess. Are you jealous?'

'Not in the slightest. She has a ridiculously handsome duke who is obviously madly in love with her... Why on earth would she want you?' Gertie had let slip the real reason, because as usual her husband was annoyingly tight-lipped about anything personal. 'Aside from your money, of course. I should imagine she is delighted to receive your *monthly* donation to her orphanage… And her soup kitchen.'

'Have you been gossiping with Randolph again?'

'Surely discussing your generosity isn't gossip? Although why you would keep it a secret is beyond me. Where I come from, people brag about how philanthropic they are.'

'A few pounds do not constitute philanthropy, Lydia.'

'Indeed, they do not—but a few *hundred* do, Owen.' She nudged him playfully with her elbow, enjoying the solid feel of his arm beneath her gloved hand a little too much. 'And before you blame Randolph for that titbit as well, I should confess I got it first-hand from the Duchess herself.' Since discovering he had suffered eight months on a hulk, Lydia had been on a mission to glean as much information about him as she could, justifying it to herself as trying to better understand the man he was now because he was so reticent about telling her anything. 'Why did you feel the need to keep it a secret when you might have known she would mention it when she extended the invitation?'

'Because nobody likes a braggart.'

'Or more likely you enjoy being a man of mystery.'

'Perhaps a little. Being mysterious has turned out to be *very* good for business.'

As if to prove him right, as they turned into Curzon Street the long line of carriages was still queueing to deposit eager gentlemen at Libertas. Fridays were always a particularly busy night, especially when the other entertainments and parties finished.

'For what it is worth, I think it is a very generous and noble thing to do.' Beneath her fingers, the muscles in his arm tightened, a sure sign he was uncomfortable with the compliment.

'It simply makes sound business sense. People like a charitable man.'

He was exasperating. 'Liar. You do it because you know how it feels to have nothing. And you know what it is like to have nobody in the world. You were orphaned at eight, Owen, and stuck in an orphanage until you were fourteen. You hated it. Especially the food. You developed a lifelong hatred of porridge on the back of it. And you were there till you were fourteen because you were too big to stuff up a chimney. Nobody would take you on as an apprentice in the other trades because you were too tall—they thought you would eat too much.'

He stopped dead. 'You remember all that?'

Why was he surprised? 'Of course I remember. Once upon a time you used to tell me things.'

'That was before we had an armistice and agreed never to talk about the past.'

Which he had taken literally, no doubt to vex her, when she had never intended the dratted thing to encompass all their past. Just the bit which always broke her heart to dwell upon. The bit she still did not want to believe, but had to accept. But how to tell him all that without reopening the wound? 'I also remember exactly where we were when you told me about it. We were in *our* spot. Behind the trees at the back of the Serpentine.'

'Hidden from the world.' She detected a distinct hint of bitterness in that statement as he started forward again as if he were suddenly annoyed.

'Why do you say it like that?'

'Because I was your guilty secret.' Which sounded dirty. 'And you were ashamed of me… Of us.'

'I was neither ashamed nor guilty. But I was mindful of the fact life would become impossible for us if anyone suspected our relationship then.'

'*Really?*' It was disbelief this time, rather than bitterness. 'It obviously had absolutely *nothing* to do with me being a stable boy who wasn't good enough and you being an earl's daughter who was destined to do better.'

'Absolutely not!'

'Then why did we creep around? Why did you beg me never to tell a living soul about us?'

'I was sixteen, Owen.' They weren't even discussing the past, yet were still arguing. Her own fault, she supposed, as she had been the one to stupidly dig it up rather than leave it buried. 'I had barely any freedom at all, if you recall!' If he was going to accuse her of being selfish and shallow, then she was entitled to defend herself. 'You know full well my father controlled everything! And I knew if word found its way to him about us, he would have dismissed you on the spot and I would have been sent to some horrible ladies' school somewhere in the back of beyond run by nuns and we would never have seen each other again.' A grim fact which had given her so many nightmares at the time. 'I couldn't bear that because—' She clamped her errant jaws shut. That was undoubtedly more information than she was comfortable giving.

Owen's step slowed and, when hers didn't, he tugged her back. 'You couldn't bear that because...?'

She fumbled for an excuse which skirted around the intensely personal truth, but there was something about the power of his gaze which wrenched it out regardless.

'Because I never wanted to be apart from you, you wretch. I adored you! I thought once I reached my majority we...' Her toes were curling inside her slippers and she bitterly regretted wandering down this cringingly awkward path in the first place. This was all too personal. Too mortifying. Too truthful. 'For pity's sake! I was sixteen,

Owen! Filled with the silly romantic notions all sixteen-year-old girls have.'

'You *adored* me?' The ghost of a smile played at the corners of his mouth and his dazzling blue eyes were twinkling. He was clearly enjoying her abject discomfort and was intent on milking it for all it was worth. '*Genuinely* adored me?'

That he doubted it made her roll her eyes. 'I was an idiot. Fresh from the schoolroom and green around the gills.' A trusting, smitten and reckless fool. 'But I soon realised my mistake.' All the hurt came rushing back then. The disbelief followed by the crushing grief of his betrayal. 'And swiftly got over it.'

'So am I to assume that once you reached your majority, you had plans to run away with me?'

She gripped the edges of her cloak and marched forward without him, furious at herself for confessing that much. 'I was sixteen, Owen!'

'But you knew then you wanted to marry me?' She cursed his long legs for effortlessly keeping pace with her. 'Were we going to elope?'

Yes.

A mad and romantic dash to Gretna Green.

Although that irony was not lost on her now. All her foolish dreams had come true—in part. This certainly wasn't how she had envisioned things. 'I hadn't thought that part through.'

She felt his hand on her arm a split second before he spun her around. 'Liar...'

His gaze locked with hers, seeking the truth, and to her utter disgust she feared he saw it. All at once, his eyes seemed darker. The irises stormy. Hypnotic. She felt exposed, vulnerable, but couldn't seem to tear hers away. He smoothed his palms down her arms until he found her hands, then tugged her closer. He dipped his head a little, then hesitated.

His warm breath caressed her cheek. Her lips tingled with awareness.

Time stood still…

'There you are!' Slugger's voice came out of nowhere from behind the parked carriages, making them simultaneously jump apart. 'Step lively, the pair of you! Gertie's gone into labour!'

'What have I done? What *have* I done?'

Randolph was pacing and, after an hour of constant self-flagellation since Gertie went into labour, was on the cusp of rending his garments.

Owen had given up trying to make him calm down, knowing from the last three labours that nothing he did was going to work. His friend would whip himself into a frenzy until he heard the babe cry and saw with his own eyes his beloved wife was alive and well. Then—and only then—would he miraculously and instantaneously become rational once again. In the meantime, he would be a wreck. Which was damned inconvenient because Owen had better things to think about.

Like Lydia's confession she had planned to run away with him all those years ago because she had adored him.

Adored *him*!

Her exact words and he still wasn't quite over them. She had said as much back then, of course, and more. But tonight he saw the truth in them.

Lady Lydia Barton could have had anyone—yet she had wanted him.

Behind the door, Gertie moaned in pain, dragging him back to the present, and Randolph clutched his own stomach in sympathy as he paced and practically howled, 'She's hurting, Owen! She's hurting! And it's all my fault!'

As technically it was, he had no words of comfort to ease his friend's guilt. Instead, Owen unfolded himself from the chair and wandered to the sideboard to pour him a brandy. 'It will all be over soon.' He held out the glass and wrapped one arm around the other man's shoulders. 'Come. Sit. Gertie's sailed through every labour so far and I've heard it gets easier each time.'

Randolph nodded, clasping the glass in both hands as if it were the Holy Grail, and swallowed the entire contents in one go before handing it back for Owen to refill it. 'I keep telling myself I should abstain… After all these years I know exactly when to avoid it… When I should sleep in another room… But I cannot help myself.' His pained expression was tragic. 'You've seen her. She's a goddess… A seductress… I can't keep my hands off her. I do not possess your willpower, Owen.'

He wasn't entirely sure he possessed it now either. With every passing day it got harder and harder. Tonight, if Slugger hadn't interrupted, he'd have kissed her. And then what?

She would know he still had feelings. Know she still had power over him. Either one gave her the upper hand and frankly scared the hell out of him.

Another moan came from the bedchamber beyond and, as Randolph threw his arms in the air and began to flagellate himself again, the door flew open.

'Any sign of the physician?' Lydia was wide-eyed and clearly panicked. The evening gown she was still wearing was hanging limply from one shoulder and half of her artfully tousled hairstyle had collapsed.

'He's just finishing up another birth on Bruton Place and will be here presently.'

This news did nothing to placate her. 'And the midwife?' Her voice was unusually high pitched.

'She is not at home…but we have a man posted there to fetch her here as soon as she materialises…' One hand reached out and grabbed his cravat.

'The baby is coming, Owen!'

His eyes swivelled to the clock on the mantel and then he smiled in reassurance. 'No, it isn't. It's much too soon. She's only been in labour an hour. We've at least another three to go.'

Chapter Sixteen

'Then perhaps you'd like to tell the baby that? Because I can assure you it's coming now!' On cue, Gertie's strangled moan cut through the pause, then she began to pant.

Behind Owen, Randolph dropped to his knees and howled, 'This is all my fault, Lydia! *What have I done?*'

'It can't be coming now.' His tone was irritatingly patronising. 'Her last labour was five hours. The one before that nine and Lottie was a good eighteen...'

Lydia pulled him into the bedchamber and pointed to where Gertie was propped on the bed, knees braced, teeth gritted and clearly bearing down. 'Look at her, Owen! Does that look like a woman with hours to go to you?'

He warily took in the scene, his eyes widening at her cry of pain, until Gertie noticed him between contractions and seemed to forget she was busy. Something she bizarrely seemed to do as naturally as breathing. 'Hello, Owen. How's Randolph holding up?'

'Oh, you know...' He smiled weakly, trying to keep his eyes on her face rather than below her neck. 'The usual.'

But when Gertie's face suddenly contorted and she groped for his hand, he was there like a shot.

'Ooh!' She squeezed so tightly the tips of his fingers

were practically purple and, at a complete loss as to what else to do, Lydia wrung out a cloth and mopped her friend's sweaty brow, all the while sending her clueless husband a pointed message with her eyes.

It took him a while to receive it. When he did, he smiled nervously and patted Gertie's hand. 'The physician is on his way. He'll be here within the hour.'

Gertie grunted again, her knuckles white as she gripped Owen's hand even tighter, then her breath sawed in and out as she pushed. 'I haven't got an hour, Owen. This baby is coming now.' Clarification which, frankly, did not require repeating as far as Lydia was concerned but which seemed to finally galvanise him into action.

'Right, then...' His panicked eyes sought hers and he gestured to the door. As soon as they were out of earshot, he rattled out a plan.

'I'll get Slugger to sit with Randolph and I'll go fetch the physician myself.'

'That's it? That's your plan?' She grabbed his lapels and shook. 'And what do you expect me to do in the meantime?'

'Well, obviously, as the only woman here...'

Her mouth hung slack before she found her voice. 'I've never delivered a baby!'

'You have the same...' his finger pointed ineffectually towards the middle of her ruined gown '...equipment.'

'Which I have never used, Owen! I don't have the first clue what to do! You're the one who's been here before. Gertie told me you've attended all three of her births!'

'Only sat outside, Lydia! Dealing with blasted Randolph! You've seen how he is! He can't be left alone.' To prove this, he flung open the door and she was confronted with the sight of the father-to-be moaning as he paced and clutched at his stomach.

'Well, you cannot leave me alone either!' It was her turn to grip his hand and she must have done it so forcefully he stared down—then his fingers curled around to encase hers. 'I need you here, Owen! Here! Where the *real* drama is happening.'

'Then I'll be here… I promise.' He glanced back towards Randolph and took a deep breath. 'Give me a couple of minutes to organise everyone and fetch towels and hot water and then I'll be back.'

She nodded, the panic lessening because he would be here and he would be in control. 'What are the towels and hot water for?'

He shrugged, completely destroying her fleeting confidence. 'I have absolutely no idea. I just recall the midwife asking for them.'

'*Ooh!*'

Lydia scurried back to her friend's bedside as Owen dashed out the door, trying to project a calmness she did not feel.

'Not long now, Gertie.'

Which from her limited knowledge of the birthing process was probably the case. The contractions seemed to be coming thick and fast, and by the way Gertie slumped back on to the pillow afterwards, they were lasting longer, too. Her poor friend looked exhausted.

'And even if the physician or the midwife don't get here, I am here with you.'

No matter how petrified she was on the inside, Lydia was determined to project a calm facade. The last thing she wanted to do was make her friend panic.

'Everything is going to be all right.'

'It's all fairly straightforward, you know.' How Gertie had the strength and wherewithal to smile was beyond her. 'Pushing the head out is the hardest bit. Once that's out, you'll just need to be poised to catch the baby. Or at least you'll likely have to catch this one. He's in a dreadful hurry to be born.'

'He? It could very well be a she, you know.'

'Mark my words, only a man causes this much trouble. You wait till you and Owen have children. You'll be able to tell the difference after the first.'

It wasn't meant as a cruel comment or a cutting jibe, but it wounded still. 'I doubt there will be a first.' She couldn't quite bring herself to say never. 'We don't have *that* sort of marriage.'

'Not yet, perhaps—but you will. I've always thought Owen would make a wonderful father. You've seen him with mine.'

She had, so couldn't deny it. Owen had all the warmth, tolerance, patience and love which had been so sadly lacking in her own sire. 'We haven't discussed children.'

Lydia hoped the next intense contraction would be an end to the conversation—but Gertie was like a dog with a bone.

'Don't you want them?'

'Of course, but…' How to put it into words delicately without blatantly spelling out her new husband would much prefer to avoid her than make babies. 'Unlike you and Randolph, we married for financial reasons.'

'So did we.'

That pulled Lydia up short. 'It wasn't a love match?' Because to observe them now that idea was inconceivable. Randolph and Gertie clearly adored one another.

'We were complete strangers when we wed.' At Lydia's startled expression Gertie giggled. 'That surprises you, doesn't it! But it's true. I met him for the first time on the Friday when he came to the women's factory looking for a wife and we were wed two days later on the Sunday.'

'That was fast.' It certainly put hers and Owen's hasty four days to shame.

'That was the way of things in New South Wales. You grabbed the bull by the horns before it ran past and disappeared over the mountains.'

'Randolph told me you were thoroughly seduced by his rugged good looks and rapier wit.' Which was such a typical Randolph comment to make, she had taken it with a big pinch of salt, but assumed he had worn her down gradually because he was so infectiously lovable.

Gertie rolled her eyes, then winced, her hands fisting in the bedsheets as she sucked in several calming breaths. 'I was...actually seduced by...' she exhaled loudly, then sank back on to the pillow '...the size of his purse and the promise of a roof of my own over my head. Things weren't easy for a girl alone in the New World. People take advantage.' Gertie's eyes clouded momentarily.

'But after a year of living hand to mouth, I decided enough was enough and promised myself when the next crop of desperate and lonely men came begging for a wife, I would snag myself the one with the best prospects. And on that day, thank goodness, it was Randolph.'

Gertie laughed at the memory while her index finger idly stroked the plain gold band she wore on her wedding finger as if its mere presence gave her a great source of comfort. 'It was funny, really. As I remember discussing it all with a friend that very morning and when I declared my criteria, I actually said, "I don't care if he's three feet tall, as long as his pocket jingles."' She grinned at Lydia. 'Life can be wonderfully ironic sometimes. I often think fate likes to play with us.'

It had certainly played with her and Owen.

'And that was all it took for you to agree to marry him?'

'As mercenary as it sounds, that was all it took. You

weren't the only one in dire straits and forced to marry in haste, Lydia. At least you and Owen knew each other before you were wed. All we knew were each other's names—but it all worked out in the end and we fell head over heels in love. Just as it will all work out for the pair of you.'

'Things would probably be easier if Owen and I did not know each other.' Lydia shrugged, trying not to feel depressed at the sorry state of her marriage. 'There is too much animosity between us.'

'Is there?' Gertie said. 'From where I am standing there seems to be a lot more between you than a little animosity. Enough that I suspect the animosity doesn't stand a chance of keeping the pair of you apart successfully for very long.'

Against her better judgement Lydia was curious. 'Such as?'

'Obvious friendship despite your differences.'

'I suppose…'

'Mutual affection…'

'I wouldn't go that far.'

'Mutual attraction. Obvious and palpable lust…'

'There is no lust, I can assure you. At least not on my part.' Good grief—was it that visible? Her friend's spontaneous bark of laughter at her lie was mortifying.

'Girl, you cannot look at him without drooling, nor he you. I cannot fathom why you're both so adamantly denying yourselves.'

'Because things are complicated.'

'Then for the love of God and for the sake of your own sanity, *uncomplicate* them as it is clear to me, and everyone else here for that matter, that a good roll in the hay is exactly what you and your idiot husband need. He's a handsome devil and thoughtful—and thoughtful men always make the best lovers. I know. Mine is *exceedingly* thoughtful.' By the scandalous expression on her face her friend was not alluding to her husband's good deeds. 'Deliciously thoughtful, in fact. I remember the first time...'

'Gertie!' This was all so embarrassing.

'Do his kisses make you melt?'

They had done. A decade ago when he had last kissed her. 'We don't have that sort of relationship... Or at least not any more.'

'Then I suspect that is the root of the problem! All that pent-up lust is fermenting and festering and sending you both daft. Take my advice. Kiss him tonight! Sprawl yourself across him and throw caution to the wind. Then tell him you want his baby... And if I'm right, Owen will happily give you one—and all your problems will be solved.' Then Gertie laughed again at her own bawdy humour until it turned into another grunt which seemed to go on for ever.

Gertie was in the midst of another punishing contraction when Owen's head appeared tentatively through the door. As he edged inside, looking every inch a man who would rather be absolutely anywhere else in the world, she saw he was carrying two steaming buckets of water and had half the linen closet draped around his neck.

'Slugger has Randolph, I've closed the club and dispatched every available body to hunt for the midwife.' She saw his Adam's apple bob nervously as he stared at the child bed. 'In the meantime I am at your service.'

'Gertie has been talking me through what we need to do.'

He smiled weakly, his handsome face bleached of all colour. 'Splendid.'

'Your job is to hold Gertie's hand and mop her brow.'

He nodded, clearly relieved he wouldn't be at the business end. 'Splendid... Splendid... I can do that.'

'And my job is to catch the baby when it comes out.' He nodded again, looking every bit as overwhelmed by the prospect as Lydia was. 'Then we have to cut the cord.'

'With what?'

'The scissors on the nightstand.'

'Scissors… Nightstand… Splendid.' His gaze travelled to the piece of furniture, then quickly returned, his brows furrowed. 'And when, exactly, do we use the towels and hot water?'

She shrugged, bewildered, just as Gertie gripped the bedstead and they both saw first-hand exactly what those items were for.

'We might also need a mop, too, Owen…once we're done.'

If he was squeamish, he didn't show it, and with stiffly squared shoulders he walked decisively to the bed. As he took Gertie's hand, she practically growled as fresh pain tore through her.

'Argh! Ooh!'

He held up his end relentlessly, his eyes intermittently flitting to Lydia's for reassurance as the contractions suddenly all seemed to merge into one. Then Gertie gripped his shirt, pulling him to eye level and snarling directly in his face.

'You tell Randolph if he ever touches me again I am going to kill him!'

'You have my solemn pledge, Gertie, if he ever touches you again, I will kill him for you.'

'Thank y— *Ooh!*' She rode the contraction and then let go of his hand long enough to point a quaking finger at Lydia. 'Ignore what I said before! Never let a man touch you! Or kiss you! Or do all the other wicked things they do so well to thoroughly seduce y— *Ooh!* Because this is what happens!'

She growled again, her nails biting into poor Owen's skin until he had to resort to peeling her fingers off one by one and reattaching them to his hand.

'I'm going to have Randolph castrated!'

'A splendid idea.' He gently mopped her brow as the contraction subsided. 'He thoroughly deserves it.'

'You'll need to be castrated, too, Owen!' He nodded sagely as she gripped his hand again.

'I'll get us all done as soon as this is over. I promise. Slugger, too.' He slanted Lydia an amused glance. 'We'll use the scissors on the nightstand.'

'You're all vile seducers!'

'We are indeed... Vile...the lot of us.'

The next fraught ten minutes were spent much the same and, to his credit, Owen endured it all stoically despite looking absolutely terrified throughout.

When it became apparent the time for pushing had properly come, at her insistence he sat behind Gertie on the mattress and supported her weight and stared diligently at the ceiling as Lydia pulled up her nightgown and hoped for the best.

The baby's head was crowning.

Each time Gertie pushed a little bit more emerged. It was hideous and wonderful at the same time. An eye-opening lesson of what her body could do.

'That's it... Keep pushing.' Remarkably, her voice sounded authoritative and confident as a tiny ear appeared. Two squeezed tight eyes. Then a nose. 'Once more, Gertie... Just once more... Deep breath...' As if it might somehow help, she sucked in a lungful of air and then saw Owen do the same, then all three of them blew it out slowly.

'Ooh!'

'That's it, Gertie... The head is out.' She smiled at Owen in wonder and he smiled back.

Because it felt like the right thing to do, she gently grasped the baby's neck and crown to help it battle its way into the world, only to feel the barrier of its shoulders preventing it.

'We need a big push now... A really big one.' Gertie nodded, her knuckles white as they gripped Owen's big hand.

This time, as he supported her through the contraction, he forgot to avert his eyes and watched transfixed as the child slithered out of Gertie's body all in one go. And to everyone's delight it was angry.

'He's got excellent lungs... You were right, Gertie... It's a boy.'

Lydia was crying. She had no idea when the tears started, but the burst of emotion was so intense there was no chance of stopping it. Thankfully, the baby was crying, too. A high-pitched, loud and noisy wail filled the room as Gertie's baby first filled his lungs. His tiny face furious at being denied the warm comfort of the womb and his perfect little fists clenched as he kicked and squirmed and complained for all he was worth.

'He's beautiful.' Instinctively, she cradled him, then, realising the job wasn't finished, gestured to Owen to take over while she helped Gertie push out all that was left.

He didn't dally. Instantly, he was at her side, gingerly wrapping his big arms around the newborn and soothing the child, his deep voice murmuring nonsense which did absolutely nothing to quieten the babe. Something about the sight of him like that unnerved her and made her yearn in equal measure, so much so she had to tear her eyes away to complete the task in hand. With much more confidence than she knew she possessed, Lydia tied and cut the cord, then cleaned her friend up.

When Owen reverently handed the squalling baby to its mother, there were tears in his eyes, too. He made no attempt to hide his emotion as he retreated from the room to fetch the father.

Seconds later, Randolph burst through the door, grinning, and soon he was also crying with complete abandon, alternately kissing his wife, then his new son, and telling them both how much he loved them.

It was such a lovely moment. Tender. Heart wrenching. Poignant. Exactly like the birth and all at once Lydia's womb seemed to clench. It was obvious husband and wife loved each other, just as it was obvious they had instantly fallen in love with their new son and she was envious of their joy and their happiness, and simultaneously devasted that she might never get to experience any of it for herself. She decided there and then she couldn't let that happen. Not when she deserved this, too.

Owen's arm snaked around her waist. 'I think it's time for a tactical retreat. And perhaps a couple of very stiff brandies.'

Lydia nodded. 'Brandy sounds good.' The feel of him wrapped around her felt better.

Wordlessly, they slipped out and clicked the door quietly shut.

'That was…quite something.' She was exhausted. Both physically and mentally. Confused and overwhelmed, her emotions dangerously close to the surface. For some strange reason she wanted to curl up into a ball and sob.

'Yes, it was.' His thumb brushed a tear from her eye. 'You were quite something, too, Lydia.' The pad of one finger traced the shape of her cheek. 'I am inordinately proud of you.'

'All I did was wait at the right end and catch.'

'You took command of the situation, mobilised the troops and completely saved the day. You even managed to look as though you knew what you were doing.'

'It was all bravado. I am actually a complete mess.' She felt her bottom lip quiver as it all bubbled to the surface and then, because it felt like the most necessary thing in the world, Lydia buried herself in his chest.

Owen let her cry, clearly sensing she needed to, his strong arms wrapped tightly around her and his chin resting on her head. He didn't offer any inane platitudes, nor did he try to hasten the process or try to get to the bottom of what was wrong. He simply hugged her tighter while her tears soaked into his shirt and all the bottled-up feelings she had kept inside for weeks spilled out in one noisy, soggy rush.

Kelvedon, Gretna, her family, Owen, the past, the present, the future... All of it needed releasing, yet practically none of it made sense.

As the racking sobs finally subsided and she still clung to him, he kissed her hair and rocked her gently. Finally, when she was sure there couldn't possibly be a drop of moisture left in her body, she pulled away a little to rest her forehead on his shoulder, suddenly embarrassed at her outburst, but not ready to completely sever the contact because she desperately still needed his strength.

Still needed him. And through all the uncertainty, that was all that made sense.

'I'm sorry... I'm a little overwhelmed.'

'As am I...truth be told.'

She could hear the emotion in his voice. Beneath her palm, she could feel his heart beating, the reassuring heat of his strong body through the soft linen of his shirt. She felt the pull of his stare and stupidly gazed up, then lost herself in it.

He dipped his head.

She stood on tiptoes.

And when his lips touched her, she sighed as the world stopped turning and then promptly disappeared.

Chapter Seventeen

Ignoring the chilling December drizzle, Owen took the long way home from his second meeting at Bow Street, needing time to ponder exactly what he did next. Engaging two Runners to investigate his case had been a big step and one he had avoided up until now because of his innate distrust of the flawed legal system which had failed to protect him so spectacularly. However, with every passing day it was becoming more apparent he couldn't let sleeping dogs lie any longer. The sand was shifting beneath his feet and things between him and his new wife were changing, too. Besides, there was no escaping the fact the Runners had resources at their disposal which he had no access to and which might tunnel a way through the dead ends he and Randolph had smacked into at every turn.

Already, they had tracked down several of the Earl of Fulbrook's former employees, including a very promising lead on Mr Argent—Owen's old stable master—who had moved to the Barton estate in Cheshire where he and Randolph had lost track of him. But after one of the Runners had travelled there to make enquiries, now they believed he had moved even further north after suffering a stroke, to reside with a daughter in the Lake District. At doubtless great expense, that Runner was headed there while the other, the older and less friendly of the two, remained in London to dig deeper into the records here. Owen couldn't say he liked the fellow overmuch, but he couldn't deny he was both dogged and thorough and as crafty as a fox to boot.

He had also given Owen a whole new angle to explore— Lydia was a thus far untapped source of information. An insider who would have seen things, heard things and noticed things no servant would have been privy to. As tempting as it was to leave everything to Bow Street, he knew it had to come from him. But for the life of him he couldn't think of a single subtle way to ask her without letting her know he was engaged in a last-ditch attempt to prove his innocence—entirely for her. Even though his chances of doing so were slim to say the least.

The Runners were right. Ten years was a long time for a trail to go cold.

He wanted to blame the imprudent and completely earth-shattering kiss they had shared a week ago for sending him on this fool's errand to more frustration and disappointment—but knew its roots stemmed much further back. The simple truth was he hated that she thought ill of him and desperately wanted to remove that destructive barricade between them.

To what end, he wasn't entirely sure.

It wasn't as if he could turn back time and change history. He wasn't the same Owen as he'd been then and she wasn't the same Lydia, so they couldn't simply pick up where they'd left off and blithely carry on as if nothing had happened. They had both lived a lifetime since and there was no doubt, in his case at least, the last decade had changed him and in many ways for the better.

He was more driven. More savvy. Undeniably less trusting and more cynical about the world, but better equipped to turn situations to his advantage. Yet as much as he lamented those cruelly stolen years, the hardships, the unfairness and the inherent dangers, he also realised he wouldn't be anywhere near as successful as he was now without them.

Two years since his return and he had real standing. Power which he never had before. A phenomenal achievement which would never have occurred without those difficult seven years ten thousand miles away, tested to the ends of his endurance and abilities and finding the true depth of his character, ambition and talent in the process.

They had sent him to the Antipodes a helpless boy, but he had returned a man to be reckoned with.

Good grief, he'd become annoyingly philosophical in the last month! Probably because the past seemed to suddenly be intricately intertwined with the present once again, wrapping itself around him like brambles, preventing him from moving forward.

All he knew with absolute clarity, and much to his complete disgust because it made blasted Randolph right again, was the heart indeed always wants what the heart needs—and his apparently needed Lydia. Clearly it had always needed her if he was prepared to risk the peaceful sanctity of their armistice to imminently reopen all those festering old wounds simply for a few answers which would probably lead nowhere.

Which he would absolutely do in an hour or two.

Or three or first thing in the morning before the Runner came knocking. Because like a coward he had done his best to avoid her since she had pulled away from that kiss and stared back at him equally dumbfounded by it—obviously torn. Lust versus disgust. The past still blatantly at war with the present. All the old wounds still raw and still festering. But a kiss to end all kisses.

They hadn't discussed it since. Not the incendiary nature of it, the hunger with which they'd both plunged headlong into it nor their mutual eagerness to escape one another once they had finally come up for air. Both preferring avoidance rather than risking the cloying armistice and jeopardising the status quo.

When they had collided, which they had with far more frequency than his shredded nerves could cope with, it was plainly obvious the climate between them had altered. One ill-conceived but unforgettable kiss had kindled the flame which used to burn so hot between them, reminding them there was undeniable chemistry and passion still lurking which a decade had failed to dampen and a month of close proximity had whipped into a frenzied inferno. It had resulted in too many heated looks, too many charged moments. Too much lust and much too much longing. So much that almost everyone who collided with them noticed, too.

And still neither one of them dared broach the subject.

Those damned brambles again—but tangling around her, too, now, and choking them both.

Yet there was something still there between them which went beyond the lust. He felt it in his heart and had seen the same torment in her eyes. Enough that he was convinced they could make their marriage work if only they could hack away all the weeds and thorns and expose the fertile ground again.

If only…

With a resigned and totally despondent sigh, he purposely went through the main front door of Libertas in case he inadvertently collided with her at the back of the property before he was ready, then sprinted up the stairs to the sanctuary of his office to contemplate tomorrow.

Two whole days thrust together at the Duke and Duchess of Aveley's castle.

If he lived through that, or emerged with his wits intact, it would be a blasted miracle.

He barely had one foot in the door when, to his abject horror, he saw she was sat in the spare chair in front of his desk. For a split second he considered making a hasty retreat and sprinting back from whence he had come. And doubtless would have, too, if it hadn't been a completely ridiculous way for a grown man to behave.

'Hello, Owen.'

If he was ever truly going to be the master of his own destiny, as well as finding a way to fix things between them, then he needed to stop hiding.

'Hello, Lydia.' *Now what?* 'How are you?'

Owen braced himself for the pithy comment, the imperious stare straight down her nose or, worse, one of their painfully polite conversations which blithely avoided everything, but alas they didn't come. Instead, she sat primly, her busy hands unable to stop fiddling with one another as her teeth worried her bottom lip.

After a prolonged and awkward pause, she briefly glanced at him and then looked away apparently horrified—which did little to put him at his ease.

'There is something we needed to discuss…a topic which is…um…personal.'

Something about the way her bottom fidgeted, almost as if she were squirming in the chair, made him similarly wary.

'Is it about *that* kiss?' As much as he dreaded this conversation, finally, perhaps sanity would prevail?

'No... Yes...' She huffed and blushed bright pink. 'Maybe.'

He found himself smiling despite the unease, utterly charmed by the sight of a thoroughly flustered Lydia. 'Then which is it, *Wife*? The yes, the no or the maybe?'

'I mean *obviously* we should discuss it...at some point...' Now she appeared to be shrinking into the chair, her shoulders curling in on themselves until she was practically a hunchback, the furrow between her dark eyebrows so deep it might have been freshly ploughed. 'But *that* is not what I came here to talk about.'

Abject relief was swiftly followed by disappointment. There would be no peace for the wicked—not that he had ever been particularly wicked. 'Then what did you come here to talk about?' The need for control had him standing straighter, his posture braced for whatever she was about to throw at him, his bland, nonchalant mask refusing to work properly no matter how much he willed it.

'Perhaps you should sit?'

That didn't bode well, and his pulse quickened. 'All right...'

Conscious he still hadn't removed his greatcoat and that nerves were making him warm, Owen shrugged out of it and clumsily hung it on the empty coat stand. On strangely leaden feet, he approached the desk.

'Should I be worried, Lydia?'

She smiled weakly, attempted to laugh it away, and when that came out a strangled mewl, looked thoroughly mortified. 'I suppose that depends...'

'Very reassuring.'

'I'd like us to have a calm and reasonable discussion.'

Those rarely ended well. Especially when he felt aggrieved and lost his temper and she got those tragic tears in her eyes which always accompanied her disappointment in him. 'Does it contravene the parameters of our polite armistice?' He wasn't ready for an argument. He was still too shaken by the acknowledgement he still had unresolved feelings for her. Still wanted her. Very probably was also still a little bit in love with her to boot.

'Most definitely—this is something we probably should have discussed a long time ago. Right from the outset, in fact. Calling an armistice with it hanging over our heads like a dark cloud was a mistake...'

Splendid. Dread settled like lead in the pit of his stomach. They were going *there*. To the impasse. The blockage. The fetid, rancid, infuriating pit of despair and frustration where they staggered blindly around and around in circles, reopening the same old festering wound which adamantly refused to heal and threatened to turn gangrenous.

But something he might be able to use to his advantage. If they were going to have an argument anyway about the terrible events from a decade ago, perhaps this was the perfect time to properly bring up the thefts at Barton House and fill in some of the blanks he had about what had been going on above stairs before he had been blamed for it all below.

'You are probably not going to like it...but still...it needs to be said.'

'Said?' Already he felt his temper spark. 'I thought you wanted a *discussion*.' He was damned if he was going to be lectured to. And most definitely not about that! 'Those usually require both parties to speak as well as listen!'

She appeared to crumple under the force of his scowl. 'You are absolutely right, Owen.' The pretty pink blush glowed crimson. 'You *do* get a say in it. A huge say.' Then she suddenly appeared defeated. 'Frankly, it cannot happen without your agreement...' She risked looking up at him and her eyes were so sad. 'Although I am hoping you will find it in your heart to say yes.'

'To what, Lydia?' He slowly lowered himself into his seat, wanting to agree to anything just to make her feel better and banish the hurt in her troubled dark eyes—but not at any cost. It would be a cold day in hell before he ever conceded any guilt.

'You see, the thing is...' Her shoulders expanded slowly as she inhaled, but her eyes dipped again to stare rigidly at the desk. 'I've given it a great deal of thought since last week...and as Gertie suggested I should approach you... and I am mindful that if you don't ask you don't get... I thought I should probably talk to you about it and gauge the lay of the land...'

Her hands were practically dancing a jig now, and because she was scaring the hell out of him, he reached out and clasped them. 'Take a deep breath, Lydia, and spit it out.'

'I want children.'

All the air left his lungs in a whoosh.

Of all the things his tortured imagination had conjured in the last few painful moments, from separate residences to divorce, that one had never entered his mind.

'Children?'

'Yes. Children.' She was blinking now with such speed she was in danger of taking off. 'Plural... But obviously we could start with just the one.'

'You want *children*?' All at once his head was filled with images. Some of them touching. Most of them carnal. 'With *me*?'

'Well, obviously! You are *my husband*, Owen! Who else could I have them with?' She suddenly sprang up from her chair and began to pace a wildly confused pattern on the Persian.

'I appreciate this might seem as though it has come out of the blue and, in view of Gertie's new baby, you'll doubtless think this is all to do with that—but the truth is I've always wanted a family. And seeing Gertie so happy and after holding little Tobias in my arms…well, it's brought it all to the fore.' Unconsciously, one hand touched her tummy. 'I'm six and twenty. In a month I'll be seven and twenty. That's practically an old maid and I thought I'd have a family by now… I need something to love, Owen. I'm so tired of feeling lonely. I want to feel a child grow inside me. I want to nurture it and watch it grow. Teach it to read… Sing it to sleep. I want noisy family dinners and little feet running over the floorboards…' She suddenly turned and stared imploringly. 'Is that too much to ask?'

He managed to blink in affirmation, but she clearly took that as a no because those awful little tears she was so adept at holding back filled her eyes.

'Do you remember when you first told me about Kelvedon? You said he was getting what he wanted and my father would get the money he wanted and you asked what I would get? And I realised it was nothing. But now things have changed and I'm married to you instead, my father has been paid and I've upheld every aspect of our arrangement so far… Don't I deserve something in return? Not necessarily immediately, of course. I'm not in a great hurry. But at some point…in the not-too-distant future… If it's not too much trouble…'

Even though his mind wasn't working, judging by the way the rest of his body below the neck was behaving, it would be no trouble at all.

'Why aren't you saying anything, Owen?'

'To be fair—you haven't paused long enough for me to get a word in.' He felt as if he was falling headfirst from a steep cliff top, his limbs flailing in the ether and the craggy rocks below approaching fast.

'I apologise… I had a speech all worked out… I thought it was a convincing one, but I am not entirely sure it came out in the right order.'

'I think I have the gist of it…'

'Good…b-because I really don't have it in me to repeat it.' She bit down on her lip and stood as still as a statue as she awaited his verdict. 'As I said…there's no immediate hurry and you probably need some time to think.'

Thinking was beyond him. Especially as simply breathing was now problematic. After an ironically pregnant pause which did nothing to stop his stunned heart hammering painfully against his ribs, he managed to moisten his mouth enough to choke out a sentence.

'You do realise that to have children at some point we would need to…'

'I just delivered a baby, Owen! I am completely aware of how it got there.'

Which still did nothing to address his biggest concern. 'But you said the thought of my touch makes you sick to your stomach!' Because he couldn't. Wouldn't…

'Oh, for goodness sake, Owen! After *that* kiss the other night, we both know that was a shocking lie!'

She exhaled and stared at her feet. 'I sincerely doubt that side of things will be a problem between us. In fact, it brings me neatly to the next issue which we urgently need to discuss before we embark on our trip to the Aveleys' on the morrow…and that is the tangible and obvious frisson which now exists between us.'

'The frisson?' Part of him wanted to laugh, the other cry at her delicate and dismissive explanation for all the yearning and craving which consumed him. 'I think that has always been there, Lydia.'

'It has.' She nodded curtly while staring intently at a spot on the wall and swallowed. 'We are both adults... Married adults...' She moistened her lips and folded her arms tightly across her bosom, looking every inch a woman who was desirous of the ground opening up and swallowing her. 'Who are clearly both struggling with... um...abstinence. Enough, or so I am told, that others have noticed.'

'By others, you mean Randolph and Gertie?'

'Cyril has also passed comment.' She could never call Slugger just Slugger. 'A rather valid one, actually...reminding me that the institution of marriage, in essence, was created to avoid the temptation of the original sin and the scriptures and our vows to one another do rather condone it all.' She chewed her bottom lip as she stared at the floor.

'Suffice it to say, it seems silly to deny ourselves *that* aspect of marriage when it is so obviously making us both... um...uncomfortable and this solution effectively kills two birds with one stone.'

'Two birds...' Procreation and rampant lust. 'One stone.' Once, while digging roads, Owen had been so overcome by the heat he had started to hallucinate. This felt similar. His head was spinning so much he was sorely tempted to lie down.

'We were always quite well suited in *that* area, I thought...and I've always enjoyed the way you...' She peeked up at him, then positively growled. 'You might try not smiling quite so smugly!' Then she spun on her heel and marched to the door, infuriated, embarrassed and utterly disarming. 'Let me know your decision in due course!'

'Yes.'

Her step faltered, and when she turned she was smiling.

Grateful! As if he were doing her a favour instead of offering him his biggest fantasy on a plate. 'Do you mean it?'

'I'm not one for games, Lydia. I want you to be happy and…the truth is, my constant and rampant lust for you aside, I've always wanted a family myself one day, too, so…' Good grief… He was going to be a father, too. Eventually. This was all too much to take in. 'This would… um…actually benefit both of us.'

And he and Lydia would finally…

All the blood pooled between his legs in celebration. 'H-how do you…propose we proceed?'

'Well, I suppose you will need to…er…*visit* me at some point.'

What a sanitised and polite way of putting it. He nodded. At this stage he was so befuddled it really was the best he could manage. The itch he couldn't scratch, the woman of his dreams, was inviting him to her bed.

'We could start later, Owen…if you are agreeable?' He'd been more than agreeable for ten long years. Climbing the walls with agreement this past month. 'Get it over with before our trip, where doubtless all eyes will be on us.'

'And we won't be able to escape each other.'

'Which will only make our current predicament worse.'

'I have got to be honest and say I have been dreading the house party—for exactly that reason.'

'Me, too.' She flicked him a part-pained, part-guilty, part-heaven-only-knew-what-she-was-thinking look and then her words came out in a high-pitched hurry. 'Would eleven suit?'

And now they were actually making an appointment. Calmly and politely. An appointment to do the deed. To slake their rampant and apparently *mutual* lust at their earliest possible convenience.

Tonight.

'Eleven…' He glanced at the clock on the mantel, the hands already pointing to nine while the most male part of his body was already excitably pointing to the twelve, then swallowed. 'Eleven suits.'

'Excellent…' Her hand flapped at nothing. 'Then I shall leave you to it.'

To what, he had no idea, but nodded anyway. She darted out of the door and quickly shut it behind her in case he changed his mind and Owen stared at it, dumbstruck.

Chapter Eighteen

Lydia had absolutely no idea what she was doing.

For the last two hours she had been a walking mess. She had managed to bathe, had brushed and plaited her hair, dabbed on some perfume and donned a nightgown. She considered climbing into bed, but that seemed too forward. She settled for turning down the covers and then waiting for him in the living room, the book in her lap a pathetic prop to make her seem entirely calm and casual, when nothing could be further from the truth.

Everything felt strange.

She was both daunted, relieved and curious. Excited and nervous. Her body felt decidedly odd. She couldn't decide if it was the lack of undergarments or the prospect of what was about to happen. Or the relentless and all-consuming desire which had thoroughly taken her over since their kiss—but she had never been quite so aware of her breasts before and the dull throb between her legs refused to go away no matter how much she tried to ignore it.

Twice, she had considered seeking out Gertie and asking advice, but couldn't bring herself to do it because this was intensely private. Between her and her husband. She just prayed instinct would prevail exactly as it had when she had delivered her friend's baby and nature would take its course.

It had always seemed to in the past.

Every time Owen had kissed her, her body had known exactly what to do and exactly what it wanted. But then she had never entirely acted upon it. And neither had he. They had been young. Fearful of the consequences of passion and mindful of the need for abstinence. There had been lots of kissing, a great deal of over-the-clothes touching, but, while she had been on the cusp of succumbing to her passions on several occasions, he had always been much too much of a gentleman to take things too far.

At the time, that had been beyond frustrating and she had lain awake for hours afterwards feeling hideously un-fulfilled. Exactly like she had after their kiss last week. Which had far surpassed all their previous kisses a decade before, sent her body into a positive frenzy of desire and made her relive the dratted event over and over again in every quiet moment since.

Gracious, that man could kiss!

He had left her so ripe and ready to be picked she could barely think straight.

But as she had plastered herself against him, a heav-ing mass of needy nerve-endings and unsuppressed de-sire, she couldn't help but notice he had a similar desire for her, too. Hard, reckless and insistent desire. So insis-tent and so glorious, she had almost demanded he take her there and then. Up against the wall with Gertie, Randolph and their newborn right behind it before she'd panicked and pulled away.

Then, of course, they had both run from it, because that was the polite thing to do when two people were sup-posed to be in a marriage in name only. Which in turn had led her to deliberate, every waking, lust-filled hour since thanks to Gertie's earthy suggestion, why the devil they were still so diligently denying each other all the forbidden fruit which their marriage had rendered unforbidden?

She did want children—that hadn't been a lie—but not quite as desperately as she currently wanted Owen.

Two birds with one stone.

Plus all those alluring and intriguing birds etched into his equally intriguing and alluring muscles...

The light tap on the door made her jump out of her skin. He was early. Fifteen minutes early to be precise.

'Come in.'

She could see he was uncomfortable. Owen always puffed out his chest and stuck out his chin when he wasn't completely in control of a situation.

'Hello...'

Had a simple greeting ever felt so loaded?

'Hello, Owen.' She slid the book to the new side table placed beside her only a few minutes before for exactly that purpose. The seductive smile she had practised shrivelling and dying before it reached her mouth. 'You're early.'

He winced. 'I'm sorry... Should I go?'

'No... No...'

'This is...' his eyes took in the room. Her nightgown. The lamps burning low. The invitingly open door which led to her bedchamber—then the bed—before settling back on hers '...decidedly awkward.'

Then he smiled the same smile he used to all those years ago and she realised everything was going to be all right.

'Yes, it is, isn't it? Do you suppose it will get better?'

'I certainly hope so. I've been staring at the clock for the past hour and discovered time moves at a snail's pace when you watch it. I was going slowly mad—so I came early.'

'Then, for the sake of both our sanities, maybe we should get it over with?'

'No painful chit-chat? No nervously sipped brandy? No last-minute cups of tea?'

'Do you think they would help?'

He shook his tawny head. 'No. They'd probably only make it worse.'

'Then we should definitely get it over with, don't you think?'

'I suppose we should.'

Trying to be dispassionate and appear both confident as well as matter-of-fact, she stood and held out her hand. 'Shall we?'

'If we must.' Her sudden forthrightness seemed to amuse him and she felt the heat of a ferocious blush creep up her neck as his fingers laced through hers. 'Lead the way, *Wife*.'

Not knowing how to stage it, she had left just one lamp burning low on the nightstand, but now instantly regretted it. Not only would he see what had the makings of an epically red and mortally embarrassed face, he would see her nerves, her body and all her carefully hidden emotions and she wasn't ready for any of that just yet.

Feeling exposed, she tugged her hand from his and quickly extinguished it, plunging the room into a darkness only alleviated by the faint glow of the fire next door.

Yet the shadows somehow felt more intimate, unsettling her further, and all her dispassionate matter-of-fact confidence evaporated like steam. Now what?

Owen sighed and she heard the bed creak as he sat upon it.

'If you are expecting me to do the necessary in a brisk and perfunctory manner, Lydia, you should know now I cannot do that.'

Which was a relief—but also not a relief at the same time.

'To be frank, I have no idea what I am expecting.' Because it seemed like the right thing to do, she sat herself beside him on the mattress. 'I was hoping you would take the lead.'

'And I was hoping you would.' He leaned a little till their shoulders touched. 'What a pair we are.' She laughed, or tried to, and rested her head against his shoulder.

'What a pair indeed.'

'It's perfectly all right to be nervous, Lydia. If it makes you feel better, I bypassed nervous a half an hour ago and barrelled straight into outright anxiousness.'

'Why are you anxious?'

'Honestly?' His hand found hers buried in the folds of her nightgown, his touch achingly gentle exactly like she remembered it. 'Because I cannot deny I might have given this a great deal of thought over the years and a great deal more since Gretna. As a rule, overthinking things is never good.'

'You thought about it with me or just in general?'

He laughed softly, his head shaking. 'With you, stupid. You were the first girl I ever kissed. And now, apparently, you are also going to be the last…so I don't want to get it wrong.' A confession which made her heart stutter. Especially as his accent had slipped again and she knew already that meant he was just being Owen.

'The last?'

'Well…we did take vows. And I cannot deny I've never stopped wanting you, Lydia. Ten years is a long time to wait.'

'You don't have to wait any more.'

'Even so… I still do not want to rush things. That would be wrong. We should take things slowly and see where they progress.'

'How slowly?' Because she feared she might burst if they delayed the necessary for too long.

'As long as it takes for things to not feel quite so awkward and at least a little bit…romantic.'

'The hard-nosed businessman and all-round man of mystery wants romance?' Her insides were in danger of dissolving into mush at the prospect.

'I know. Call me old-fashioned…' His smile this time was less pained and more boyish. Shy, even. 'Maybe we should start with just a kiss? Ease ourselves into the proceedings.' He mimicked the accent of the innkeeper from their embarrassing wedding night. 'As I recall, we were very good at that.'

'As I recall, we became quite proficient at it.'

'We did.' His thumb was gently stroking the back of her hand and just that simple touch was making her yearn. 'Do you remember our first kiss? We were in Hyde Park, shrouded by trees.'

'In our little spot. Near the Serpentine.'

He nodded. 'I was nervous then, too. So overwhelmed, I hesitated…'

Not once, she remembered with a smile, but at least a hundred times when the perfect opportunities presented themselves all those lazy Thursday afternoons that heady summer—and she had been unsubtly hinting for a good two weeks beforehand. Was on the cusp of kissing him out of sheer desperation, she suddenly recalled, the longing had been so intense and she was already head over heels in love with him by that time.

'You didn't hesitate. You panicked as I recall.'

Because, with the benefit of hindsight and behind his cocky bravado which he always strapped on like a mask, any fool could have seen it wasn't just her first kiss, but had obviously been *his* first kiss, too.

Innocent, clumsy, magical and utterly perfect.

Beneath her palm his heart had raced so fast, neither

of them had a clue what they were doing and he had been the one to pull away looking, she now remembered, utterly terrified to have overstepped the mark. Worried about his job, his home, his references, her reputation, the ramifications of stepping above his station if their forbidden romance was ever discovered.

It had been Lydia who had dragged him back then, not giving a fig about any of his natural concerns, who couldn't wait for each Thursday to roll around so they could spend all afternoon kissing in the dense thicket of trees. And it was also she who had convinced him to creep into her bedchamber in the last few weeks of their romance to do more of the same when she simply couldn't wait for Thursdays to come around any longer. It came as a shock to suddenly realise, with unnerving clarity, that if anyone had done the seducing all those years ago, it had actually been her. Owen had always been the cautious one. Probably because he had the most to lose. Just as he continued to be cautious around her still. His face was inches from hers, but he didn't close the distance.

But what did he have to lose now?

He must have seen the question in her eyes. 'I fear you are going to have to kiss me first, Lydia.'

Her anxiousness made her clumsy and she practically threw herself against him. He refused to be rushed. His lips brushed over hers like a whisper, the pad of one finger tracing her hairline and then her cheek until she practically melted into it.

He took his sweet time in deepening it, tasting just her mouth as though it was the sweetest exotic fruit until her palm cupped his cheek and she gave in to the urge to run her fingers through his hair.

By the time his tongue softly tangled with hers, her body had remembered exactly how much she had always enjoyed this and just how much she needed it. Needed him. Nobody had ever kissed her like Owen Wolfe and with the blurring and passing of time, he thankfully didn't disappoint. It was exactly the same—only better.

A confident man's kiss rather than that of the gauche stable boy.

Lydia's arms coiled around his neck and she pressed her body against him, sighing when his arms looped around her waist and anchored her in place. Owen was absolutely right. They shouldn't rush this. It was such a decadent kiss, it deserved to be thoroughly enjoyed.

She allowed herself to be carried away by both the romance and the sensations. The sublime feel of his mouth on hers. The strength of his arms. The erratic beat of his heart. The impressive breadth of his shoulders. The enthralling feel of his big hands on her waist, her hips and then the possessive fervour as they finally settled on her bottom and the kiss became more intense.

'Do you still feel awkward?'

She felt his answering smile against her mouth. 'Not so much any more. You?'

He deserved the truth now that she knew this mattered to him. 'I've always adored kissing you, Owen. I've missed it.'

'Me, too.'

His lips and teeth knew all her sensitive places as they slowly made their way to her ear and then her neck, but this time, undoubtedly because she wasn't hampered by the bonds of what was proper, she wanted to feel them everywhere. Boldly, she gave in to the urge to explore his body, running her palms over his back and along the taut muscles in his arms. And when that wasn't enough, it was Lydia once again who tugged them to lie down on the mattress; she, too, who pushed his coat from his shoulders, needing to be closer to him.

Needing more than just a kiss. 'Let's not go too slowly.'

'Well, if you want more, *Wife...* I'm more than happy to oblige.' Laughing, he rolled on to his back, dragging her to lie above him, and she felt his desire through the layers of their clothing, hard and insistent and welcome against her tummy. The promise of things to come. Only this time no longer forbidden, but necessary.

So very necessary, she deepened the kiss and writhed against him in obvious invitation.

But again, he wouldn't be hurried. As her eager fingers undid the long line of annoying buttons on his waistcoat, he unwound her plait until her hair encompassed them like a curtain, all the while kissing her as if she were the most precious thing in the world.

She moaned when those hands cupped her bottom again, then slowly began to explore her curves over her nightgown while his talented mouth continued its deadly assault on her lips. 'I've dreamed of this... Dreamed of you, Lydia...' His voice was laced with desire and perhaps emotion as he paused to stare deep into her eyes through the darkness and, to her surprise, she realised she wanted it to be both. His desire and his emotion. Exactly as they had had before—but he kissed her instead of elaborating and she had to make do with what she thought that intensely intimate and searing kiss meant rather than hearing it come from his mouth.

Until it didn't matter. Nothing mattered beyond her and him and the shared passion which engulfed them. As always, when she was thoroughly overwhelmed with Owen, time stood still. She had no idea how long they kissed for. It could have been minutes. It could have been hours. All she knew was that with each stroke of his tongue her desire for him built until she feared she might explode from the wanting.

She needed his hands on her skin. Needed to feel his bare skin against hers. And because he was being too much the gentleman still—and she didn't know how to ask him—she tugged the hem of his shirt from the waistband of his breeches and allowed her greedy palms to explore his chest as she pushed the fabric upwards. His skin was hot and smooth, the light dusting of hair intriguing as it narrowed over his stomach. With the absence of proper light and because she was too consumed with him to be shy, where her fingers went her lips followed and she revelled in the way he seemed to unravel at her touch.

At her insistence, he pulled his shirt off, allowing her to explore his shoulders properly with her needy palms, teeth and tongue. Then his arms. She could feel the slightly raised outline of his tattoo in the darkness. The way his nipples pebbled and he shivered at her touch. Every gasp. Every sigh. Every quiver of pleasure.

But still it wasn't enough and she needed to be closer, needed him to stop being so respectful in the way he touched her. Because only mindless naked flesh against naked flesh would do, she kissed him like a starving woman, wrenching her nightgown up until her bare breasts were pressed flat against his ribs.

Yet still he held back.

'Why won't you touch me?'

He tore his mouth from hers then and she could just about make out his stormy irises as he stared intently into her eyes.

'Because I need to know you are sure.' His voice was ragged, thick with desire, and it made her feel powerful and feminine and sinfully wanton. 'I need to know you truly want this, Lydia…that you want me.'

It was his hesitation that did it, combined with the longing in his voice. He wasn't immune or cold or vexing in his hesitation. He was vulnerable. This mattered to him. She mattered to him.

'I want you, Owen. All of you.' Then, because it was true, she said what she sensed he needed to hear. 'I always have.'

His next kiss was gloriously carnal. He sat with her astride his lap, his hungry mouth barely leaving hers for a split second as he dispensed with the barrier of her nightgown. Then his hands went on a slow exploration of frustratingly still-unchartered territory, smoothing possessively along her thighs, her hips, her ribcage before he finally filled them with her aching breasts and she moaned aloud, his thumbs tracing lazy circles around her taut nipples as he groaned into her mouth.

'You're beautiful.'

And she felt beautiful.

Because she could feel how much he wanted her. It was obvious in every laboured breath, the tense cords of his muscles and in the intriguingly insistent press of his hardness against her body. And Lydia revelled in it all, her back arching as his clever mouth found her breasts and his teeth tortured her nipples while she clung to him for dear life, but still needed more.

At some point during his complete assault of her senses, he must have turned them over, because suddenly she was under him and while her fingers fumbled with the buttons on his falls, his began another lazy journey downwards to the soft curls at the apex of her thighs. Then lower still.

Not only was she powerless to stop him, she needed his touch, moaning her own encouragement as he uncovered, then caressed an outrageously sensitive bundle of nerves which seemed to have the power to obliterate all rational thought.

'I dreamed you'd be like this...' Her shameless passion seemed to fire his desire further—which liberated her, banishing all her inhibitions.

Her body felt slick and so very sensual, and each achingly gentle and tender caress freed her to truly feel it all without the need for propriety and decorum. She didn't care that she was naked. Didn't care that she was wanton. He clearly adored both and that was all that mattered. As the delicious sensations built, Lydia gave up trying to remove the rest of his clothing, her hands fisting in the sheet as he continued his relentless yet magnificent siege on her body.

Her hips rose wildly when his mouth replaced his fingers and for a while she feared the delicious pleasure he was inflicting with nought but the tip of his tongue might kill her if she allowed him to continue. But if death was the price, she was happy to pay it. She called out his name, her fingers tunnelling into his hair as the world was reduced to a pinpoint of unimaginable ecstasy before it exploded like stars behind her eyes.

Rendered entirely boneless, she lay panting on the pillow, her limbs shamelessly splayed in invitation and watched fascinated as her shadowy lover stripped off what was left of his clothing, his staccato breathing as impatient as he was.

Unshackled, the male part of him was much bigger than she had imagined, but she wasn't scared. How could she be scared when this was Owen and he was looking at her with such heat—like a man possessed and consumed entirely by her?

And unbelievably, she discovered in that pivotal moment her thirst for him wasn't quenched. There was more to have and she wanted it all. Every last impressive inch.

She tugged him back to kiss her, her hand boldly reaching out to explore him, feeling wicked and sinful and all powerful as Owen held himself rigid while she learned the shape of him. Warm, hard, fascinating—

Entirely male.

Entirely hers.

And when she snaked her arms around his waist to drag that necessary part of him against her, he carefully covered her body with his and kissed her with such poignant tenderness it brought tears to her eyes. 'It's not too late… we don't have to…'

'Yes, we do.' Lydia pressed her lips against his mouth and entwined her legs around his hips. 'I want you. Can't you see that? It's only ever been you, Owen.'

His answering sigh was like a benediction. 'It's only ever been you, too, Lydia.'

'Then for the love of God have me, *Husband*, because I cannot wait a second more.'

There were no nerves or anxiousness any longer as he smiled against her lips. Instinct and desire for this man had taken over her body and she marvelled at how perfect it felt to feel him gently edge inside her—to feel how that sublime invasion affected him, too. Feel his muscles bunch beneath her hands as he fought for restraint.

But she was too hungry and too impatient for him to hold back, so used her legs, hands and hips until he filled her to the hilt.

Then he paused, his forehead resting on hers, giving her time to become accustomed to the intrusion, and she felt his heart beating against hers, as she suspected it was always meant to.

And when they gazed as deeply into each other's eyes

as the darkness would allow, she had felt such a connection, such an intense and all-encompassing sense of rightness, she almost told him she still loved him.

Had always loved him, truth be told, regardless of everything.

But the intense emotion left her astounded and she hesitated, then he began to move inside her and the moment was lost in a raging torrent of fresh desire, all consuming and wonderful, before he swept her away all over again and they finally saw the stars together.

Chapter Nineteen

The loud crash of thunder outside was strangely apt, but nowhere near as loud as the thunderbolt which had struck him last night. That prophetic sound still rang in his ears alongside the words which had caused it.

'It's only ever been you, Owen.'

Words he had wanted for ten long years, but hadn't realised he'd been waiting for.

But did that mean he was the only man she had ever wanted in the physical sense or was it more than that and she had been alluding to her heart? The not knowing was sending him insane when he already knew he wanted the spiritual, temporal and emotional far more. Now that his body had possessed hers, he wanted to possess her heart, too. Because she had his. She had always had his.

He had, in the overwhelming heat of the moment, almost said as much aloud.

Twice.

Once on the back of her confession. And the second time as he had gazed at her beneath him, not daring to speak. Not daring to move. So humbled to be inside her and overwhelmed by the rush of emotion which their joining had unleashed.

Boom! Another damn thunderbolt—but this one the most powerful yet.

And one, which quite frankly, had scared the hell out of him.

So much so he had thoroughly lost himself in her body, then extricated himself from her bed as soon as it seemed polite to do so. For his own safety he had avoided her since. Something he regretted now Slugger was loading the carriage with their luggage and they were on the cusp of leaving for Aveley Castle.

'Are you all right?' Randolph came in, frowning. 'Only you've been in the strangest mood all morning.'

Owen briskly closed the ledger he hadn't had the where-withal to be working on. 'Yes... Perfectly fine. Merely dotting the i's before I go away.'

'Because if something was bothering you, all jesting and teasing aside, you could confide in me...' His friend's expression was uncharacteristically serious. 'I am always here for you.'

'I know that.'

'So there is nothing you want to discuss? Nothing pressing you need to get off your chest? No advice you need from your oldest, dearest and wisest best friend? Marriage advice, perhaps? *Romantic* advice? Or *personal* advice?'

'Honestly, Randolph, I am in need of no counsel whatsoever.'

'Really? Then if we ignore the alternating soppy and panicked expression which keep marring those handsome features of yours after what was undoubtedly a night of long-awaited and unbridled passion, I have absolutely no clue why there is currently a Bow Street Runner here to see you. Yet he is downstairs for his *prearranged* appointment and clutching papers which you apparently have to see *before* you go away.'

'Ah…'

'*Ah*, indeed.' His friend climbed on to a chair and folded his hands in his lap. 'Which begs the obvious question—what is going on, Owen?'

'Nothing that concerns Libertas.'

'I didn't think for a second that it did. You are much too honest to be up to no good and I'd have to be blind as well as stupid—both things I plainly am not—to fail to see this is all to do with Lydia.' He settled back in the chair and huffed out a breath. 'Now, because I am your best friend, because Gertie and I care and because Slugger is so aggrieved the long arm of the law appears to be after you, or me, or him—or any one of our many loyal former criminal employees, for that matter—he may very well throw that poor Runner bodily from the premises if I dally much longer. So for the love of God, tell me what is going on!'

'I've reopened the investigation.'

'Why?'

He considered fudging it, but knew there was no point. What his friend lacked in stature he made up for in brains. 'Because the past is in the way, damn it!'

'You've acknowledged that you love her, then?' Sometimes Randolph was annoyingly right. 'That's a good start. And have you sorted *everything else* out?' As if everything else were that easy. Completing the twelve labours of Hercules would be easier.

'I have acknowledged I have *feelings*…and that I would like to make a proper go of things…and have a proper marriage with Lydia. As to the other things…'

'Do not tell me she still requires proof of your innocence before she will similarly commit?' His friend was outraged on his behalf. 'Surely she has seen enough of your character now to know you were incapable of those crimes?'

'Probably... Maybe...' He found himself wincing under his wily friend's exasperated glare. 'We haven't discussed any of it since we called the blasted armistice.'

'You have an *armistice*? With your *wife*?'

'It was the only way to stop us arguing.'

Randolph blinked, his mouth hanging slack. Then he was all animation. 'Good grief! I've never heard anything so ridiculous in all my life! You've been married a month! A month! How do the pair of you even function with all that nonsense still lingering in the background?' He dropped his head into his hands.

'When I pointed you in the direction of a marriage of convenience, I assumed it would force the pair of you to sort out your differences once and for all. I knew you still loved her and hoped she might still have feelings for you, and between you, both of you would come to realise that love conquers all. That you'd both been given a second chance! And that you could both discover that the past no longer mattered because you had a future—a rich and exciting future with each other, Owen! Not a blasted armistice which can only possibly serve to keep you both apart!'

'We've been getting on rather well as it happens...as last night is testament to.'

'You've merely built a bridge out of matchsticks! And it will not last five minutes unless you are honest with each other and talk about things!'

Now there was a sobering thought. 'It'll be easy to talk about it all with proof in my pocket. And before you ask, no, she doesn't know I've engaged Bow Street to help find it. At this stage, that's...'

'A little too revealing?'

'Exactly. And probably a fool's errand in the grand scheme of things.'

'Which will put you right back at square one.' Randolph shook his head. 'So just to clarify—because Gertie won't believe this—the past is getting in the way of your relationship.'

'It is. It's always there. Hovering. Like a bad smell. She still thinks me a thief and I'm still furious that she could think it and wounded at her betrayal.'

'And you thought it more prudent to engage a Bow Street Runner and *then* bed her rather than perhaps discuss that pressing issue first?'

'The two weren't linked. I engaged the Runners—there are two of them, by the way—and then…' Owen felt his brows furrow. 'Wait…how do you know what happened between us last night? Did Lydia say something to Gertie?'

Hell's bells! Did she regret it already? Had she reminded herself he was a scoundrel of the first order, a filthy thief who'd pinched her dying mother's blasted pearls and battened down the hatches again as if last night didn't matter? When it obviously mattered. Obviously meant something.

Even more proof he had to unearth the past. Neither of them knew where they stood.

'She didn't need to.' Randolph flapped imaginary wings. 'She practically floated into breakfast this morning all a-flutter, lips all kiss swollen, sighing like a loon…' Then he broke into a knowing grin. 'It didn't take a genius to work out she'd finally stripped the wolf out of his sheep's clothing.'

Owen did his best not to look incredibly smug. 'She seemed all right to you, then? Happy?'

'Exceedingly… Was positively doe-eyed with distraction and most definitely delighted by it all.'

'Delighted?' Now that was promising. He felt the tension in his muscles ease at the thought.

'Nauseatingly so. Which begs the obvious question.

Why didn't you tackle the difficult subject once the deed was done? It was the most favourable time!'

'It really wasn't.'

That comment earned him a stunned scowl. 'Of course it was! Women are always at their most receptive after they have *blossomed* and we gents are demonstrably more magnanimous—and, quite frankly, it is ridiculous that the pair of you continue to avoid it. Especially as the stakes have been raised and you have both clearly been speared mortally by Cupid.' His friend slid off the chair to pace in frustration.

'The conversation isn't going to get any easier, idiot! If anything, the longer you put it off is only going to make things more difficult as all the poison becomes entrenched and continued avoidance makes it worse. Be honest. Lay your cards completely on the table while the pair of you are away—because if she cannot see your innocence for herself and you cannot ever prove it, you will never be able to move forward.'

Owen nodded, trying to focus on the positive. 'Do you really think she's been struck by Cupid, too?'

Randolph threw his hands in the air. 'That's it? That is the only part of my impassioned, wise and imploring monologue you heard?'

'I heard it…' And the miserable truth was difficult to swallow. 'But if the Runner has found something, then it won't matter.'

'Because she will know she has always been wrong and she'll fall at your feet in tragic remorse, begging for forgiveness?'

Something like that.

'My name will be properly cleared and she will stop thinking ill of me.'

'Never mind she'll feel dreadful and riddled with guilt

and will likely never get over it—you will feel superior. And if they find nothing, just as we did, then what? Are you happy to go through life with a woman who thinks you genuinely stole her mother's jewellery for your own ill-gotten gain? What a tremendously healthy start to a marriage that will make.'

Randolph jumped back up on the chair and grabbed him by the lapels. 'People make mistakes, Owen. But true love means seeing past them. No matter what. You and Lydia will never be happy until you both accept that. Stop building a house of cards and lay some solid foundations. You can't hide behind your pathetic armistice for ever.'

Before Owen could respond, Slugger crashed through the door and jabbed an agitated finger in his face as well. 'Is that slimy Runner friend or foe, Owen?'

'Friend.' And hopefully a less vexing and astute one than blasted Randolph.

'Then get the blighter out of my hallway! He's making me nervous!'

Chapter Twenty

Idly, Lydia traced one of the intricately drawn birds inked into his biceps, feeling thoroughly decadent and thoroughly adored. After two hours of travel to Aveley Castle, followed by hours and hours of socialising, dinner and parlour games, they had fallen into each other's arms the second they were alone in their allotted shared bedchamber.

Making love with the lamps still burning had been as scandalous as it had been educational and, with their new familiarity with intimacy, everything about their second coupling had been better. Exquisite, in fact. Lydia still felt drunk on the back of it. Or perhaps that had happened when he had awoken her at dawn to make lazy love to her again? Now, tangled naked in the sheets together, neither of them seemed in a particular hurry to move despite the day's packed schedule.

'What is the story behind these birds?'

'They are swallows.'

Hardly an explanation. 'Then what is the story behind these swallows? There must be one.'

'Maybe I woke up one morning and decided I fancied a flock of swallows tattooed on my skin.'

Lydia propped herself up on her elbow and pretended to glare at him and in return he twirled one finger in her hair. 'Do they, in some way, contravene the terms of our armistice?'

'I got them in Port Jackson.'

'I guessed as much.'

'We all had them.'

'Swallows?'

'No.' He smiled, looking every inch like a man perfectly content with where he was. 'Tattoos. Different pictures meant different things. Some had names of loved ones, lost loves or permanent declarations of new. Randolph has Gertie's name emblazoned on his chest and wrapped in a big heart. But some had broken hearts, too, alongside a few pierced with knives for betrayal. Mermaids and ships were all about the long journey we took…the flags are pretty self-explanatory. Weeping willows were popular because they symbolised grief.'

'Did many people die there?'

'No.' He paused for a moment, as if debating his answer, then she felt him exhale with resignation. 'Sometimes. Things could be very hard. But the willow was more a symbol of grief for all that they had lost rather than an actual death. When you've been exiled to the other side of the world with scant chance of ever coming back, those last goodbyes to those left behind might as well have been a death. Families were torn apart. Parents separated from children, husbands from wives…' He tugged her back to lie upon his chest. 'Those things leave an indelible mark, so I suppose that's why we added them to our skin.'

'Like Cyril's tears?' Those three etched droplets had always bothered her. 'What do they symbolise?'

'He'll tell you they are for his late mother if he's got a drink inside him, or to put the fear of God into his boxing opponents if he's stone-cold sober, but neither of those is entirely true. He fell hopelessly in love with a free girl in Parramatta and, between you and me, she led him a merry dance. But as is so typical in matters of the heart, love is blind and poor Slugger was the last to realise she wasn't anywhere near as devoted to him as he was to her.'

'She met someone else?'

'Ran off with someone else, actually—the true father of the child she was carrying a week before she and Slugger were due to wed. It hit him hard and for reasons best known to him, he decided to immediately mark the sentiment with tears that will last for ever. He probably regrets them now, but it seems insensitive to ask.'

'Poor Cyril.' Clearly the man did have a gentle artist's soul after all. Her gaze wandered back to the swallows and she realised he must have been the artist. 'And what do your swallows mean?'

'A safe return...back to here. I always wanted to come home. It was everything. So every year, I reaffirmed that vow with another bird.' He waited for her to count them.

'Seven.'

'It was almost eight—but fate intervened.'

Lydia had no clue how he had earned his pardon other than he had done something heroic. Knowing Owen as well as she did, she also knew he would have stepped up to the mark regardless of the reward at the end of it. It was the way he was. A noble soul and a born rescuer. 'Will you tell me that story, then?'

'We were working at the barracks, the stable actually, and there was a fire. Being winter and therefore, conversely, hotter than hell in New South Wales, it spread faster than people could evacuate. Some were still trapped in the stores and we helped them escape and then managed to douse the flames.'

'We?'

'Randolph, Slugger…and me.'

Such a typically Owen response to a supreme act of bravery. 'And that's it?' When she knew he might add himself last to the list, but would have been the first to run into the flames. 'Was anybody killed?'

'We got all nineteen out…thank the Lord.'

Which suggested, even if they had shared the burden equally, he was responsible for saving the lives of at least six of those lucky people. What sort of strength, bravery and fortitude did that take? To risk your own life, very probably over and over again, to get everybody out from a raging inferno?

'You really were a hero.'

He shrugged it off, uncomfortable with the compliment. 'As a thank you, the governor pardoned the three of us, so we sold our little hell and came home.'

Lydia made a note to ask Gertie for all the pertinent details he had left out as soon as they got back. Pushing him to brag about his achievements would glean nothing. However, seeing as he was finally opening up, she decided to push her luck. She needed to know everything about this modest, brave and complicated man she had married.

'How did you cope with *that* boat journey?' Because yet again, and despite the rainstorm which had followed them all the way to Aveley Castle, he had still ridden alongside the carriage.

'Better than I did on the way there. But as a paying passenger I could decide whether I stayed in my cabin or not and it was a cabin. Not a cupboard.' Then he hesitated again, almost as if he were making a decision about something important, before he surprised her.

'On the hulk and then on the transport ship over, we were all crammed into the tiniest space possible below deck. During the day it wasn't as bad. They removed the chains so we could work or take a little exercise, but every evening after they fed us, they would chain us back up and lock us down below. I hated it. I hated the lack of freedom, the heat, the stench, the humiliation of it. Most of the time I could block it out, but at some point I must have given away my fear to one of the guards and, from that point on, he used my damn bunk as a punishment whenever he felt I was being too insubordinate.' He laughed without humour. 'I never did properly learn my place, Lydia. As you know.'

Her heart wept for him so she kissed him. 'Hardly a surprise, then, you cannot abide confined spaces.'

'No…hardly a surprise, I suppose.' He took another deep breath. 'But it got worse. On the passage to the Antipodes, somewhere in the middle of the wild Pacific, there was a horrendous storm. Heavy rain, huge gales. Waves so tall and angry the ship could barely stay upright.' Beneath her palm she could feel his heart begin to race.

'It lasted for three whole days and nights and they chained us to our bunks for the duration.' And that was the real reason why he feared confinement now. 'For everyone's safety, they said, but what they really meant was for theirs. If we went down, and for a while it seemed highly likely that was a certainty, the navy didn't want to have to fight a couple of hundred convicts for the few measly rowing boats which might save their lives.'

She kissed his cheek and hugged him tightly and he hugged her tighter right back.

'The ship took a battering, the hull began to leak badly and as we were being tossed about I was powerless. Devoid of any control and rendered insignificant. I honestly thought I would die there. Chained to a hard bunk as the vessel was sucked beneath the waves. I've never been able to stand being closed in since.' He shivered involuntarily.

'Another indelible mark…' A deep one. But she was humbled he had finally deigned to confide in her. 'But enough of all that maudlin talk…' He kissed her thoroughly before he pulled away. They both knew he was escaping the memories and felt awkward at sharing them.

'You've made me dally long enough, *Wife*.' His eyes had darkened to a stormy deep blue, blatantly drinking in the sight of her still lounging on the pillow and making no attempt to hide the effect she had on him. 'If I laze here any longer thinking all these sinful thoughts, I shall be late for the Duke and that won't do.'

The men were spending the morning shooting and had an early start. The ladies were breakfasting later and then were going to ride the grounds, then visit the village. As she watched him pad deliciously naked to the washstand, Lydia realised that while he was probably happy to be escaping her questions, she wouldn't see Owen again for hours.

'If I feign a headache and skip the market this afternoon, do you think you might also be able to slip away?' In case he missed the passionate invitation in her eyes, she stretched on the mattress like a cat, allowing the remaining covers to shamelessly expose her bare breasts because she knew he was particularly partial to them.

Those stormy eyes swept the length of her. 'You're trying to kill me, aren't you?' She could see the evidence of his desire as he snatched a fresh shirt out of his trunk and wielded it at her like a weapon. 'What sort of a witch are you to tempt me and give me ideas which will likely haunt me all morning and put me off my game?' Then he gestured to the impressive state he was in below the waist. 'I'm going to have to wash in cold water now! I hope you're happy, *Wife*.'

'So you'll creep away, then?'

'How does two suit?' He splashed water into the bowl, grinning.

'Two suits—unless you can make it at one. Because I shall be here at one. Resting…' She sat and stretched again, running her hands through her hair like the most practised of courtesans. 'Very probably naked…'

Owen soaped his chin with a growl. 'You are a minx, madam.'

'But you like me anyway.'

He shot her another heated look and for a moment she thought he might tell her he more than liked her. Instead, he smiled and snapped open his razor. 'For the record, I should like it noted I rather like these little appointments we have taken to making.'

'So do I.'

'I also like the new spirit of…honesty which seems to be developing as well.' Suddenly he was using a measured tone rather than the playful one of a second before. 'So, if you are agreeable…this afternoon perhaps we could also make an appointment to *talk*?'

'About what?'

'About…us, perhaps, and the way things seem to be going between us.' He was staring diligently in the mirror, avoiding her gaze, apparently concentrating on shaving, but Lydia wasn't fooled.

'I think things seem to be going well, don't you?'

He dunked the razor in the water before he answered, making her slightly nervous he'd felt the need to gather his thoughts before replying. 'They *are* going well…very well…' He scraped the blade along his jaw again. 'And in that spirit, I should like to lay my cards on the table.'

In case it was bad news, she pulled the sheet around her body and braced herself, wondering if things were moving too fast for him or he felt the need to reaffirm the rules of their arrangement. She could cope with the former, but sincerely hoped it wasn't the latter. Not now that things had moved on and her heart was fully engaged once again.

'You see, the thing is…' He still didn't turn around. 'I've decided I don't actually want what we originally agreed to.'

Then it was the latter. Lydia's throat constricted as her poor heart absorbed the blow.

'Oh…'

She wished she wasn't naked. Wished she hadn't just offered herself again on a plate. Somehow both made her humiliation worse. Fortunately, Owen was concentrating too hard on cleaning his razor again so didn't see her obvious disappointment.

'When I first suggested marriage I convinced myself it was because I was rescuing you from Kelvedon—but that was a flimsy lie. I suppose, in part, it was…' He began to drag the blade over his opposite cheek, still completely focused on the task. 'But the real reason was…' The blade paused and he finally flicked her a glance. In that moment she saw he wasn't anywhere close to being as calm and collected as he had wanted her to believe. 'I still harboured feelings for you. Strong feelings…which just seem to get stronger with every passing day.'

The cords strangling her throat instantly relaxed and she felt the corners of her mouth pull into a smile as she exhaled the lungful of air she had been holding.

'And for quite some time now I've hoped that perhaps our marriage might become a proper marriage in every sense of the word.' He was back to staring in the mirror again, only this time he failed to appear close to being matter-of-fact. He was a little jumpy, his Ts less pronounced and his vowels flatter. And both were music to her ears.

'I should like that, too.' Why make the poor thing suffer when he was obviously in turmoil? 'We have certainly made some headway in the last two days.'

'Things are moving very fast.' Instead of smiling at her admission, he seemed troubled by their progress. 'Making me fear we are running before we can walk...which is what we need to talk about, Lydia.' There was no doubting his expression was pained. 'We can't keep blindly stumbling forward until we have squared off the past.'

'That doesn't matter, Owen.' She didn't want to argue any more. Never wanted to feel all those awful feelings which the past dredged up. Not now they were happy.

'It does. I wish it didn't, but it's lurking like a giant pothole in the road, just waiting to keep us apart.'

'One we have managed to avoid so far.'

'Have we?' He swiped the last of the soap from his face with a towel, then tossed it in the corner to snatch up his shirt. 'I know it's there. You know it's there.' His fist tapped his chest. 'It's eating away at me, Lydia. I know we agreed to ignore it, but we can't ignore it for ever because one of these days we are going to fall in that pothole regardless. Then what do we do? We'll start to hate each other again and that would break my heart.'

Just as it would break hers. 'You think reopening the wound will make it better?' Because she knew it wouldn't. Every time they kicked that hornets' nest it ended badly. 'When we have been getting on so well and moving forward?' One step forward and two steps back.

He had already got into his breeches and was thrusting his arms through his shirt. When his face appeared it was frowning. 'How far forward can we go dragging all that poison along with us? We need to discuss it, Lydia. We need to work through it. Let's give our marriage a fighting chance. I...' He closed his eyes and clenched his fists briefly, then his intense blue gaze locked with hers. 'I care too deeply for you to settle for half measures. Because it turns out I want it all!'

That flash of temper told her all she needed to know. He cared. Truly cared.

'Are you trying to tell me you still love me?'

He waited a beat, then grabbed a cravat, turning his back on her again to wind it impatiently around his neck. 'I care...deeply.'

Lydia allowed that to settle for a moment, revelling in the warm, overwhelming sense of rightness his clumsy declaration created within her. 'That's a start.' And all at once that was enough.

'We need to cancel that damn armistice!' His big hands were making a dreadful mess of his knot. 'And once this stupid shooting party is done, at precisely one o'clock, we are going to talk. Even if it means we argue! I can cope with shouting. I can even cope with your tears! But I cannot go another day without chopping back those blasted brambles!' Then he ripped the ruined strip from his neck and shook it. 'I hate these blasted things!'

'Oh, Owen...' She threw the bedcovers aside and walked towards him. He cared for her still. So deeply he was getting himself in a state. 'Let me do it.'

He stood as still as a statue as she wound a fresh cloth around his neck, but his breathing was erratic and his eyes kept dipping to her naked breasts. 'Do you realise that when you are flustered your accent slips?'

He winced. 'I'm trying to lose it.'

'I wish you wouldn't. Around me at least. I've always liked it. It reminds me of the old Owen I fell in love with.'

'And how do you feel about the new Owen?'

She couldn't resist teasing him a bit. 'He is growing on me.'

'That's *a start*, I suppose.' He couldn't resist looking a

little pleased at the news. 'One that gives me something to build on. Then maybe—after we have tackled the past— you might consider *adoring* me again.'

'I think we both know I adore you already.' She finished the knot and looped her arms around his neck. 'So much so I fear I may need to monopolise all of our appointment later showing you exactly how much.'

'We really do *have* to talk, Lydia.'

'No. We don't.' She pressed her lips to his. 'Because, as I said, the past doesn't matter any more.'

'It doesn't?' He was finally smiling, too, now, hope swirling in his eyes, confirming this was the absolutely correct thing to do.

'Of course it doesn't.' If the past was holding them back and upsetting him so much, then she had the power to banish it all. 'Because…'

'Because?'

She couldn't resist kissing him again to draw out this most significant of moments.

'Because… I forgive you, Owen.'

He stiffened. Pulled away. All the cosy intimacy and heartfelt confidences suddenly blasted away by an Arctic gale.

'You…*forgive* me.' The usually stormy irises of his deep blue eyes hardened into ice crystals.

He shook his head, briefly looking uncharacteristically broken and beaten down before the usual pride and bravado had him standing taller. 'God, I'm a blasted fool!'

Like a whirlwind, he grabbed his boots and his coat and, while she stood there impotent and shocked to her core, marched to the door. Lydia had never seen him so angry. Usually he waved his arms about and created lots of bluster—but this was different. It was quiet fury. Molten. All-encompassing.

As he grabbed the door knob, he spun around, his expression livid. But his eyes…

His eyes were pained. There was hurt in them. So much she could hardly bear it. Unthinking, she took a step towards him, needing to make it all better, but he stayed her with one coldly raised palm, all the heat and desire of a moment ago replaced by utter disgust.

'You can take your blasted forgiveness, madam—and you can go to hell!'

Chapter Twenty-One

Owen was still fuming several hours later when he learned the Earl of Fulbrook was dead. One minute he was doing his damnedest to look like a man having a good time in front of his host while internally screaming at his blasted wife, the next he was flying through the Aveley woods desperate to get to her.

He found her in their room overseeing the last of the hasty packing. She looked pale, shocked and so very alone it broke his heart.

'I suppose you've heard the news.'

He nodded. 'His heart.'

'Ironic, really, as I never realised he had one.' She stuffed an impatient hand in a glove. 'Is it normal, do you suppose, to feel nothing? Because I am numb, Owen. Almost indifferent.'

'He wasn't an easy man to love.'

'True... He was much easier to hate. Yet now I do not know how to think.' She reached for the letter on the nightstand and handed it to him. He recognised Randolph's ostentatious sloping handwriting on the front. 'Word was sent to the club late last night. He died alone. Maybury found him.' She exhaled loudly. 'A depressing end, all in all.'

One Owen uncharitably felt was fitting. 'The carriage is ready. We can have you home in a matter of hours.'

'Justin will need me to organise the funeral. He's not good at that sort of thing.'

'But I am. I can do it all for you.'

'And wouldn't that be ironic, after everything that's happened. I do not fool myself dear Papa had any affection for me, but I know he hated you. He wanted you hanged, Owen—yet you would still offer to plan his funeral?'

'For you, Lydia. Not him.' She was lost, not herself and in dire need of someone to take control, so he held out his hand. 'Come…let's go. Then we'll work out what needs to be done.'

She allowed him to lead her to the carriage and sat there staring blankly at nothing while he arranged everything around her. His men had saddled his horse, but he couldn't leave her. Not when all the light had dimmed in her eyes and all her fight was gone.

'Tie him to the back.' A decision he would undoubtedly regret when cold droplets of sweat were already trickling down his spine. 'I will ride with my wife.'

Owen sucked in his last lungful of fresh air and pulled open the door, only to have Lydia blink back.

'What are you doing?'

'I'm not leaving you alone.' To prove that fact to himself as well as her he flopped heavily on to the bench next to her, slammed the door shut and bashed on the ceiling. His stomach lurched at the same time as the carriage did and he tried to ignore the oppressive walls closing in. He was bigger than four blasted airless walls.

She must have sensed his discomfort, but said nothing as they rattled out of the Aveley stable yard and on to the long gravel drive. By the time they finally got to the end his blood was pumping so loudly in his head he could barely think. Then he felt her hand. Like an anchor. Sure and solid and clasped around his.

'Would it help if we opened the windows?'

Owen wanted to smash every pane. 'It's freezing outside.'

She ignored his flimsy stoic protest to release the catch on both and then retrieved two thick blankets from beneath the seats as the frigid December air buffeted them both. He refused his with a curt shake of his head, relieved he could at least breathe now, but feeling ridiculous to be in such a state. Here she was in her hour of need and he was a panicked mess. Instead of being nauseatingly noble, he just felt nauseous.

'Before you crucify yourself for feeling scared, know that I appreciate the gesture. I really don't want to be alone.' When she found his hand this time she laced her fingers through his. 'It means the world you are here.'

'I wouldn't be anywhere else.' It was true, even if he could barely breathe.

'My head is spinning. So many disjointed thoughts and memories all bombarding me at once. I can barely make heads or tails of them.'

'I'm happy to listen… They might take my mind off things.' Although the solid comfort of her hand was helping. That and the knowledge she wanted him by her side.

'His last words to me were, "Do your duty." Not "Thank you" or "I'm sorry" or anything even mildly placating to make me feel better. Just, "Do your duty, Lydia." Then, once he had his money, he washed his hands of me. For the life of me I cannot fathom how he justified all that. Do you suppose he regretted it all? Do you think, in his last moments, he even spared me a thought?'

'I am sure he did.'

'And I am sure you are lying. In those last moments I

think he was only capable of thinking of himself. Nobody else ever really mattered to him.'

Sadly, Owen did not doubt that.

'When my mother died, I recall he behaved as if it was all a dreadful inconvenience to him. How awful is that?' She didn't seem to want an answer. 'But then he was going to marry me off to Kelvedon and completely disregarded all my pleas to spare me that fate, so I suppose I shouldn't be surprised he was so heartless. Now, all I can feel is guilty.'

'Whatever for?'

She squeezed his hand. 'Because he is dead—my last remaining parent is gone—and all I can think about is our argument this morning.' For the first time since he had heard the news about Fulbrook, there were tears in her eyes. 'Why did my forgiveness upset you so?'

'Let's not do this now, Lydia...'

'Why not? You wanted to talk and now seems as good a time as any. I already feel wretched. You already feel trapped. I sincerely doubt we could feel any worse. And you are right. The past is in our way and I so want to move forward. I thought that would be a way through it. A way to stop it all.'

She glanced up at him, her beautiful dark eyes so filled with sorrow they made him forget the carriage walls. 'I know your character now. I even admire it. You are an inspiration, Owen. Good and kind and so very noble. Deep down, I have always known that there must have been a very good reason for you to have done such a thing. Unless it was a silly, rash mistake, the sort we all make when we are headstrong and young and think we know everything...' She gazed at him with such longing. 'To err is human after all...'

'And to forgive is divine.' For a moment, he seriously

considered accepting her forgiveness. That would be the easiest and quickest way to get on with their future exactly as she said. It would make him the bigger man. But he knew he would be doing them both a disservice to settle for that. It would eat away at them both. Him in particular. She would still think ill of him and he would always feel aggrieved at that. As if she had settled for second-best when he wanted to be her everything. 'But I cannot accept your forgiveness because I did nothing wrong, Lydia. I need you to see that. I need you to know it.' He pointed to his chest. 'In here where it matters.'

He watched her features crumple and forced himself to harden his heart against it. They both had to face the past. Had to have the tears, the anguish and the arguments. It was the only way. 'But I saw it with my own eyes, Owen…'

'Just for a moment, try to forget what you saw. Because you saw exactly what you were supposed to.'

'I don't understand.' Yet he could see that she wanted to and that meant the world to him.

'People often don't believe what they see, Lydia—but they always *see* what they believe. You saw what someone wanted you to believe. And they did a very good job. If I hadn't been the victim, I would have been entirely convinced of my guilt. The scene was so…calculated.' The damning evidence had been hidden. Part of it beneath the mattress which had been stripped from the frame by the time they had brought him there. But then, when both Lydia and her brother had been summoned to the scene to witness his arrest, the constable found more. The two worthless candlesticks had been stuffed at the back of his only, tiny cupboard. Behind all his meagre worldly possessions.

'You still want to convince me it was a conspiracy?'

'No.' His own voice sounded desperate now. Only some

of that was to do with the confined walls of the carriage. 'I want you to view it all with your head and your heart—not your eyes.'

'Now I really don't understand.'

'When you are clearly happy to forgive me, what possible reason could I have to perpetuate the lie?' He gently turned her face to his, needing her to see the truth in his eyes.

'I have my life back. A pardon. A successful business. My own fortune. The woman of my dreams is now my wife. I would have to be a fool not to grab your forgiveness with both hands…if I truly were guilty.'

She was silent.

After the longest, most significant pause of his life, he pressed his fingers to her breast bone. 'What does your heart say, Lydia?'

Another pause, one made more tragic by the single tear which spilled out of her eye and trickled slowly down her cheek. Then she huffed out a sigh. 'My foolish heart has never believed you were guilty.'

He sagged with relief. 'Then help me prove it.'

They spent the rest of the journey discussing the events surrounding the thefts. Owen asked her question after question and, while she answered every single one of them as accurately as possible, recalling all manner of minutiae, every passing moment which had been buried over the years, all she could properly focus on was the one which was the most important.

What possible reason could I have to perpetuate the lie?

Because there truly was no reason. Not that she could fathom.

That, combined with his ferocious, angry reaction to her heartfelt forgiveness this morning, seemed to point unequivocally to his innocence. Somebody must have set him up—exactly as he had always claimed. But why anyone would do something so cruel was a mystery.

Owen had said he had always suspected it had something to do with her, but couldn't put his finger on why he felt it other than it was what his gut told him. Which in turn led to a swirling cauldron of hideous emotions at the thought of all he had suffered because of a gross miscarriage of justice which she might have inadvertently helped cause. And if that were indeed the case, how would they move past it? Was love enough? Could they both forgive and forget or would a part of him always be disappointed that she had ever doubted him? Because she was thoroughly disappointed in herself now.

But before they tackled that huge obstacle, Owen wanted a blow-by-blow account of everything and everyone she could remember from those fateful last weeks to help him piece together what had happened properly. Her testimony was the missing link, the other side of the coin, and he was correct in his assumption it had never been heard. Nobody had asked her a damn thing in the aftermath of Owen's arrest. She had been left to deal with her sick mother's rapid decline while her menfolk were obsessed with the trial, both oblivious to the other heartbreak she was struggling to cope with all alone.

His barrage of questions churned up all sorts of painful memories of the past which she had not revisited for a very long time, the emotional toll of her mother's illness being one of them.

When she hadn't stolen those scant few hours a week with him, Lydia had been at her mother's bedside. What had begun as a bad chill in the early spring had rapidly declined into a long-standing malaise her poor mama had not been able to shake. Just before she met Owen, they had travelled to Bath together so she could take the waters. The excursion did initially alleviate her symptoms—but they had all returned by the end of the summer and things took a dire turn for the worst the week after Owen's arrest.

The same week he had been sentenced, her mother had died, turning a hideously dreadful time into a living hell. The black pit of despair had taken Lydia a good six months to start to emerge from. Was it any wonder she had buried it all? Yet now she had to face it. For him.

For them.

She had promised to write it all down, to create a post-humous diary which he could then compare to the extensive notes and investigations he had made already, to see if there was another clue which might lead to the real thief.

And on top of it all she also had her father's death to cope with, combined with fresh guilt and turmoil concerning Owen. It all felt overwhelming.

By the time they pulled into Berkeley Square, she was as wrung out as a dish towel and more confused than ever.

Bleakly, she stared at her father's house. As it was too soon for the funerary hatchment bearing the coat of arms to have been prepared, the door had been tied with black ribbons instead. Then the door opened and a sombre May-bury wearing both black gloves and a mourning armband waited, head bent, while a footman rushed towards the carriage door.

Beside her Owen moved to leave with her, and she shook her head.

'I should probably do this alone.' There was no telling what sort of state her brother would be in and she didn't trust him not to exchange a few ugly words with her husband in the heat of the moment. She would need to prepare the ground first. Clear away the obstacles of the past to make way for the future. 'Just this first meeting. There are personal family things which will need to be discussed and my brother does not know you…yet.' Although now that her father was gone, she hoped that he would.

He nodded, understanding, but still helped her down. 'Would you like me to wait?'

'No… I could be hours. I shall see you at home.'

For a moment he appeared ready to argue, then stepped aside, but she saw how hard that was for him to do and felt a wave of love for him wash over her. She had married a good man. The absolute best.

'Then I shall leave you the carriage. If you need me, send word and I will be here in a flash.'

He kissed her hand, a polite nod to propriety in this, the home of it, then watched from the pavement as she climbed the three white steps to the house and she sensed him lingering even after the butler closed the door. Owen's presence gave her strength, exactly as it always did, which was just as well because she would need it. The next few days would not be easy.

Chapter Twenty-Two

'Is my brother here?'

'He is, my lady. In the drawing room.'

'And my father?'

'Laid out in his bed. I expect you would prefer to visit him first…to pay your respects.'

'Thank you, Maybury.' At least she would get that over with first and perhaps see if she would feel something beyond the numbness which was all she seemed able to muster regarding his death. 'Can you have some tea sent to the drawing room and tell my brother I shall be there presently.'

As was customary, a footman stood guard outside her father's bedchamber. He bowed and opened the door, closing it quietly behind her as Lydia stepped inside. With the heavy velvet curtains drawn, it was dark, but even so the room still felt unfamiliar. Even when his health declined, she had only been invited in there a handful of times. This was very much his space, like so many rooms in this depressing house which no longer felt like home.

On the bed, still dressed in a nightgown, was the shadowy outline of her father and she walked towards it, waiting for some feeling, some remorse or grief to sting her, but when none came stared dispassionately at his corpse on the bed. Owen was right. Her father had been a difficult man to love. Impossible, in fact. In death, his face still appeared cruel and soulless. Deep frown lines were etched into his skin, a memorial to everything about life and people which had always disappointed him so.

Lydia allowed a minute to tick by, wondering how she was supposed to pay her proper respects when she had so little respect for the man in the bed. There were no tears. She was yet to shed a single one. Perhaps they would come later? And perhaps not. She was old enough to know duty and love were two entirely separate entities. As a Barton, she had always known her duty. As a daughter, she wasn't sure she had ever felt love.

So many memories of this house flooded her mind—yet none of the scant few truly good ones involved him. All she could recall of her father seemed predominantly bad. There had been no laughter that she was sure of. She had never shared a joke with him, never whiled away a pleasant hour in conversation or they hadn't even taken a walk together. He had never taken an interest in her and she knew better than to seek him out as that rarely ended well. He had been largely absent for so much of her childhood that as a girl she had always felt him a stranger. As an adult, she often wished he was still a stranger as she could only recall his disdain or his distance. He had never been a natural father.

Thank goodness Owen was. Seeing him with Gertie's brood always brought a lump to her throat. And now they were lovers, perhaps one day soon she would be able to watch him with his own children. Perhaps that would help to heal the wounds in their past—although she could feel them already healing. This morning was a bump in the road, not a pothole...

With a sigh, she realised contemplating Owen was not what she was supposed to be there for and forced herself to stare back at the man who had fathered her for the last time. She didn't hate him. How could one hate a stranger? She was detached. Indifferent. Eager to be gone.

In the hope she might feel some connection, she took his hand and still felt indifferent, the only thought entering her head was that she had no recollection of ever touching him before. His skin was papery, cold and alien. Not all of that could be blamed on death. If his blood ran through her veins, surely there would be something? But there wasn't.

Then all at once the numbness lifted. Beneath it was still some residual anger for the shoddy and neglectful way he had treated her, but to her complete surprise, all that was being overshadowed as pity crept in. Not for all her father had suffered—more for all he had missed as she realised how dreadful it must have been to live a life completely devoid of love and laughter and joy, and all of that entirely self-inflicted. He had been too dictatorial. Too unforgiving. Too consumed in his own world, needs and ambitions to venture outwards to embrace anyone else's.

What a sad waste of a life.

'Rest in peace, Papa.'

She replaced his lifeless hand on his chest, thankful that she had failed to inherit any of those traits. She would have love and laughter and joy in spite of him and, thanks to this perennially detached and unsympathetic man, she would share those things with Owen. The one good thing he had done for her, for which she would be grateful to him for ever, albeit completely by accident. 'Thank you.'

Respects, such as they were, paid, Lydia left him. Closing the door felt symbolic. Another pivotal moment. The decisive ending of her old life and a bold, fresh start to the new. In an odd sort of way it was like a weight being lifted from her shoulders, reminding her what was done was done. The past could not be altered, but the future could and *would* be shaped differently.

Back downstairs, she located her brother in their father's study rather than the drawing room, rifling through the desk and, like her, he did not appear to be in the throes of deep mourning either.

'I literally had to prise the key to this desk out of his cold, dead fingers, so hoped for a pleasant surprise or a hidden stash of money that he might have miraculously put by.' He huffed and tossed a handful of papers to one side before he came towards her and kissed her cheek. 'No such luck. Nothing but nonsense and more responsibilities. It's going to take for ever to sort out.'

'I could help if you wanted?'

'Unless you have a spare thousand in your reticule, there's nothing you can do... Although you could be the one to receive any visitors and show them Papa.' He shuddered. 'The sight of him dead turns my stomach.' Then he glanced back at the papers as if they too greatly inconvenienced him.

'Of course, he was too miserly and too suspicious to pay for a secretary, so he has left me a disorganised shambles to sort through on top of the shambles of the estate affairs he passed over to me when his health first failed. I suspect most of that is for the bonfire. Our father kept everything, it seems. Invitations and letters from eons ago. Every receipt and every bill. Everything, it turns out, except the thing we need the most—cold, hard cash to pay for his funeral.' Twice in that unfeeling sentence he had alluded to the need for money. Did he expect her to lend him some when he hadn't even had the decency to enquire after her health in the month she had been gone? Or to ask Owen when he couldn't even utter her husband's name without showing his complete disdain for him?

Before it showed on her face, she banished the irritation. Justin was her brother and therefore completely entitled to speak plainly. Knowing their father, he had left him a huge mess to sort out and her brother was probably not asking for a loan at all, merely venting out loud to the one person he could be entirely honest with.

'There is bound to be some money, although I doubt he kept it lying around the house. It's probably in a bank somewhere.'

'Unlikely. He distrusted banks almost as much as he distrusted his family.' There was no denying that. 'But enough of that. Let's have tea. I haven't seen you in ages.'

It was on the tip of her tongue to respond with a terse "whose fault is that?", but today wasn't the day. Instead, she followed him into the drawing room. Unlike her husband, her brother would never dream of pouring the tea, so she took charge, all the while pondering how odd it felt to be back here. This house had been her home for six and twenty years, yet she had no attachment to it. It was bleak and soulless in comparison to her new home, the mantel clock ticking loudly in the void left by the distinct lack of conversation. It was staggering how distant they had become as adults when as children they had got on so well.

'How are you, Justin?'

'As well as can be expected given the circumstances.'

'I suppose you will be moving out of the Albany now that you are the Earl of Fulbrook?'

'Yes. I shall have my things transferred back here while we are away. To inconvenience us as much as possible from the hereafter, Papa stipulated Cheshire as his final resting place, although Lord only knows why. He hated the dreary place and it takes for ever to get there. Not to mention how expensive it is going to be to deliver him there. I cannot imagine what he was thinking.'

'It's where Mama is buried.' Lydia had only been back once since that funeral. Her father had little time for the family seat and had always resented the expense of opening it up for her mother every summer. In view of the debts he had burdened them with, his thriftiness concerning that huge Tudor manor now made perfect sense. 'And all his ancestors.'

'Still—it's a dreadful inconvenience. And costly. Burying him here in town would be much cheaper.'

There had been so many hints now, she couldn't ignore it. 'I could ask Owen to lend you some money if funds are short.' Although why funds were still short when Owen had already paid all her father's debts was a concern. It had only been a month. And how Owen would take it, when he had already coughed up thirteen thousand pounds to bail the family out of trouble, she had no idea. Not well, she assumed. But she would ask if she had to, knowing he would help simply because she'd asked.

Justin looked appalled. 'Oh, he'd love that, wouldn't he? I'd rather borrow from a backstreet money lender than give that scoundrel the satisfaction! And while we are on the subject of your husband, I shall say plainly he is not welcome at either this house or the funeral.'

'That is a bit harsh!' Her brother might well have some prejudices against him—all, it seemed, were unfounded—but he was still her husband, one who had alleviated her family's huge financial burdens considerably. 'While I am not blaming you, I do think we have misjudged him. Owen is generous of nature. Very thoughtful and with more humility and understanding than I fear this family deserves. Why, not ten minutes ago he offered to arrange Papa's funeral for us, to save us the burden.' His humility, decency and ability to let bygones be bygones was humbling.

'I'll bet he did! He does *so* enjoy publicity.'

'He absolutely does not.' If anything he was the exact opposite.

'Not a day goes by without some story splashed all over the papers aggrandising his achievements. He's a shameless self-publicist and slimy social climber.'

'How dare you!' Lydia shot up from her seat. 'I shall only grant you the benefit of the doubt so far, Brother! He is my husband, has been nothing but decent and kind to me since our marriage, and I will not sit here and listen to him maligned. If the newspapers publish stories about him, that is hardly his fault. His good reputation precedes him.'

'*Good* reputation!'

'Yes. Good. He's defied all expectations, built a business from scratch and impressed a great many people since his return and that is admirable.' He had certainly impressed her—but more with his character than his fortune. Owen was not like any of the men she was used to and absolutely nothing like the males in her family. He wouldn't be moaning and griping were he in Justin's shoes—he would roll up his sleeves and do whatever needed to be done to fix the mess he'd been left with. And he would do so without complaining and still be the one to show visitors to their father's bedchamber.

'He runs a gaming hell, Lydia. A den of iniquity.'

'It's a gentlemen's club, Justin. No different from White's or Brooks's and nobody would call those hells. And as for it being a den of iniquity—nothing could be further from the truth. I should know. I do live there. All the staff adore him.' She doubted her brother would understand why she thought that detail important, but it was. It said everything one needed to know about the excellent character of Owen Wolfe. 'The truth is the newspapers do not know the half of it. Nobody knows how philanthropic he is. He keeps all that quiet and never brags about anything. He left the Antipodes a hero. The governor himself praised him as one of the best men he had ever known.'

Her brother rolled his eyes and it took all her strength not to shake him by the shoulders. Instead, she took a deep breath and tried to make him see reason. He was the last of her blood until she and Owen had children. Families were supposed to stick together. Like Owen's, who did not have the luxury of blood to bind them. 'Give him a chance, Justin. Get to know him. I think you will be pleasantly surprised…'

'Oh, good Lord!' The patronising and dismissive tone galled. 'He's seduced you into believing he walks on water again, hasn't he? That he is completely above reproach… the Messiah. Or more likely Machiavelli!' He stood, too, and waved a disapproving finger at her as if she were a naughty child.

'He is the master of deception and manipulation! A puppeteer of the worst sort who uses his charm, good looks and silver tongue to get precisely what he wants as the success of his filthy hell is doubtless testament.'

'That's not true.'

'Now you are his willing marionette once again, Lydia.' He had the audacity to smile as he patronised her. 'Didn't you learn your lesson last time?'

'And what is that supposed to mean?' Although with a sinking feeling she knew exactly what was coming. Her brother had known about them.

Justin scoffed and then shook his head. 'Our mother's jewellery? Or did you think nobody realised you had practically led him into her bedchamber when you carelessly invited him into yours?' He stared at her stunned face, eyebrows raised, then shook his head in disappointment.

'I let it slide then. You were young, impressionable and I knew full well Papa would throw you out if he knew the extent of your involvement. As your elder brother I couldn't let that happen. People in glass houses and all that… And who hasn't dallied with a servant to relieve the tedium? But you'd have to be a complete imbecile to be hoodwinked by the blackguard again. Wolfe cannot be trusted, Lydia.'

His finger waved imperiously again, his tone and mannerisms more akin to their father's now than the brother she wanted. 'He is such an arch manipulator, he almost walked away scot-free. Did you know that?'

She hadn't.

'He defended himself and practically had the judge eating out of his hand with his practised falsehoods. Circumstantial evidence be damned! And he'd have got away with it all to if we hadn't—' He suddenly clamped his jaws shut.

'Hadn't what, Justin?'

He pulled himself up to his full height, bristling, as if she had no right to question him. 'Given the court a cast-iron witness who could prove your dirty little secret a barefaced liar.'

Dirty little secret. Guilty secret.

Owen's words, too. Words that had wounded him deeply just as they did her now.

'What witness?'

'Argent. The stable master. Saw him creeping out of the house with a sack full of loot.'

'I don't believe it.' Her heart denounced it as a shocking lie. 'Mr Argent obviously perjured himself in court.'

'Are you so bewitched you can no longer see the truth, Lydia? He is a fraudster. A crook. A dirty thief and a callous manipulator. You used to hate him.'

She had never hated him. Because her heart had known. 'Do not insult him. He is my husband!'

'Not of my choosing. I begged you not to marry him. Since you have, I absolutely refuse to suffer his presence or his interference.'

'It was an offer of help.'

'You can call it help if it makes you feel better, but I see it for what it is. Just another bargaining chip. One he'll ultimately use against me, like he did with Papa, and I'd sooner take myself on to the streets than give him the satisfaction of feeling superior and turning me out. I know full well he is merely waiting for the perfect moment to pounce as it is. Wolf by name, wolf by nature. And your wolf wants his revenge because we bested him and dared to call a spade a spade.'

Lydia turned on her heel and marched to the door. She couldn't believe how quickly things had deteriorated. All the vitriol and malicious spite coming out of her brother's mouth. He was no better than their father!

Which made her pause.

These were fraught circumstances. Papa hadn't been dead twenty-four hours and her brother had been left with a mess. He had never been good in a crisis. Never been good with responsibility. Now was a time to pour oil on troubled waters and mend things—not inflame them. Justin was usually a placid man. A weak and impressionable one who was clearly not himself. For the sake of what was left of her family, she had to try again.

'This is nonsense, Justin. I cannot believe we are arguing about Owen or that you would speak of him in this way when thanks to him you have a fresh start. We should forget the past, for the sake of our family, and try to make amends.'

'Amends!' Again he scoffed, flatly refusing to be placated. 'I will not dance to his tune like you or Papa. I refuse to be blackmailed by a jumped-up servant with ideas far above his station. He is not my family, Lydia. I want nothing to do with him.'

'Blackmail?' Her brother wasn't quite himself—he had clearly gone mad. All the stress of their father's sudden demise and the need to take on the mantle of responsibility had given him temporary leave of his senses. 'He offered more money, Brother, and our father greedily took it. That hardly constitutes blackmail.'

Justin paused in his searching and stared at her as if she were mad. 'He held us to ransom, Lydia. Either we gave you to him or he took the house.'

'He paid the mortgage, Justin! He gave you back the house.'

'He owns the damn mortgage, Lydia. And whenever he wants something he waves the damn deeds in our faces!'

Chapter Twenty-Three

'Slugger said you were back.' Owen came quickly into his office, ridiculously pleased to see her, then stopped dead.

Lydia was sat at his desk, papers strewn everywhere and glaring at him as if he disgusted her.

'You are investigating my family!' A statement, not a question, because she was holding the file the Runner had delivered yesterday. A very damning file. One he should have locked away rather than tossed carelessly in the drawer. 'How could you?'

'I am investigating the thefts…it is impossible to do that without looking into your family history, too.' He raked an agitated hand though his hair, cursing himself for his stupidity. 'To be fair to me, I merely engaged the Runner. I didn't tell him to dig up all *that*.'

While the contents of the thorough dossier did not lead him in the direction of the real thief, they were still damning. Beyond damning, in fact. Documenting a sordid tale of Barton hedonism and debauchery which he had intended to spare her from.

'I have sisters, I see. Two of them I never knew about. By two different women to boot. And apparently a nephew, too.'

Both her father and her weak-willed brother had a habit of paying off mistresses instead of debts. And the list of hidden debts the dogged Runners had uncovered was frankly staggering. Mind-boggling, in fact. Justin Barton had racked up gaming debts at every unsavoury and undesirable gaming hell in the capital and, as he had initially suspected, gone to some very dubious money lenders to help pay for them. He sincerely hoped she hadn't reached the page which listed his penchant for brothels who catered in quite particular perversions. No sister should know their brother enjoyed such depravities in the bedchamber.

And then... *Oh, God*! There was all the Kelvedon stuff. Owen winced. 'I knew nothing of it all myself until yesterday.'

'Yesterday? Before we left for Aveley Castle?' After they had made love for the first time and before they had done it again for the second. That made him wince again. He should have said something. 'What do you intend to do with it?'

'Nothing.'

Her bitter laugh was without humour. 'More blackmail, I presume, seeing as that has proved so fruitful.'

'Blackmail? Of course not.' He touched her shoulder, only to have her pull away as if he had slapped her. 'Lydia... I'm sorry you saw all this. Genuinely I am. I am just trying to get to the truth.'

'No, Owen. You are *trying* to control everything and everyone. Using whatever makes the best leverage— exactly as you did before.'

'Where has this all come from?' Because this wasn't the woman he had made love to this morning, nor the one he had bared his soul to in the carriage. But in the hours since he had last seen her, she had been with her brother. 'Has Justin put all this nonsense into your head?'

'We both know it isn't nonsense.' She stood, took herself to stand on the opposite side of the room and then hugged her arms tight around her body in defence. 'You have been blackmailing my family.'

'I really haven't...'

'Do you deny you used the mortgage deed to force my father into giving you my hand in marriage?'

He should have told her about that at least. He'd had ample opportunity these last few weeks. 'Only because I couldn't bear the thought of you marrying Kelvedon! You know how I feel about you, Lydia.'

'Do I? Only you've never actually said it out loud.'

Only because it frankly scared the hell out of him. For a man who feared being controlled, it was the ultimate weapon. Or rather she was.

'Then I'll say it now... I love you, Lydia. I've always loved you. Right from the first moment I saw you and that blasted thunderbolt knocked me sideways. I never stopped loving you. It's why I came back. Why I was desperate to come back.' He had seven damning swallows tattooed into his skin to prove it. Each marked a year and renewed his desire for a safe return home—to her. He now knew it had all been for her. 'It is why I immediately sought you out as soon as the ship hit the shore and why I couldn't leave you alone afterwards.

'You must have realised. Must have wondered why I just happened to be in the park when you rode there? Why I always sought you out at balls and parties?' He edged towards her and, when he was close enough, reached out his hand and gently caressed her cheek. She didn't pull away this time. 'Why I married you... All those damn thunderbolts! They keep striking me out of nowhere. Knocking me sideways. It was never business... I love you, Lydia. So much it terrifies me...and I think you love me, too.'

If she didn't, he was well and truly doomed. 'I hope you *love* me, too.'

There were tears in her eyes. He was baring his soul, but she still looked down her nose at him. 'Did you use the mortgage deed as leverage to get back my clothes?'

'I did… I had to. Your father wouldn't budge otherwise.' Owen should have come clean then. 'I tried to tell you…' He couldn't lie. 'That's not strictly true. I *wanted* to tell you, but… I knew it would look bad.'

'It does look bad.' Yet she still didn't pull away. 'And all of that…' he gestured to the desk '…also looks bad. So much so, I really don't know what to think or who to believe any longer.'

'What does your heart say?'

She stared deep into his eyes, then took a step back. 'I don't think my heart has the best judgement. Not when my head knows categorically you possess all that damning knowledge.' Her gaze flicked to the file on the desk. 'And you still own the deed to the Berkeley Square house.'

'Then allow me to simplify things.'

He unlocked the safe and pulled out the deed, then handed it to her.

'It's yours now. To do with as you please.'

'Even if that means gifting it to my brother.'

'So he can mortgage it all over again and likely lose the house within the year?' Owen shrugged. It wasn't as if he was ever going to see his three thousand pounds again anyway. Justin Barton owed twice that and most probably more. 'Yes. I'll even summon a messenger so you can send it express or we can deliver the damn thing together right now. And as to all that…' They both glanced to the messy pile of damning papers. 'Let's throw it all on the fire.'

'No…it might turn out to be important…for your investigation.'

'I'll call off the investigation. It doesn't matter.'

'It absolutely matters. You have a right to know the truth. After all you have been through, I wouldn't deny you that. Any more than I can deny the truth of what you've discovered. It's right there in black-and-white, after all. Your Runner has been very…thorough.' That she didn't condemn it all as lies was testament to her great strength of character. Unless she already had some doubts about her brother.

'Then you keep it. Put it somewhere safe until you decide what you want me to do with it.'

She stared at it, obviously shocked at the gesture, but still not completely convinced of his sincerity. 'I need to think about things.' She clutched the beribboned deed to her chest like a shield. 'There seems suddenly so much to think about… So much that I do not understand…when last night I thought I knew absolutely everything I needed to know.'

Last night they had made love for hours. Randolph's words of caution had been ringing in his ears and he had blithely ignored them and built his house of cards anyway, selfishly avoiding the past for just a little bit longer so he could enjoy the present. Deluding himself it didn't truly matter when it did.

Idiot.

Even today, when they had talked in the carriage, he had held back. Censoring the past to suit his own purpose and forgetting he hadn't been the only one to live it. In his determination to uncover the truth he was hurting the thing he loved the most. Looking at the enormous weight of the world suddenly on her shoulders, he wasn't quite so sure any more it was worth it.

Ignoring the pile of papers, she walked to the door, their whole future in the balance.

'Just remember…above all else, Lydia…please remember that I love you.'

'Enough to pay my brother's debts if I ask it?'

If he sold his half of Libertas to Randolph he could just about cover them all. 'Yes.' If that is what it took to keep her affection.

Her fingers grasped the handle, slowly pulled the door open, then she hesitated and turned around, the oddest expression on her face. 'For me there was no thunderbolt…' Of course there wasn't. 'For me…time stood still.' She offered him the ghost of a smile. 'It has an annoying habit of doing that around you.'

Chapter Twenty-Four

Yes.

No pause. No hesitation. She had asked him if he would pay her brother's debts as a test of his sincerity and he had agreed in a heartbeat, even though she knew from Gertie he had spent almost all his savings paying her father. Owen was prepared to bankrupt himself for her.

Purely because he loved her.

Through all the chaos this dire day had thrown at her, only that seemed to matter.

As pivotal moments went, it was probably the most significant moment in her life. She had been lost in the fog, ambushed by secrets and rattling skeletons from the past, feeling betrayed and bereft and so crushingly alone, expecting him to disappoint her, too, and he hadn't. He had held his hands up, admitted he had been wrong, spoken directly from the heart and handed it all to her without a second thought.

Why on earth would he do that unless she was his entire world?

Then he had given her space to digest it all—not that it had helped—and she had sat for hours next to her fireplace, staring at the flames and wondering what on earth she was supposed to do next. Then another two had passed as she stared at the ceiling.

When she had flung open his bedchamber door in the small hours and fallen on his mouth hungrily, he had sensed she wasn't ready to talk and simply needed passion. Being Owen, he had given it unreservedly, just as he always gave her everything she wanted. Taking her lead, there had been no preamble, no lazy journey of discovery, no need for explanations. It had been hot and fast and completely uninhibited.

When he repeated his assertion that he loved her, she could see the truth of it in the stormy blue depths of his beautiful eyes, so she told him she loved him, too. And he had thanked her.

Thanked her!

As if she had just given him the most precious gift in the world when she had only been admitting to a truth which had been self-evident for ten long years. She loved him. Needed him. And believed him completely.

Not that that had helped her to sleep either. While Owen slept the blissful sleep of a man who genuinely hadn't done anything wrong, Lydia's mind was racing. The past, so long buried, was suddenly coming back in a flood. Events which had seemed insignificant. Details she had forgotten. All of them needed to be examined and dissected and put into their correct order.

All through that summer, and largely ignored by Lydia because she was too busy being head over heels in love, items had been going missing from the house. She remembered that now. Alongside her mother's treasured pearls had been three jewelled stick pins belonging to her father, a valuable antique ormolu clock which had lived in the morning room and several small pieces of silver—snuff boxes, pill boxes, hip flasks and the like.

At the time, she had thought nothing of it. Servants had a sporadic habit of stealing things in the Barton household for the exact same reasons as they hastily left its employ— because their wages were so bad and they had such little regard for her father. But as she reluctantly recalled it all now, those thefts that fateful summer were different because they weren't sporadic. In fact, they had become so frequent, her father had decided to get to the root of things himself and unmask the culprit. And like most things he did in self-righteous ill temper, he became obsessed.

They all knew he wouldn't rest until he caught the perpetrator. The entire household was in uproar because of it. Therefore, it stood to reason, it was entirely plausible the real guilty party might have panicked and implicated Owen to save himself from imminent discovery and her father's revenge. Her husband wanted to know who might have been capable of such a heartless fraud, yet she was struggling to remember all the servants' names at that time. There had been so many over the years, she would probably have to resort to the household account books to list them all. Or talk to Maybury, the only retainer who had lasted the course.

One of those many long-forgotten servants had to be the culprit. But who?

Who?

Then, as she dug deep to try to force it all out, her fevered mind suddenly wandered further back still, to the weeks before she had met Owen, and all at once everything slotted into place.

Her racing heart threatened to beat out of her ribs as she stared at her father's house.

'Do you want me to come in with you?'

'No.' As dawn was yet to break, and because he knew

the still-sleeping Owen would be furious, she had walked through the dark streets all alone except for Slugger, who had accompanied her. 'But I would be grateful if you waited here for me, Cyril...in case things turn nasty.'

A laughable statement when things were guaranteed to turn nasty.

She took one last calming breath to steel herself, then knocked on the door.

'My lady?' Poor Maybury was flustered, not all the buttons on his waistcoat yet done up in his haste to get dressed. 'What brings you here at this hour?'

'Urgent business. Inform my brother I am here and tell him I need to speak to him immediately.' There was no point skirting around the issue. Things needed to be said and the truth needed to be uncovered.

'He didn't retire till very late, my lady...'

'It cannot be helped. Kindly inform him that if he is not downstairs in five minutes, then I shall be coming up.'

The butler must have seen the slightly manic and determined expression on her face because he nodded and practically ran up the stairs. Left alone, she decided to take the opportunity to search her father's study herself, just in case she might find something which might prove her unthinkable new theory incorrect.

Less than five minutes later, that was where Justin found her. He was wrapped in a robe, his hair on end and his eyes dull and bleary. Probably, she realised dispassionately, from drink. Justin liked to drink. It was one of his many vices, apparently. Looking at him now, she realised she had given him too much leeway in recent years and made too many excuses for the way he behaved. He was a weak-willed, pathetic specimen of manhood. Spoiled, arrogant, self-absorbed and ultimately spineless.

'What the blazes is going on, Lydia?'

She had trusted him. Thought him on her side. Yet all along he had been in cahoots with their sire. He had never been a decent brother at all—merely a liar. A cowardly wolf in sheep's clothing.

'Where to start? That is the more pertinent question.' From her reticule, she pulled out the folded letter she had hidden when she had first found it in Owen's office and handed it to her brother, then watched him warily scan it.

'Where did you get this?'

'The smelly Marquess of Kelvedon gave it to a Bow Street Runner.' She wanted to slap him for his deceit and his greed and his treacherous duplicity.

'What are Bow Street doing talking to Kelvedon? Did you put them up to it?'

How dared he be outraged! 'Surely your first response should have been to drop to your knees and beg my forgiveness for your treachery, Brother! All the while I believed you were trying to save me from marrying that lecher, but I now realise it was you who brokered the deal in the first place. You suggested Kelvedon to Father, didn't you? That is your handwriting, isn't it, Justin? Your seal on the front?'

'Father needed a certain amount of money and the field of potential candidates was slim.'

How typical of him to pass the blame elsewhere rather than apologise.

'And why did he need that money, Justin?'

'You know full well why! Papa put us up to our eyeballs in debt!'

'Which brings me neatly on to *your* debts.' She retrieved the second pilfered sheet from her bag and watched his face pale as he read the damning list.

'It's funny what you remember sometimes.' And since she had been dredging up and trawling through her memories, things she had once believed almost without question no longer held up to scrutiny. 'But I now see how a passing comment, something I had no reason to think was significant, suddenly becomes incredibly significant. Like Papa's comment on the night he informed me I was to marry Owen when you argued against it. He said, "You've done *quite* enough already, boy…" He was referring to this, wasn't he? Your gambling debts. Your loans. Harlots. Hedonism. Avarice. The money *you* paid your mistress to leave the country with *your* illegitimate son. Your mess, Justin. On top of his. And you both sold me down the river to pay for it all.'

She had rendered him speechless clearly, because he gaped like a fish. Although what she expected him to say, when there really was nothing he could say which would justify his actions, she had no clue. 'We've had three poor harvests in a row, Lydia! I was desperate!'

Lord, he was pathetic. A lily-livered, selfish liar to the end.

'Those debts go back to Cambridge, Justin.' And the root cause of some of them disgusted her. Her beloved brother really was just the mirror image of their horrible father. She'd had her suspicions over the years, but quashed them. Felt guilty for her disloyalty for even thinking them, but had refused to believe what was right in front to her eyes.

Not believing what she was seeing—but seeing what she wanted to believe. Exactly as Owen had cautioned.

Justin and their sire were two peas in a pod. He was just as callous. Just as pompous and unfeeling. Just as entitled and heavy-handed in getting exactly what he wanted and to hell with everyone else.

Now she knew the truth, she did not have to see the

proof in black and white—she felt it in her heart. Almost
as deeply as she felt the dagger in her back.

'I have been doing a great amount of thinking since
yesterday, reminiscing on the past, and in so doing I have
had to re-evaluate many of the things I believed to be true.
Especially around the time of Mama's death. And all those
thefts.' Warily, he took a step back, his lying eyes darting
everywhere while Lydia felt sick to her stomach.

'Then about an hour ago I remembered something I
should *never* have forgotten. Concerning the morning
Mama and I left for Bath…' She walked towards him, her
facial muscles hurting from the force of her scowl. 'The
carriage had been loaded and I was sat in it, waiting for her.
I waited for twenty minutes, Justin…because she couldn't
find her pearls.' She paused then, because of all the hideously pivotal moments in her life, this one deserved some
gravitas. She lifted her finger and pointed at him.

'They had been stolen before we left, hadn't they?' He
shook his head in immediate denial, but his eyes were
wide. 'We were gone a whole month…don't you remember, Justin? And Owen didn't start working for our father
until the day before we arrived back home.'

Like the mythical Janus, he had two faces. The one
which might leak the truth was hidden now by his de-
ceiver's mask. A disguise she had fallen for time and time
again. 'I have no idea what you are talking about, poppet.
I was at Cambridge then. Don't you remember?' That he
could look both amused and worried about her at the same
time was testament to his skill. 'Surely you aren't trying
to suggest I had a hand in it?'

Why had she never noticed her brother was dead behind
the eyes before? They were as soulless and selfish as her
father's. 'I am not suggesting it, Justin. I know it. Without a shadow of a doubt. You needed money and because

Papa was so stingy with it you took it in other ways. After all, who would expect the heir to steal? What do you say to that…*poppet*?'

'And what proof do you have for this egregious falsehood?'

'None—bar what I feel in here.' She thumped her chest. 'But I will have! I know you put a witness on the stand to condemn Owen. You told me so yourself. I will find Mr Argent and I will pay him twice what you did to tell the truth than you did to have him lie.'

He smiled. *Smiled!* And shook his head. 'Argent is dead, Lydia. He died of a stroke some years ago.' Like a chameleon, he went from relieved to concerned. 'You are clearly overwrought to be inventing such nonsense. Or has Wolfe planted these poisonous seeds in your head?'

'It makes no difference. Because I remember! I remember you being there next to me when they arrested Owen. I remember you wrapping your arms around me, telling me you always suspected he was a bad lot. From the outset you were the one putting poison in my head, making me doubt what I knew inside… You probably fed the same poison to Papa and he would have lapped it up. He loved to look down on people. Loved to feel superior.'

He reached out to take her hand and she stared at it like a snake. 'Wolfe has always been able to control you and now that Papa is dead he wants this house and he is using your good nature to get it.'

The deed seemed to pulse inside her reticule, but she did not need the reminder. 'You sent an innocent boy to the other side of the world to pay for your crimes, Justin, tried to get him hanged.' She went for him then, couldn't stop the rage from turning violent, pushing him and slapping him as tears streamed down her face. 'How could you, Justin? When you knew I loved him?' He scrambled away and put the desk between them. 'I am going to Bow Street.., I am going to tell them exactly what you did and let them investigate your crimes!'

'No!' Panic made his voice high-pitched. 'You cannot do that! I am innocent!'

'You are as innocent as Owen is guilty.' She snatched his letter to Kelvedon from the desk and shook it at him. 'If it took the Runner less than two weeks to uncover this, he'll have found enough evidence to have you arrested and charged within a month!'

'But I am your brother!'

'You had a young man transported for a crime he didn't commit while you committed fraud, theft, perjured yourself in a court of law and broke our dying mother's heart when you stole her pearls. She never got over the loss of them. We both remember that, don't we?'

The real Justin appeared as his mask crumbled in panic. 'It wasn't like that! I only borrowed them…'

'Pawned them, more like!'

He grabbed her hands and stared beseechingly. 'With the intent of getting them back, Lydia, I swear it…but I was led astray by bad people and in danger… I had no choice…'

Even looking at him, watching him squirm, made her sick to her stomach. She tugged her hands away because his true character made her skin crawl. 'Is nothing ever your fault, Justin? Since when is theft borrowing? Since when is it acceptable to pawn somebody else's possessions without their consent?'

'I was going to get them back! Things just got out of hand. Papa wanted someone's head on a pole…'

'And you gave him Owen's rather than admit it was you!'

'I gave him a servant, someone I assumed was of no consequence…' His head reeled sideways at the force of her slap, and he whimpered, clutching his cheek as blood dripped out of his nose.

'He was of consequence to me! You knew that and used it to your advantage.' Just as she knew he would have happily told her father of their romance if she'd had the courage to speak out, then used that, too, as further proof of Owen's guilt. 'You callously thought it all through and with malicious calculation, you planted evidence. Paid a witness…'

'You cannot prove that. Nobody but you heard me say it and if you betray me—your own kin—and go to Bow Street, I will deny it all till my dying breath. It will be your word against mine. A peer versus a scoundrel's wife! Nobody will believe you!' His face had contorted into a mask of hatred now. Selfish, self-serving, desperate hatred.

'While I might not be able to prove it yet, that makes no difference, because I know without a shadow of a doubt that whatever happens next, you will already go to hell for it!'

Chapter Twenty-Five

Whoever had coined the phrase *Be careful what you wish for...* clearly knew a thing or two.

'What are you going to do?' Randolph's troubled expression undoubtedly matched Owen's.

'What can I do? This will break Lydia's heart.' The second Runner's report was more damning than the first. And even when presented with proof of her brother's debauchery and downright duplicity regarding her, she had still asked Owen to pay his debts. If he sent the blighter to jail, she'd never forgive him.

'You have to tell her.'

'No, I don't.'

Because it wasn't worth it. He saw that now as clear as day. Her father wasn't yet in the ground, she had just learned her brother had sold her off to Kelvedon. Owen wouldn't be responsible for shattering what was left of her world.

'I'll let sleeping dogs lie.' Better to be the bigger man than the vengeful one.

'Then the past will always be there—hovering in the background.'

Not if he accepted her forgiveness. He knew in his heart

she would still forgive him. She loved him and that would be enough. 'I'll simply tell her I stole those blasted candlesticks in a moment of weakness and have been too ashamed to tell her.'

His friend rolled his eyes. 'And her mother's precious pearls?'

'No... I shan't admit to those. I'll deny all knowledge of the pearls because they matter too much to Lydia.'

Randolph threw his arms up in the air exasperated. 'This all matters, Owen! Just because the truth is unpalatable doesn't mean Lydia doesn't have the right to hear it!'

'He's right, Owen.' The so far silent Gertie stroked his hand. 'You were determined to find the truth. You've hunted for it for years. Now you have it, you must see it through to the end. It isn't fair that we both know it and your own wife doesn't. That's not the way to build a good marriage.'

She was right. They both were. He knew it just as he suddenly knew so much more. Enlightenment had made him very philosophical all of a sudden. It was staggering how clear things became when one was stood on the moral high ground. From the summit he could now finally see everything and no one was more shocked than he was to discover it had altered his perspective.

Owen knew he should be angry. Knew he should be howling at the heavens and kicking furniture all around the room at Justin Barton's horrendous crimes, or at least savouring the moment of being completely exonerated, but instead all he cared about was how it would affect Lydia.

And selfishly, how it might affect him by default.

Them.

Could there ever truly be a *them* if he had her brother arrested? The new Earl of Fulbrook was the only family she had left. She adored the snake. And while she might be currently furious at him for arranging her betrothal to Kelvedon, she would not want to believe Justin capable of committing such a betrayal, nor thank him for appraising her of the fact, and Owen loved her too much to put her through the ordeal of another trial. Another sentence. Another banishment to whichever miserable English prison they sent peers to while she was left to pick up the pieces. There would be more scandal and enough misplaced guilt to crush her spirit.

Two wrongs did not make a right.

But, as usual, blasted Randolph had a point. There had been enough lies and he would not add to them. That wasn't the way to start a marriage. 'I'll tell her after the funeral.' Which she was currently in the midst of planning because her wastrel brother didn't have it in him to organise anything which did not benefit himself.

Or at least that was where he assumed she was. He had awoken all alone and, with the reliably watchful Slugger mysteriously missing, too, found nobody who knew where she had gone. They had both been gone all morning.

Gertie was pouring him a second cup of tea when he heard Lydia on the stairs and Owen rushed out to greet her. Except it wasn't Lydia. It was Slugger.

'Where is my wife?'

'The same place she's been for the last three hours—sat on a bench in Hyde Park. Staring at a bunch of trees.'

'At the back of the Serpentine?' Alarm bells started ringing. 'What's she doing there?'

His big friend shrugged. 'She went to her father's house, stayed there less than half an hour, came out looking distraught and then went to the park. I can't get a squeak out of her and, while I was loath to leave her all alone, I can't deny I'm worried. Something's wrong, Owen. Very wrong. You need to go fetch her because she will not listen to me.'

He didn't need to be told twice, dashed down the stairs, sprinted down Curzon Street and, when his legs weren't carrying him fast enough, did the unthinkable and hailed a hackney to take him as close as he could get before running again.

His lungs were burning by the time he reached the Serpentine. In the distance, there indeed was Lydia, still sitting on the bench, her shoulders slumped as if the weight of the entire world now rested on them.

'Lydia.' Her head snapped up, her expression suddenly so tragic he couldn't bear it. 'What's wrong?'

'I've been thinking about the past…and what you said about it being like brambles. And I understand now, because I feel as though they are choking me.'

All his fault. He'd kicked the hornets' nest. He couldn't let it lie and now she was suffering.

'About that…' Gingerly, he sat next to her on the bench, deciding there and then it was his job to protect her from the truth. She didn't deserve to feel this wretched. Nor should she have to choose between him over the only living relative she had left. 'I am calling off the investigation. I've decided I don't care what happened. All that matters is now.'

'Liar.' It was barely a whisper. 'You know my brother did it, don't you?'

Owen was silent, trying to work out how she had learned what the Runner had relayed to him at eight this morning when she had been gone since dawn. He considered denying it, considered confessing to the crimes himself, then dismissed both foolish ideas because neither would be fair. 'Who told you?'

'Nobody. I remembered something. Something significant. My mother's pearls…' She shook her head, then stared back down at her hands, clearly lost in her own personal pit of despair. 'They were missing weeks before I first met you. She lost them before we went to Bath, which coincidentally was about a week after my brother came home from Cambridge. He had been summoned back by Papa for overspending his allowance and, according to your file, he already owed a thousand pounds of gambling debts by then. I confronted him this morning…'

He reached for her hand. Through the soft leather of her gloves, he could tell it was frozen solid. 'Come… Let's go home. It's freezing out here.'

She refused to budge.

'My heart always knew you were innocent. That's the real tragedy I cannot get over. I didn't want to believe my eyes, but…'

'I know, Lydia. It doesn't matter.' And in that moment he realised it didn't. Randolph, damn him, was right again. In the grand scheme of things this was in the past, set in stone and ultimately irreversible. Therefore, it was best left there. He wouldn't allow it to taint his future now that he had a future with her. 'It really doesn't matter any more.'

She turned to him then and he could see she was thoroughly devastated. Guilty and ashamed. Broken. 'I should have said something, Owen. I should have spoken out. Defended you. Then perhaps…'

He placed a finger on her chilled lips. 'There is no perhaps. There is nothing you could have said or done which would have changed the outcome. I would still have been arrested. Still sentenced. Still sent to the other side of the world.'

'You don't know that.'

'Yes, I do.' He wrapped his arm around her and tugged

her close. 'I had this notion that when I came home, I would give you irrefutable proof of my innocence and then I would forgive you and it would all be made better. I really wanted to savour that moment and I suppose feel superior because of it, but I don't want that now.'

In fact, all things considered, it was now the last thing he wanted. 'As I see it, you have nothing to be forgiven for either. We were both powerless to change things, Lydia. Neither of us had a voice. I was a nobody and you were just the sixteen-year-old daughter of a man who never noticed you. We were both victims. We both lost out. Were both unfairly punished. If you had tried to defend me, admitted you knew me, then your father would have sent you away in disgrace, I'd have definitely hanged and your mother would have had nobody with her when she died.' He kissed the top of her head, feeling bizarrely lighter than he had in years. The truth—the whole truth—had truly liberated him from the past more effectively than he could have ever imagined even a few days ago. Like an oppressive weight had been lifted, those damn brambles hacked away. 'With hindsight, it could have been so much worse and all we lost is ten years.'

'Thanks to my brother.' She pulled away, squaring her shoulders, so determined to be brave. 'He bribed the stable master to testify against you in court.'

'I know.'

'The stable master is dead.'

'I know that, too. Mr Argent died of a stroke two years ago. But his daughter is alive and well and living in the Lake District...'

She sighed, her clever brain piecing it all together. 'I suppose he made a deathbed confession and she is prepared to testify as much in court.'

'She is. But I am not going to bring charges.'

* * *

'That's ridiculous!' Lydia blinked back at him, completely flabbergasted. 'My brother blamed you for a crime you didn't commit. Had you transported! Tried to have you hanged!'

'He did.'

'Don't you want retribution? Justice? Revenge?' Because she did. She had been sat here for hours, debating whether to head straight to Bow Street to tell them of his treachery or to head back to Libertas to beg for her husband's forgiveness first and see if he could find it in his big heart to want to remain properly married to her when she could have saved him. She should have remembered that one pertinent detail sooner.

Ten whole years sooner!

'I've never been one for revenge. I've always prided myself on being the bigger man. Randolph calls it my most nauseatingly pious trait. While I wasn't born *a* noble, I was born intrinsically *noble* and I rather like the irony of being the obviously bigger and better man in this case.'

'Please don't be noble for me!'

'I'm not. Not entirely. A tiny part of me cannot bring myself to have your only living relative arrested, that is true, but bizarrely, and for the life of me I cannot explain why, I am quite content to be noble. He knows he is guilty and he also knows we know he is guilty. He'll get his comeuppance eventually. It is as predictable as night following day. Fate has a funny way of squaring things off—as our marriage bears testament to. Besides…' He looped his arms around her waist again possessively and kissed her, smiling. 'The very best revenge is not to let his petty cowardice and self-preserving selfishness win now that we finally are bound together for all eternity as we were always meant to be.'

'After everything, you are going to allow Justin to escape scot-free?' He really was the biggest of men to allow that. And most possibly the most foolhardy. 'I want him to pay, Owen!'

'He will. And handsomely. Because I have another plan. One he will not see coming.'

This sounded more like it. It might be vengeful and mean-spirited, but she wanted to see Justin suffer. 'What is it?'

'I thought we'd give him the deed to the Berkeley Square house and wash our hands of him completely.'

If the sky suddenly fell down or pigs sprouted wings and started to fly above their heads, she couldn't have been more surprised. 'That's it?' Lydia could barely lift her jaw from the floor. 'You want to gift him the house! That is your plan? Why on earth would you want to give him the deed?'

'Because, as you rightly said, my love, to err is human and to forgive divine.'

'How could you possibly even suggest forgiving him?' Because she never would. Her eyes had been opened wide to what he was and, more importantly, she felt it in her heart. Her brother was dead to her and deserved everything he got. 'He's a monster!'

'He is. But we are better than that, Lydia, and, more than anything, I have decided it simply doesn't matter any more.'

'How can you say it doesn't matter?'

He smiled at her—beamed, in fact. 'Because he didn't win.' Something which seemed to please him immensely. 'He threw everything at us, lied, schemed, cheated, plotted, separated us by ten thousand miles and seven long years— yet here we are regardless. Still together. Still madly in love. It's taken the truth for me to finally realise that that is really all that matters to me. I have everything I've ever wanted and nine-tenths of that everything is you.'

'That is all…' Her heart was positively melting at the way he was looking at her. There was so much love and joy in his eyes. '… Lovely… But I still do not understand why we should give him the deed. Not having him arrested for his crimes is one thing—but giving him the house is rewarding him for his treachery when he deserves to rot in jail.'

'Do you want that house, Lydia? Because I certainly don't. Whenever I see it, I remember the day I was dragged away from it in chains. It's filled with nothing but bad or tainted memories and the debilitating, depressing ghosts of the past—and I think we are both done with all that. It will only hold us back as all thoughts of revenge always do. Let him have it, with my blessing. If you want a house, give me two years to save and I'll buy you one. A better one. Certainly a happier one. If we give him that one, then we can cut all ties with the dreadful Bartons for ever—and move forward.'

More proof she had married the perfect man. Loved the perfect man. He was giving up his rightful, hard-won justice—for her. 'He'll only lose it.'

'That is inevitable.'

'But it is your three thousand pounds, Owen! And I am mindful you have already lost ten.' Almost everything he had. Each penny earned with his blood, sweat and tears, ten thousand punishing miles away. All diligently saved for the future he longed for, but could only dream of having while her brother squandered his away.

'I didn't lose anything, my darling.' He pulled her up, grinning. 'Because ultimately I *won*. So much more, ironically, than I bargained for. So much more than I ever dared hope for.'

He kissed her again. A gloriously passionate and public kiss that left her completely breathless. 'And don't let this go to your beautiful, vexing, stubborn head, Wife, but I'd have happily paid twenty, so I think I've got off lightly.'

'You didn't have twenty.'

'I'd have found twenty. I'd have sold my share in Libertas in a heartbeat…for you.' Before she could find the words to speak, he took her hand and entwined his fingers through hers. 'Come—let's get that toxic deed and give it to him now. His face will be an absolute picture. Then, let's have a wonderful life purely to spite him—and your miserable father and anyone else who looks down their nose at us. Let's savour every moment, Lydia, build a million wonderful memories to make up for the ones that were stolen and thank our lucky stars that fate was *always* on our side. Because it won't be on his. Your brother is doomed to live the rest of his miserable, loveless life looking over his shoulder for all the numerous others he has cheated, robbed and maligned over the years. All of whom will not be as forgiving as this better and bigger man. And unless he has an epiphany, which I fear he is incapable of having, he is doomed to die a miserable and lonely death one day—just like your father. A proper life sentence… Whichever way you look at it.'

What a truly noble man he was. 'Clearly I married a mad man, but if that is what you want…' She tapped her reticule in defeat. 'The deed is in here. Alongside the list of his debts and the letter he sent to Kelvedon. I was going to take it all to Bow Street and ask them to arrest him.'

He seemed momentarily surprised and then touched until both emotions were replaced by cheerful resignation. 'I dare say it is only a matter of time before they do—so let's save ourselves the hassle and leave that up to some other poor wretch. All the interviews, statements, the trial…the scandal and publicity…' He made a face. 'Having been through all that before, albeit from the other side of the dock, I'd rather spend the time productively making up for lost time. Or making those babies you were so adamant you wanted.'

'But he wronged you. Stole seven years from you.'

'He did. But his arrest won't change any of that. I cannot turn back time. I will never get those years back and neither will you. They are done and dusted. But our love endured.'

'And you are not angry?' Neither did he look it. 'I don't understand why you are not shouting and waving your arms about?'

He kissed her nose, grinning. 'Clearly marriage to a good woman has mellowed me. Perhaps I have become even tempered all of a sudden?' He shook his head, smiling as if such a thing was indeed a miracle.

'But to allow him to get away with it hardly seems just! Are you sure you don't want to press charges, Owen?'

'Bizarrely, never surer. We can't change the past, Lydia, any more than we can run from it. But we can come to terms with it. It happened. It wasn't fun. But we emerged out the other end stronger people. In a strange sort of way, I wouldn't be where I am now if your brother hadn't cheated me. I wouldn't have Libertas, or Randolph or Gertie and all their annoying children—or very probably you. We were so young and naive, Lydia, and our situation next to impossible. We might not have stayed the course.'

'But what if we had?'

'Let's not kick *that* hornets' nest. Neither of us could possibly ever know what might have been. Only what was and what is.'

'You are very philosophical all of a sudden.'

'I am. Perhaps it will become my newest, most nauseating trait?' He tugged her away from the Serpentine and, feeling decidedly off-kilter and confused, she allowed him to lead her briskly to Berkeley Square. While she hoped he might come to his senses, he showed no signs of it and beamed as he knocked loudly on the door.

The butler answered straight away, looking every bit as wary as he had on the day she had been left standing on the doorstep.

'We have come to see my brother, Maybury.'

He swallowed nervously. 'I shall see if he is at home, my lady.' Then he tellingly closed the door rather than inviting them in.

'Care to make a wager he is suddenly out?'

'He wouldn't dare!' Lydia would knock the damn door down herself if he tried it.

'Cowards always hide.' Owen's deep voice was carrying, enough that several of the people around them slowed their pace to watch the spectacle. 'Especially when they are in the wrong.' In a show of impressive bravado, he sat on the top step, facing out to the square, arranging his long legs in front of him and crossing them at the ankles as if he hadn't a care in the world. Then he winked and patted the stone beside him. 'We might as well be comfortable while we wait.'

It was funny—sat next to Owen and watching the sea of curtains twitch all around them, she didn't feel the least bit humiliated. If anything, she felt empowered. By the time Maybury returned, looking completely terrified, she had the makings of a plan all worked out. Owen might well be noble and determined to be the bigger man—but she was a woman. His woman. And she felt no compunction to be the bigger person at all.

'I am sorry, my lady, but His Lordship is indisposed.'

'Is he, indeed? Well, that is embarrassing…' She allowed her voice to carry, too. There was no feeling of mortification this time. No cringing embarrassment. In front of the whole of Berkeley Square she fully intended to cause a scene. 'It puts me in the dreadful predicament of having to conclude my business with him here on the street.' Slowly, she stood and made a great show of rummaging in her reticule.

'Kindly give him this, please, Maybury. It is the deed to this house, which my dear husband bought to save my feckless brother and miserable father from complete financial ruin. Tell him that against my advice and despite my cowardly brother's shoddy and ungentlemanly behaviour towards him, my beloved and noble husband has decided to gift the deed back to him.' She unfolded the enormous piece of parchment and practically held it aloft so that any onlookers could indeed confirm at every social engagement they happened to be gossiping at it appeared to be every inch a legal document before she imperiously handed it to the butler. 'And can you also kindly inform the new Earl of Fulbrook that, henceforth, we wash our hands of him and his further *six thousand* pounds' worth of gambling debt.'

The poor fellow blinked back at her for several seconds before he finally found his voice. 'I will, my lady.'

'Furthermore, please tell him that while my sainted husband is benevolent enough to forgive him for his treachery, I am not. When Bow Street come knocking—and both they and the bailiffs will come knocking one day very soon—I shall happily give them statements as to his character and *all* his past transgressions. All of them, Maybury. Be quite specific in that.'

Poor Maybury gulped. 'I shall, my lady.'

'And do let him know I've now found all the *evidence*

I need and I shall keep it until such a time as I deign to use it.'

The butler simply nodded this time, his eyes as wide as saucers.

'Splendid.' She reached out her hand and hoisted a quietly impressed Owen back to his feet. Out of the corner of her eye she could see she was drawing quite the crowd, as suddenly, and a tad predictably, half of the residents of Berkeley Square all felt the overwhelming need for some fresh air and were taking a hasty walk. Better still, every carriage seemed to have stopped and, despite the flurry of activity all around them, it was eerily silent. The perfect opportunity to remove the dagger from her back and plunge it further into her hideous sibling.

'And might I also suggest—because I have always had a great deal of time for you, Maybury—that you find yourself another employer, as I cannot see this particular job lasting for much longer because the Barton coffers are as empty as my cowardly brother's heart. Your loyalty has been admirable, but we both know it has been severely misplaced. This is a dreadful house, Maybury. Owned by a dreadful family of selfish men who have no regard for other people, or indeed the law.' She smiled and, to the old retainer's shock, leant forward to squeeze his hand.

'Goodbye, Maybury. I shan't be back, so you'll never have to leave me standing on this soulless doorstep again.'

'I am sorry about that.' Looking embarrassed, the butler bowed. 'Good day, my lady... Mr Wolfe.'

She turned until the distinction made her pause. While she had an audience, she might as well make the most of it.

'Actually, Maybury, I am not a Barton any longer.' Thank goodness. 'I am *Mrs Lydia Wolfe.*' The name she had wished for a decade ago. The name which felt exactly right. The name she said loud enough for all the curious inhabitants of Berkeley Square to hear and which she might well have tattooed on to her skin in an intimate place which only Owen would ever see. An indelible mark symbolising an indelible truth. 'And I am very proud to be so.'

She took his arm and beamed up at him, the world slowing to a standstill as he smiled back.

'And what, pray tell, was all that about?'

She shrugged, unrepentant. 'I am human. I erred. And it felt divine.'

'I see.' But he was smiling. 'Now that you have got that off your chest, are you ready, *Wife*?'

'For anything, Owen—as long as you are always beside me.'

'I am never leaving you again, woman. Make no bones about that! You are stuck with me for ever, *Mrs Wolfe*.'

'A life sentence.'

'With absolutely no chance of a pardon, I'm afraid.'

'That all sounds positively splendid… *Husband*. Do lead the way.'

And without looking back they stepped forward, finally leaving the past behind where it belonged, towards the bold, bright and wonderful future they were always destined to have.

Together.

* * * * *